Rituals

Like A Song

By

Ryan Hastings

Table of Contents

It's Raining

Oh, how the world itself is writhing in pain. The conflicts it has endured over the millennia…bathed in the blood of angels, celestials, and humanity. The magnitude of malformed monstrosities and titans of hell quickly led the mortal race to engines of war that would become fibers of their very existence here. War is a constant.

Dom'rel's rebellion militarized the universe, leaving humanity especially vulnerable in those early hours and days. Originally, "Heroic Gifts" were responsive to a sudden and violent turn in history, a way for mortal men and women to combat a rapidly encroaching darkness. Three-quarters of Harth's population was ultimately lost in those relatively brief moments, leaving survivors to pass the Gifts along through biology and for us to continue to pass them through our own methods.

The engineering marvels of Harth can be attributed to what I would call "pissing matches" between evil forces. Larger and fiercer beasts kept being bred everywhere the wicked took refuge.

So, greater and more powerful weapons had to be developed. Technology had to be developed. And frankly, it had to be given in some instances. What can I say? Some of us enjoy the light shows.

Speaking of light, the Child has been born to Lady Firebourne. Honestly, it was a bit eerie, as something of a "hush" briefly befell blackened places. A mortal boy with an angel's name like many infants, He was a new hero for the world...yet to be another combatant. The birth of Iman'el Firebourne had come on a quiet night, bringing The Light into Shiro. Even this misty-eyed fool was in attendance, kneeling alongside a handful of my kin. Others will chronicle Iman'el's life more directly. My focus remains on our dear friends.

Beautiful anomalies pierced even the darker skies that night, a sign to those who had little of anything else left...giving peace to some who lay bloody and dying in those moments and hope to those clinging to survival. Swae remained in Dan-hali, meditating in full radiance on a beachhead, facing in the direction of Malene, one of three major continents. Miri'el did the same at Zufa'Zuf, levitating above the grand temple there. Asheya, a central area of Zuhetta, glowed even brighter for several hours, with its amethyst light reflecting from the clouds over the continent Zuhetta.

A crystal sky and the bright stars and wonders in the heavens were easy to see from Parraeysia, and bright moons gave the island a soft glow of its own. The Light's prophesies were kept close among the Ma'ji in the dragonkin homeland, as they raised many prayers and songs that night. Rayne, a broodmother, remained in a peaceful stasis, with her prismatic scales shining in the light-filled night.

The darkness stood still for a time that night, though it remained in the many foul places that had become of Harth. This abysmal war now saw a new warrior born into its battlefields. Humanity had retained its footing.

On this particularly rainy day, Yana, a summoner, was responding to a mandatory summons for an evaluation. Her icy-blue eyes were leering away from the door that she was expecting the doctor to walk through. With her arms folded, Yana quietly scolded Dehza, the Destroyer Celestial.

"I'm probably here because of you. If it has anything to do with me, your lack of situational awareness is to blame," Dehza replied, at a normal speaking volume that prompted the receptionist to briefly glance about. Yana's right eye twitched ever so slightly from frustration. Otherwise, her demeanor was unchanged.

The door opened. Thulo, an owl and a former shaman, popped his feathery head out of the doorway.

"Shit," Yana dejectedly stated.

"This way, young lady," Thulo kindly said, beckoning with a wave of his wing. Yana uttered as she passed by the receptionist.

"You work for an owl?" The receptionist smiled and nodded.

Yana closed the door behind her and plopped down on a couch. "There really isn't anyone else?" Yana asked.

"Actually, shamans are too few these days," Thulo replied. "We try to focus on the healing aspects of our gift and partner it with doctoral degrees."

"I bet there's at least one shaman that still has hands around here," Yana said with a gentle smile.

Thulo sighed as he perched on an adjacent chair.

"So, what's up?" the summoner asked.

"While evaluations are standard procedure, I was specifically assigned to you," Thulo answered.

"Why?" Yana inquired.

"Because I'm the only shaman that's on your level," Thulo proudly answered.

The summoner laughed out loud. "I'm sorry, I'm sorry," she said through some laughter.

"You really still have magical powers?" she asked through more laughter.

Thulo waited a moment for Yana to get it out of her system. Finally, the summoner finished.

"I'm sorry," she said, still bearing a cute smile.

"Laughter is good, even if it's at my expense. How has your sleep been?" Thulo inquired.

"It's been pretty good lately," Yana said, clearly having trouble keeping a straight face.

"Sleep does the body better than most give credit, but I suppose it's just as healthy to keep a good sense of humor," Thulo said, glancing down at some notes.

Continuing, Thulo asked, "No thoughts of harming yourself? Suicide?"

Yana shook her head, instantly regaining her composure.

"Truthfully?" Thulo asked.

"Of course," Yana assured.

"Wh…who gave you all those notes?" she asked curiously, but without any hostility.

"Several people close to you, including those who could give me more history," Thulo replied.

"You're the only summoner on Harth, Yana. Your mental state is important to many more outside of yourself." Yana nodded.

Her demeanor was soft.

"Now, while I was able to attain valuable data about you, there's a bit more to this process," Thulo mentioned.

"Process?" Yana echoed.

"Have you been hearing voices, Yana?" the owl rather bluntly asked.

"What? No!" Yana rebuked, her eyes grown wide.

"Yana, this will work better if you're honest now," Thulo sternly replied.

Yana gasped and made a run for the door, only to find that it had been locked from the outside. She began to cast a spell to blast it open, but Thulo cast elemental bonds that weighed down her hands, thus preventing her spell motions. Yana looked at the owl in awe. "No way," she exclaimed.

Thulo flapped his wings once to send a gentle drift of magic-infused air across Yana's face, inducing a sleep spell.

"N…no way," the summoner yawned, as she slowly and gently slumped over.

Thulo hopped down and walked over to the slumbering summoner and boasted, "The powers are in the soul, despite the kind of body."

He placed his wings on either side of Yana's head and closed his eyes. He may have still been a legendary shaman, but he certainly was not ready for what he found among the nether; that is, the image of Deth--the destroyer and also known as Dehza--in all his fury and terror laying waste to a dying star. The spell made the vision all too real for the shaman. He quickly broke away, flapping and hooting in horror around the office.

When the receptionist saw the owl huffing in the corner and the summoner still sound asleep, she flung the door open. After a moment, Thulo said, "I saw a ghastly spider." The receptionist curiously nodded and closed the door once again.

"What in the world?" Thulo uttered.

"Perhaps it's best that we have a chat, shaman," Dehza remarked.

"Good Lord," Thulo gasped, "am I hearing things now?"

"Undo the wrap on her left hand," Dehza said.

Thulo inched forward, hesitantly removing the wrap with his beak. The owl took a small hop back at the sight of the fiery eye that manifested from the scar. "Unbelievable," he uttered.

Dehza went on, candidly explaining the situation thus far. It was never his purpose to infiltrate the summoner, he said. "She's where she needs to be," he explained. "Though she is a powerful weapon, she is mortal and warrants extreme protection. The time of war will come for her again; but, until such time, she is prohibited from leaving the consecrated ground. Understood?"

"I will relay your message," Thulo affirmed.

"Call me a source. I can't have my name just being thrown around. Is this also understood?" Dehza added sternly.

The owl saluted. "Good, this concludes our session," the eye remarked before returning to a glowing scar.

Thulo took a moment before speaking the spell words to recall the magic.

As Yana slowly woke from a nap, she tried not to seem too concerned when she noticed her wrap was undone. There was an awkward pause as the shaman and summoner looked at each other. "Quite a mind you have, miss," Thulo stated with confidence. "Everything checks out. Do stay on a good regimen."

"Yeah," Yana curiously replied, grinning a bit at the owl. "I'd like you to have some follow-ups—once a month should suffice," Thulo said. "I'll have a prescription sent to loyal herbalists," he added.

Waking from the spell, Yana was careful to stand, supporting herself as her body still felt a bit funny. Kindly smiling, she affirmed the shaman's words.

"Yana?" Thulo asked.

The summoner stopped and looked back, replying, "Hmm?"

"How much does your husband, Bael, know about your past?" he politely asked.

Yana was not offended at all by his question. She grinned and replied, "Not enough."

Thulo nodded, replying, "Simply food for thought."

Yana agreed as she continued on her way out of the office and towards the door. The receptionist cheered her on.

"Bye, Yana. We all love you."

Yana smiled, replying with a soft, "Bye."

The summoner, exiting to a covered walkway, noticed that the rain seemed to have slowed the usual bustle of Rime. Yana slowly put a skunkweed cigarette between her lips but did not even have time to conjure a runic flame before a marked military car came to a halt in front of her.

Sapphira, Yana's friend, waved from the driver's side. "Wanna go to the airfields?" she asked.

"Why am I not surprised to see you here, Sapph?" Yana answered with an accusatory but otherwise friendly tone.

"Can't blame a girl for caring," Sapphira innocently replied, as she opened a passenger door for her friend.

Yana got in, lighting her cigarette as she did. The vehicle gently pulled away, heading due northeast along relatively empty streets. The country's soul was in a strange melancholy as the inevitable specters of the future continued to present themselves.

"Ready for your big show?" Sapphira happily asked.

"Always," Yana replied with a wink.

"They seem really confident. I mean…technically, a handful of badass dragons and a celestial have airpower," Sapphira said with growing excitement.

"But, this would be like partnering humanity with them. That's so cool. Is this like the spell Galai'el, the angel, taught you--the one you used on the ship?"

"It's a cleaner version of that spell, yes," Yana replied in a relaxed manner.

"You should go there sometime. I'm sure you'd have the clearance," Sapphira remarked.

"We'll see," Yana sighed. "I have a feeling certain individuals aren't particularly ready for me to do much traveling."

"Bael?" Sapphira asked.

Yana chuckled. "He'd be fine as long as he could go, too."

Sapphira shrugged. "Anyway, we'll figure it out. I'm not sure why these individuals would be so concerned about you going there."

"It might be a lot more dangerous than here," Yana commented.

"Didn't seem too bad when we went," Sapph replied quietly. "Certainly, nothing like it would be, going back into the dwarf kingdom Ramm.

Some miles later, the vehicle was bypassing the perimeter of Shiro's ever-expanding airfields. Airpower was officially a commodity, and production had plenty of catching up. The influx of minds, gifts, and workers to Shiro did well to balance the demands on the alliance capital. Even in such rain, varying scopes of projects continued. Yana could not help but give an impressed whistle at the larger gunships steadily growing in number. Their vehicle eventually came to a stop inside a massive hangar, at which time the two ladies exited and approached some stacks of cargo where Eli and Skarg were playing a game of cards. Eli Darius, a pilot and sky commander, was clearly winning, with a noticeable stack of cash on his side of a crate.

"They have enough?" Sapphira inquired, greeting Eli with a kiss.

"Everything's good to go," he replied.

Yana pulled up a chair beside Skarg, her friend and dwarven male.

"You haven't aged a bit since this all started, lass," Skarg remarked with a grin.

"It's good to know you'll be safe here." Yana blushed, gently smacking the dwarf and replying, "Don't talk like this is all some kind of goodbye." Skarg, maintaining a semi-serious expression, said, "I'm bein' truthful, lassie; it warms me to see ya doin' so well," he said.

Eli took the sentimental moment to scoot the money from the table. "Just keep each other safe over there," Yana said softly to the group.

"We'll be fine, ma'am," Eli replied with refined confidence.

"It should be like shooting very disgusting fish in a very gloomy barrel. We're just waiting on some manner of reinforcements from Zuhetta," he added.

"Reinforcements?" Yana repeated in kind.

The reinforcements being referenced are the darkdancers, albeit there are only two of them at present. Since they had been declared essential enough to stall the first deployments for a couple of days, they would be plugged into the allied forces going into Ramm. Few, outside of certain Zuhettan circles, even knew of the darkdancers' existence.

Eli gave Sapphira the respective paperwork as he glanced at Yana. "You ready to impress the world again?"

The summoner smiled, affirming with a thumbs up.

Eventually, the girls took the documents back to Blackwolf Keep, the main fortress of Rime in Shiro. They were greeted by

Thalis, a human male warrior, as they passed each other going down the steps.

With an innocent look in her eyes, Sapphira stopped in front of the man. "Where ya heading?" she asked happily.

"What'd you want?" he sighed candidly.

Sapph held out the covered papers.

"Take these to the commander of the infantry, General Nix?" Thalis looked at her with exasperation.

"You can't?" he asked.

"He doesn't like me," Sapphira said timidly.

Yana simply watched the exchange, paying no mind to the rainfall.

"How on earth could that man not like you?" Thalis sarcastically asked.

"He thinks I'm a bad influence on Eli--that I feed his ego," Sapphira uttered, glancing away.

"You are, and you do," Thalis chuckled.

Yana had to struggle not to giggle as well.

"You won't help me?" Sapphira groaned.

"Nope," Thalis replied, once again departing on his merry way. "It'll build character," he added.

Yana parted with Sapph at the general's door. Yana was on her way to see Lady Firebourne, the mother of *Iman'el, the Child.* Sapphira knocked on General Nix's door and poked her head in.

"Airship reports, sir," she said with a smile.

General Charles Nix was a hardened veteran, a gifted frost caller, and a military tactician. He was wide-shouldered, bald, and had an impressive grey moustache. Sapphira held out the papers. The general gently took them in his hand as he put on some spectacles to glance over the reports.

Sapphira stood at attention and waited. Nix set the reports down and lit the remainder of a cigar.

"Anything to drink? You're almost off the clock, right?" he asked through a puff of smoke.

Sapphira stuttered for a second but agreed to have a glass of whiskey. The general motioned for her to have a seat.

"You volunteered to go into Ramm…you wouldn't mind my asking your reasons?" he inquired.

Sapphira was certainly not ready for such a question and returned the inquiry with a somewhat blank stare.

The general chuckled and said, "I'm not trying to trap you, girl--just a quick chat that I'm having with a healthy number of spouses ahead of this deployment."

"It's the right thing to do now," Sapphira replied, turning her eyes to the glass in her lap.

"I believe you, but I know that's not the only reason why," Nix stated. "I'm just keeping everyone's interests in mind--like what losing you would do to him."

"Are you asking me not to go, sir?" she asked.

"I'm asking people to prepare themselves for this endeavor of ours," Nix replied.

"Eli is one of my top admirals, and you'll soon be assigned to communications. I need everyone to be able to put professionalism ahead of anything else, no matter what might happen on the other side of those mountains." The general's tone remained solemn and firm.

Sapphira nodded, quietly replying, "I hadn't heard about a reassignment. Is this a promotion?" she added.

"You have friends in high places," Nix chuckled.

"It's not a promotion, but you'll have some new perks and a fancy title. You'll also be working frequently with one of our smaller teams. I actually don't know much about whoever is on the said team just yet, but I'm sure you'll find out once you're on the other side." Sapphira downed what whiskey was left, then stood and saluted. Nix returned the salute.

The summoner had come into the royal courts, looking about for Lady Firebourne, a descendant of one of the ancient bloodlines. There were a few dozen individuals shopping in various businesses, Kora being among them. Yana went over to the snow-white wolvyn, inquiring about the Child.

"She's probably nursing about this time," Kora commented. "Oh, well then, I won't disturb," Yana replied. "I was just sort of in the area."

"You look to be at peace," Kora kindly remarked. "It's so nice to see you this way, even if you're a bit wet."

Then there was a deep booming vibration that shook the very floors and walls. Some in the room were initially concerned by the phenomenon, Yana being one. Others seemed accustomed to it, Kora being one.

"Don't worry about it, ladies and gentlemen," a ranking cog calmly hollered.

"It's just progress being made."

"Quite a motley bunch in the labs, milady," Kora remarked.

"I insisted they could've done this elsewhere, but The Keep laboratories are designed for such madmen," she sighed.

There were two more booms in close succession.

"How long does this go on around here?" Yana asked.

"Luckily, the troll's machine can't last long," Kora replied. "It'll do a couple of dozen in a day. Otherwise, I believe the military is taking over the project relatively soon."

"Presumably a bigger and better location?" Yana rhetorically asked. Kora nodded happily.

The summoner made her way to the sublevel labs of Blackwolf, still receiving respectful nods and salutes from the persons she passed. She knew she was getting close when there was dust swirling about a darkened hall, and she heard Kira's voice shouting, "Wait! Wait! WAIT!"

Then another boom and flash followed, sending more dirt and dust down the hall.

Yana conjured To'to, a violet ethereal falcon that perched on her shoulder. Its aura parted the particles and gusts around her as she continued walking. The spirit calmly glanced about, barely making a sound.

"Did you not hear the girl, To'to?" Vega, a female Ma'ji humanoid, scorned.

"It still worked," To'to replied casually.

Yana could see a number of small devices glowing with void energy on a table, with dozens more that appeared empty.

"Hey, big sis," Kira, a warrior, greeted and hugged Yana, her sister-in-law.

"Come to see our little project, have ya?" Morgan, a human female necromancer, nodded at Yana, as she continued stabilizing the flowing energy.

Four other research officers and two cogs were also present in this rather small space, but they seemed to be managing.

Vega slapped To'to atop his head and then came to greet the summoner. Her fur was a bit sullied by soot and dirt. Yana tried not to laugh at the Ma'ji's windswept look from the blasts. Vega tried to fix some of it as she approached.

"How are you, Yana?" she asked lovingly.

"I'm well," Yana replied. "I guess I haven't been in The Keep during one of your sessions."

"I would hardly say that I have much to do with this," Vega commented. "I suppose I'm here just out of morbid curiosity, or perhaps as medical assistance should something go wrong."

We've done alright," Morgan chimed in, as she performed the void syphon with a small grid to collar-like devices that had been designed to contain such portions of voidlight. Kira handed one that was already nearby to Yana, putting another device around her own neck. Kira exited the room and went to the end of the hallway where Yana had entered.

The summoner put the collar on, fitting a ring around her left ear. *"You can hear me, right?"* Kira asked, her voice vaguely distorted among the nether.

Yana was clearly surprised and impressed. *"Y...yeah,"* she replied in subtle awe.

"Once the amplifiers are made, these things can reach over a thousand miles," Kira stated excitedly, hurrying back towards the chamber.

"We're hoping to find a way to make it global," Vega added with a grin, "so that armies and people can communicate instantaneously with a voidkeeper on Harth…hoping that it can become a reality."

What is the transition between these two paragraphs?

The darkdancers from Zuhetta were greeted by Stella, the voidkeeper; Amon, the dwarven king; and Delia, an Aka'rah and Yana's friend. Delia leapt at the opportunity when she heard the name of those who had rescued her. Stella was also pleased to accompany the two shadows, Delia and Amon, to Ramm.

Both shadows had retained their bloodlines and the respect that came with them, and both had been given tremendous resources. Delia pledged her resources to their new comrades. Amon was keen to pledge his resources to his allies. By Delia's added request, Amon halted the deployment to Ramm to wait for these shadows.

Rather than being deployed to Ramm, Enysa, a human female darkdancer, was to remain in Shiro in an attempt to grow the house. Because of that, she was a bit pouty.

Trova, a human darkdancer, joined the group. He indicated they needed specifically a cog for their intended mission. Instead, A'mi, a human female alchemist, was quite eager for the experience and was selected to accompany Trova to Ramm. Enysa was quickly learning the shadow's accomplice's alchemical art along the way, hoping to soon submit her papers regarding a scholar's degree. Stella would be aiding the development of the void-tech. Enysa had many questions to ask Trova but remained refined in asking them until the proper time.

"We can give you a run-through of one of the armories before you're on your way," Amon stated. "You all have access to everything our elite would have, no matter the time or reason."

"Much obliged, majesty," Trova replied.

"Maybe I can find a big-ass scope to help me spot candidates better," Enysa uttered sarcastically.

Enysa took a satchel Trova handed her as they walked. After glancing inside, Enysa saw the remaining vials of blood.

"Wait…why are you giving me this?" Enysa asked, coming to a curious stop.

"They should stay with you. Hopefully, you'll want them," Trova replied, motioning for her to continue. Enysa saw this gesture in several lights, but most were for reasons she did not want to think about. "You mean, safer?" she asked. "Well, yeah," Trova replied plainly. His comrade understood the responsibility, but the fact still made her uneasy.

"Since you'll be staying here, feel free to bunk anywhere, lass," Amon remarked while glancing at Enysa. "There's any variety of options for someone of your status. Trust me, there are plenty of unique folks to make friends with."

"I've actually got a nice little place," Delia remarked happily. "It has a wonderful view. I'd enjoy being a sort of base for all of you."

"If you insist, your majesty," Enysa replied, with a dash of awe.

Delia smiled at the darkdancer.

"You can be a bit more laxed. Royalty means only so much here," she said kindly.

"Yeah…but the Aki'rah name is the last name of a great ancient bloodline that you hear about across the world," Enysa answered humbly.

"Indeed, I remember reading about Aki'rahni airpower in very early wars," Stella chimed in. "My father was always fascinated by foreign armies and battles."

"Well…that history has been drastically changed," Delia sighed; "Shiro and the people here are all that's left of Malene."

They parted ways when the group came to an intersecting point in Rime's streets. Stella would return to her quarters in the research division. Enysa and Delia went west, while A'mi, Trova, and Amon went east to join the others. Enysa would soon discover that Delia's residence was hardly a "little place." The vehicle ascended into the cliffs that overlooked the city, stopping outside of a mansion that still bore signs of construction. Enysa was breathless when she saw the design of the place. It was luxurious in all respects.

Their steps echoed in the vast entryway. Very nice furniture was still randomly set about the place.

"Is it just you here?" the darkdancer inquired, her eyes looking up and around at the beautiful interior.

"Amon kept me company for a while…and Jeeves, the skeletal butler and companion of the darkdancers, has been a delightful addition," Delia replied. "Honestly, it's a bit much; but, if you're trying to grow a brand, you'll need the facilities to do it."

"This is so kind of you, ma'am," the darkdancer stated.

"I owe my life to the darkdancers, as do a few others located here," Delia reminiscently remarked.

They ascended a grand staircase to the third floor, coming out onto a large balcony. Delia was accurate in her statement about the view, and she smiled happily at the darkdancer's awe-filled expression.

"The lights go forever," Enysa remarked.

"There will be more of them soon enough," Delia added, joining the darkdancer by the railings. "This city, this country, is mending and growing by the day."

Enysa could see the areas of Rime that were still heavily damaged, where lights faced towards the buildings and not from them. Among other things, she began to wonder about the battle that had taken place before.

"Oh, here," Delia remarked, seeming to remember something. "If you're hanging around Shiro, maybe you want to swing by the old chapter house at some point," she added, handing the darkdancer a folded envelope. "I've already done some snooping, but maybe something else will catch your eye. There's no rush."

Enysa peered at the contents and put the envelope in her satchel.

"We're both a little far from where home was for us," Delia said softly, gazing out over Rime; "but, I really hope you can think of this as one."

"I think so, ma'am," the darkdancer replied contently.

"Welcome to Malene, Enysa," Delia said kindly.

Trova had come to the entrance of the massive tunnel highway that led into Ramm. The industrial lights that lined its interior were shut off. Amon firmly gripped the darkdancer's hand and shook it. "We'll see you on the other side, lad," he said respectfully.

The darkdancer gave a casual salute; then shadowstepped into the abyss. King Amon, the dwarven warrior, waited several moments, then signaled for the lights to be restored.

Bright lights once again clicked on, eerily echoing down the miles of tunnel. Amon took a deep breath, fastening one of the void collars to his neck and saying, *"Time to go."*

Engines from airships came to life, as did the roar of tanks and vehicles nearby. The king climbed aboard one of the massive battle armors as it rolled by, heading onward into a new breach.

Following Wolves

Three wolvyn hunters had been deployed into Gol, now coming into a brazen range of Evermore itself. The city of Gol is consumed by demons. Jovuk, a black-furred alpha, ripped his blade from the back of a wraith lord. The hunters had ambushed a platoon of undead and demons with enough sleek precision as to dispatch such a high-value target. The wolvyn were running out of space for the trophies and communique they had captured.

"Think they'll give us a title for killing that one?" asked Holen, a tan-furred wolvyn mastiff.

"You're always so concerned with titles," replied Shoshana, a grey-furred wolvyn gamma, looking down the scope of a rather large rifle. "Titles, titles, titles."

"At least they're something to go on your grave," Holen remarked.

"If you're lucky enough to get a grave these days," Shoshana chuckled.

"Anything looking down won't be able to see us through this blizzard," Jovuk grunted, as he lay down next to Shoshana.

"Hopefully, we have better eyes from this distance."

"Indeed so, boss," Shoshana answered. "Actually, quite a bustling place."

"Anything we didn't see in Rime?" Holen inquired, toying with his repeater crossbow.

"Hard to say, but they're definitely mining from where that undead dragon appeared," Shoshana uttered, continuing her spying.

She did her best to follow what seemed to be supply routes, taking note that the south appeared to be the direction of choice.

"Vae'yir," Novak grumbled. "They're moving their manufacturing farther from Shiro."

"Untouchable," Holen remarked.

"For now, at least," Shoshana sighed, with disheartened agreeance.

Then the gamma's ears perked up as she saw a more human-looking individual come into her field of view. Her comrades grew still and silent, practically anticipating the threat Shoshana seemed to sense. A dozen dark portals opened before the figure, and several dozen cloaked humanoids stepped through. Then the lot of them exited from her sight.

She subtly slid back from the soggy mound, saying, "I think we have enough to take back."

The pack agreed, taking their leave from the position as quietly and quickly as they had come. Thankfully, their journey to and across Shiro's border was uneventful. They took off their wet and putrid equipment, warmed up, and soon were transported north. The trip across the small country would serve as a well-deserved rest for the three hunters coming to their destination in the city around sunrise.

As luck would have it, Azotus, the wolvyn warrior chief, was sitting outside The Inn, enjoying a bit of breakfast when the vehicle pulled up across the way. The war marshal could easily see the three wolvyn slumped forward and backwards, still sleeping.

A fellow soldier woke the three, and they each came around, stepping out from the truck. They came over to Azotus and greeted him with salutes, which the war marshal returned.

"You know the menu around here; my tab is still open," Azotus commented.

His hunters certainly took advantage of their chief's generosity, filling up three tables with their orders. The war marshal sat back while his comrades inhaled their meals. The conversation could wait as far as he was concerned.

As the three hunters seemed content enough to sit back in their chairs, Azotus said, "Well, you stayed beyond your assignment. Hopefully, you do have something to say with the bit of worry you caused. You need to see your wife after this, Holen," the war marshal added. Holen lowered his head and ears, nodding. "Sorry, sir."

"Won't happen again, war marshal," Jovuk stated respectfully, "but we surely didn't return empty-handed."

Azotus grinned, motioning for his friend to begin his debriefing. The account of his hunters kept the war marshal quite attentive. He sat quietly and simply listened. If pit forces in Gol were moving anything away from Shiro, it proved that they were planning an inevitable alliance raid on Evermore.

The city of Vae'yir was far out of reach for current military strengths and would be utterly suicidal no matter how one sliced it. Airships were now a precious supply, and none of the standard designs were nearly fast enough to fly bombs in and out. This also seemed to solidify the idea that Shiro could otherwise remain at rest, since everything of the pit's posture in Gol was defensive. However, if allied forces were going into Ramm, it made sense that other plays would be made in response.

When his comrades were finished speaking, Azotus pondered for a moment. "Go and rest," he stated. "I'll send for you in time. You're officially the first of any scouting party to blaze that far into Gol. I'll see that you're equipped a bit more effectively before doing it again."

His hunters saluted him and took their leave. Azotus soon began his leave as well. He left a hefty pouch of coins on a table, though his tab was always open here.

Yuri, the inn attendant, whistled and shouted at the war marshal. "Oye, Azo,'" as he held up the money.

"I'm not the one cleaning that mess," Azotus hollered over his shoulder.

"You're a good pack of hounds to feed, sir," the cook responded.

The war marshal continued down the street, reflecting during the morning breeze and thus concluding that he should speak to Stella, the voidkeeper.

Stella came to Azotus' office in Blackwolf Keep, responding to a cordial summons.

"Please take a seat, ma'am," he kindly grumbled.

The war marshal discussed what his comrades had told him and eventually laid out two prototype airship blueprints. These aircraft were drawn up with void engines in mind, which clearly created a divide in the voidkeeper. Azotus expected Stella's hesitancy and was by no means being pushy.

Visions came to Stella's mind as she examined the blueprints. They were brief but vivid. Her pinkish, purple eyes looked up at Azotus with a subtle hint of sadness in their gaze. Embattled by the idea, a few quiet moments went by as the voidkeeper thought on the notion.

"How long would they take to build?" she quietly asked.

"To get one of either in working order would be quicker than you'd think, as resources and personnel are ready to be allocated," the war marshal replied. Stella clenched her fists, coming to a resolute and bitter decision.

"Begin the work when you can," she humbly stated. "I will provide any level of output that is needed."

The war marshal nodded ever so slightly, aware enough to know this was a slippery slope.

"Sky swords?" Stella uttered, her eyes returning to the drawings before her.

The inevitable future presented itself quite plainly. Then there was a knock on the door. Kora entered as she cradled the infant, Iman'el. Stella and Azotus both came before the babe and knelt respectfully. The infant enjoyed being carried by Kora. Her flowing white fur made the boy smile and laugh.

"Where's his mother?" Azotus asked curiously.

"She's tending to a few minor political matters," Kora replied softly, "so he gets to be my pup for a while--quite an easy job I must say."

Indeed, even in the presence of a wolvyn alpha-like Azotus, the Child simply cooed and looked about. Stella felt a small measure of peace come into her conflicted self, smiling as the Child held her finger.

"What journeys have arrived with you, little one?" she thought to herself. The glow of the void within her glass scars became a shade brighter.

The visions that came to the voidkeeper were of victory and defeat. Indeed, this new generation of aircraft would be a turning point in Harth's history. On one edge of the sword, it was the sort of aerial superiority that would be an equalizer for years to come and, ultimately, an asset to humanity. The other edge was of future conflicts, at which time this technology would be a courier of death between mortal kin.

I always thought it was clever how they held onto some definition of "weaponize." I will give credit where credit is due. Humanity does not literally make a void bomb for a thousand years or so, but I digress. I applaud the voidkeeper for her maturity in advancing such matters, myself quite eager for these machines to be taken to Harth's battlefields.

A forward operations base would quickly be established at Ramm's side of the border as airships continued to touch down barren highways that diverged from the border crossing and as tanks continued to roll into the frostbitten swarmlands. The build-up would be swift and without resistance. The insect hordes of the pit were now reliably clustered in a shelter for warmth. The most concerning matter was the lack of an underworld presence. Alliance forces were educated enough by now regarding the world viper and his capacities.

Trova had gone ahead to a rumored location in Stellahelm, the site of a darkdancer battle that seemed to have ultimately cleared the city of infestation. There was a readily available amount of frozen swarm corpses to confirm the rumors. Some were dead by impressive wounds…others by the cold. The noted refinery was in ruins. It had been leveled and was now covered by the elements. The darkdancer, occasionally glancing around the quiet and snowy place, began to document his findings.

Some static accompanied Amon's voice through the nether. *"Any news, comrade?"* he asked.

"It's secure, but the damage is catastrophic." "To say the least, getting resources in working order here would be a hindrance," the darkdancer replied.

"Dammit," Amon uttered. *"Well, do what you need to do and head back. At least we know we have a bit of room to breathe."*

"Confirmed," Trova answered. The darkdancer went on his way through the streets, simply observing the decimation. As the scale of the conflict became so tangible, Trova found himself struck by a sinking feeling. The darkdancer could practically feel

the fear of the masses who perished here as their screams passed through his mind.

Before continuing a brief expedition of Stellahelm, Trova knelt and offered a prayer for the departed and living alike. There truly was not much to be reported or brought back as evidence in any manner. The city had been sacked quickly, leaving only lackluster remnants. It was a sad and simple situation, which was representative of many dwarven cities and settlements. The darkdancer marked a few points of interest where defenses and fortifications could be advantageously placed. Anything else, he simply marked Stellahelm as "uncontested."

"Blackbeard's Legion" is the name of an elemental mechanical army that rested beneath a military base in Lok'rom, which was about 200 miles northeast of Yarimheim, the capital city of the dwarven kingdom Ramm. Taking "Blackbeard's Legion" was Amon's primary objective, even though he knew it would be the operation that would eventually make them most vulnerable. Open settlements could literally be flattened by artillery and airpower. However, even to contest one of the major cities imbedded in the mountains would truly test alliance efforts.

Only Amon himself--one of royal blood--could activate the million armored soldiers, as well as access the vaults in which they were located. But even the exterior of these vaults was ideal for hives to form. Every route the alliance could take into Lok'rom was suitable for the swarm to still be sheltered. Yarimheim would have to be captured beforehand. The swarm was still a part of an army, and one is wise to remember such a fact. Their soldiers must be stationed at strategic positions.

Blackbeard's Legion was fueled by an old and powerful blood spell. That is, the king's blood would convert into runic energy, proportioned to charge each soldier for a hundred years. In order to retake Ramm, it was an accurate assessment that this legion needed to be secured.

Sapphira, a human military communicator, had summoned A'mi. Standing by Sapphira was a wolvyn mastiff. Sapphire introduced the wolvyn to A'mi, who appeared to be a bit repelled by the wolvyn's naturally ferocious appearance.

"This is Kasslow," Sapphira said with a smile. Kasslow saluted the alchemist. A'mi looked the large wolvyn up and down, curious about his attire.

"I don't mean to be rude," she said timidly, "but you're the first one of your kind I've seen with pilot ranks."

"I'm a quick learner, miss," Kasslow replied humbly with a hardy and accented voice.

"Eli wanted wolvyn pilots for these operations, especially for smaller crews and ships," Sapphira explained. "They're naturally suited for the terrain and conditions and are ideal for the sort of deployments here."

"It'll be fun, comrade," Kasslow added happily. "Our ship has guns and everything else needed for our mission." A'mi sighed and gently rolled her head around, cracking her neck.

"You're the only wolvyn pilot?" she uttered.

"Yes, I am the only wolvyn pilot," Kasslow replied. Shifting her eyes away, Sapphira remarked, "It's an ongoing program, but Eli hand-picked Kasslow for you two."

"I've heard that you work with a darkdancer. That's totally awesome," Kasslow said, giving a thumbs up. A'mi couldn't help but smile at their large furry chum.

"So, how does a wolvyn get so comfortable with aircraft?" the alchemist inquired.

"I was an engineer with Gizmo when I was on the island of Chelsea," Kasslow replied. "I'm familiar with crazy machines."

"Gizmo, the runt cog?" A'mi thought to herself.

Dragons and Gifts

The sanctum of Parraeysia was undergoing its own modernization sweep, a constructive and restorative project. Gizmo found plenty of competent and talented workers among the Ma'ji, although he was often short in his temper with their overall lack of mechanical exposure. Lifts, bridges, and power grids were steadily in the works throughout the great city and broader island. They were scheduled to be completed when Rayne, now a broodmother, awakened from stasis.

Among the growing archives of recovered texts and materials was a sort of guide.

Majim'ati Ma'ji were stewards of a respective dragonkin brood. For a young dragonkin generation, this was a title and position of the highest ranking by Ma'ji historians, caretakers, and instructors. Intellects, warriors, and every discipline in between would be required of anyone entering the Majim'ati ranks. Over the coming months and years, almost half of the existing Ma'ji population would become studious to this cause.

Even with all of the hustle and bustle of returning to Parraeysia, there came an altogether new breath of life. Ma'ji spellflingers, who could only once conjure a few sparks, were finding themselves in control of combative-strength magic. Warriors and bladedancers now commanded increased strength and agility while ghostdancers and shamans received healing hands that could reach into the very spiritual planes. Further, the Skybourne bloodline had once more returned the light to this sanctuary.

Rayne literally stood beside herself, with an astral projection of her mortal body next to her slumbering draconic form. She was in a bit of a daze as she came out of an otherwise indescribable sleep. She was nervously smiling as she laid her hand on the massive dragon. "The dragonsoul blossomed well," remarked a familiar voice. Rayne turned to see Aron Skybourne, an ancient paladin, who was armored in an angelic plate that was a shade brighter than the rest of this phantasmal plane.

"A sturdy, well-rounded figure," the paladin added, glancing about the dragon that dwarfed the two specters. "And about as close to a primordial dragon as I've seen in quite some time. You should be proud, child," he added.

"I doubt I had much to do with it," Rayne replied.

"You'd be surprised," Aron answered. "The vessel spirit is like a mother in and of itself, passing traits on to the dragonsoul."

"Traits?" Rayne inquired curiously.

"Primordial dragons are likened to Celestials Raey of Light and Deth, the destroyer. They are balanced archetypes of their kind," the paladin explained. "For your dragon to resemble such specimens, we can only conclude that it represents balance out of

universal chaos...the sort of balance that was there at the beginning." Rayne looked at the paladin with dumbfounded eyes. Aron stroked his beard and chuckled, "Luckily, the dragonsoul knows its hosts better than they know themselves."

"I still have so many questions," Rayne said quietly. "I could barely tell you what heroes did when all of this began for us."

"And now you're the mother of a resurrected dragonkin nation," the paladin kindly slighted. "Complication has been the name of the game since the fall. To say the least, it made a royal mess of things. The good news is that you'll have ample time to catch up on all that history you've missed."

"Meaning?" Rayne asked. "Well, you're sort of locked in your room for the duration of this," Aron replied, motioning around the massive stasis chamber. Rayne sighed and plopped down on the ground.

Aron conjured a number of ornate tomes before Rayne. "Bloodlines" and "The Gifts" were among the titles. The artistry of the tome, The Gifts, caught Rayne's eye. She reached over and slid the rather hefty text towards her, opening it to the index. "A fun choice, especially to start," Aron remarked. Rayne read down the list and found herself surprised at the actual number and variants of the Heroic Gifts. The Warrior class alone was comprised of twelve branches, with Paladin being one of those branches.

Aron took a seat adjacent to Rayne and began reminiscing in his own way. He noticed Rayne's legitimate interest in "Harth's Heroes," as she continued to skim the pages. "I had four childhood friends that were particularly dear to me throughout my youth," the paladin began.

"I was gifted as a warrior, but I didn't have control over divine energies until Bol'rel, the second-born archangel, bestowed them on me." Rayne looked up, attentive to Aron's story.

The paladin smirked. "He saved my life, and I hated him for it for a while."

"Why?" Rayne asked.

"Because he called me out on my stupidity and for my arrogance that got three of my friends killed," Amon replied, "and he reminded me that I failed in my duty to protect them. While these gifts have strengthened humanity among these conflicts, they call their vessels to unspeakable danger and nightmarish deaths. So many heroes have met their end, alone, battered, broken, humiliated, and desecrated. Countless others that survive horrific encounters have simply slipped into the crowds, their will too scarred to ever rejoin the ongoing battle." Rayne closed the tome and gently set it aside, pausing before she softly asked, "Did you avenge your friends?"

"Regardless of what my intention was, it was dwarfed by the damage I had already caused," Aron replied humbly.

"Heroes have families and loved ones too. These tragedies make waves, child. The girl that survived, disappeared. She rejected everything about the Light after that day, and she was never able to be recovered." Rayne's heart sank as she recognized the magnitude of Aron's statements.

"The dragonsoul is a gift, Rayne," the Paladin reassured. "You have openly accepted it, and soon you will be a medium for it to reverberate throughout the world. You can save many."

It was a mild night as Gizmo lay in a hammock on the grand pavilion where the reflection of stars floated on the waves below. Twitch, a spider-like mechanical body, built by Gizmo, was off elsewhere with the shifts of workers for these hours. Radagast, a male wolvyn priest, was attempting to find anything salvageable in the ancient kingdom of *Azkelon*. Several Ma'ji scholarly types were still about the place as well, categorizing and organizing what was turning out to be a relatively healthy stock of survived information.

The shattered land of Azkelon has long been obscured to even legendary seers. The former continent's annihilation left a noticeable blip in Harth's timeline. The situation on whatever fragments of land remained was entirely unknown to the mortal realm, and no knowledge had been handed down to humanity in any such regard. It was a place of myths, even foolishly sought out as a place of some hidden fortune. Truthfully, the scary stories were the most accurate--a place where angels still gave their mortal forms in combat--a place of chaos, torment, and bending realities.

One story says that the very gates of the pit opened among Azkelon's kingdoms and that a massive dragonkin army was sent to aid every manner of righteous soldiers and beings there. But the corruption of the evil broodmother, Mwyrryn, and her betrayal painted a much darker picture that day. Perhaps there is a mission that remains to be completed?

Zeit, a dragonkin alpha warrior, had become the instructor to a number of awakening heroes, particularly those on the melee side of the spectrum. He was a fine master from whom warriors could learn. Omoori, a lightweight warrior and keen on protective discipline, was among the blossoming heroes. Omoori and four other Ma'ji were currently sparring with their dragonkin sensei. Realistically speaking, the dragonkin alpha's size and speed were unmatchable. The up-and-coming Ma'ji heroes were quickly learning what it meant to freeze in the face of such a monstrosity in combat.

The dragonkin would stop his heavy glaive within an inch of a hero before reengaging his other opponents. The student would step away so that another could enter the melee. Even aspiring spellflingers were able to truly explore their powers against the dragonkin's mighty armor. The plate pieces were custom fit for Zeit and were designed by Gizmo as anti-freaking-everything. The weight of the armor was balanced, which provided maximum protection without hindering the dragonkin's impressive agility.

A young, red-maned Ma'ji stepped into the ring, nodding towards a fellow hero who had died. Besuu Umsook, a promising and ferocious warrior, charged the dragonkin. His two broadswords met Zeit's glaive with a sturdy ring. Besuu began an offensive that certainly had Zeit's attention. The dragonkin knowingly took the bait, curious to know how his other opponents would seize the room to breathe.

An impressive flurry of a dozen strikes was exchanged between Zeit and Besuu before the dragonkin came in for a clench. "Hurry!" Zeit happily grumbled. Besuu found himself near the edge of the ring. His eyes were scanning to see if the other heroes would help. Zeit broke the deadlock, throwing his glaive at a mage who was on the verge of releasing a powerful fireball. The student had to escape from the ring, and he shouted in frustration as he brushed himself off.

The glaive returned to Zeit like a boomerang, just in time to parry another onslaught from Besuu. Again and again, their steel met. It became a duel…a spectacle for a few moments. Besuu was truly gifted with impressive strength, but Zeit was correct in his suggestion. The Ma'ji alpha fought well, eventually beyond his body's own ability. His sword simply slipped from his hands. Besuu staggered as his muscles practically shut down. Zeit held up his armored claw, motioning for the session to cease.

Dehza

The sun barely began to peak over the horizon when Yana came out to sit on the balcony. Her bare body was draped in a sheet, and smoke was streaming from her skunkweed cigarette. The balcony faced east, where, in the distance, the jagged peaks of Ramm were quite visible. The summoner simply looked towards the swarmlands. Her kind, azure eyes were complimented by the rising sun.

Bael, whose assignment was to assist with rubble removal in a portion of Rime for the day, was dressing into civilian clothes. Rubble removal was a common duty for reapers. "Where are you headed today?" Yana inquired from the balcony.

"Southeast merchant sector," Bael replied, with a sly grin on his face as he fastened his belt. Yana continued to gaze out over the town, puffing the cigarette every now and again.

"You were talking in your sleep last night," Bael remarked.

The summoner's eyes widened as she glanced over her shoulder to see her husband confidently leaning against the balcony doorway. "Who is Dehza?" he asked, with a smirk across his expression.

"Nothing," Yana replied plainly.

"Nothing? Or no one?" Bael rebutted in kind, putting his arm around Yana as he sat beside her. The summoner, staring back at Bael, kept herself tightly bound in the sheet. The reaper sighed, subtly taking some of the sheet in his fingers.

Bael, with one swift motion, stole the sheet from around Yana. He positioned himself in front of the doorway, blocking the view of the naked summoner. Yana crouched down, hiding behind the bench and out of the view of people below. "Bael," she quietly exclaimed, "what the fuck?"

"Take off that pretty wrap around your hand and show me your scar, and I'll give you the sheet back," the reaper casually replied. Yana huffed and quickly undid the silk covering.

"You could've just spoken up," she grunted, as she revealed her left palm.

The glowing scar flashed, and a fiery dragon's eye opened in the summoner's hand. Bael knelt and covered his wife with the sheet. "A deal is a deal," he said, clearly in awe at the sight.

"I'm friends with a bunch of nosey people," the summoner uttered, leering away from the other two.

"I definitely understand why you didn't want to use this hand for certain things now," Bael remarked. Yana blushed.

"That's how you're going to start the conversation?" she asked, rather furiously.

"Hello, Bael," Dehza said. Bael was a bit surprised by the childlike voice that manifested from the fiery eye. He nodded back at the eye in response.

"You really didn't intend to keep this a secret for long, did you?" Yana frustratedly uttered.

"Of course not. Humanity is awful at keeping secrets," Dehza replied, "but the lack of attention has allowed me to better settle into these surroundings."

"I haven't heard your name before," the reaper said. "I'm better known by my celestial form, Deth," Dehza answered.

"The one that was going to kill everybody?" Bael remarked.

"Yes," Dehza affirmed.

"Interesting," Bael muttered.

"He's using me to hang out on Harth," Yana plainly stated, and added, "that's pretty much the relationship."

"I assumed your composure would remain relatively unphased in our present situation, Bael," Dehza said.

"You're a fine partner for Yana." Bael raised an eyebrow and replied with a slightly confused, "Thanks."

Yana seemed a bit insulted by the friendliness of the exchange but was easily disarmed by her husband's reassuring smile.

While the summoner and the celestial have had a variety of conversations up until now, Dehza's influence over Yana's physical body had been the topic more than once. Only once did he try to take over what portion he could, and that was for a legitimate experimental exercise. I have to say, as I am thinking about how to explain this, there are many colorful ways to describe the occasion. Aside from the slight shapeshifting of her hand, just watching the girl wrestle her own wrist into a chokehold was noteworthy of that evening.

Dehza could, in fact, manipulate the summoner's entire left arm, but there was no need. He had been honest enough with Yana thus far.

Bael continued preparing for his work, chuckling to himself. "I guess I should be glad that you're laughing," Yana said, ultimately relieved by the overall situation.

"I wasn't necessarily expecting this. I'll say that much," Bael replied. "Maybe something to do with your gift. But, harboring a celestial?"

"Like I asked for this," Yana mumbled.

"What have I given you to complain about?" Dehza rebuked.

"The fact that I have an eye in my hand, to start?" Yana proclaimed.

"You're too sensitive," Dehza sighed.

"TOO SENSITIVE?" the summoner hollered. Bael kissed Yana and headed for the door.

"We can have a nice Q&A about this later," he said with a wink. Yana, with a cute and pouty expression, leered at the dragon's eye.

"I love you," she quietly said.

"Love you too," Bael happily called from the doorway. There was a moment of silence while the remaining two stared at each other.

"Are you going to try to strangle me again, Yana?" Dehza asked.

"You're such a dick," Yana sighed, lying back on the pillows.

"Is that what you're upset about? Always having a dick in your hand?" Dehza replied plainly. Yana looked at the fiery eye with exasperation.

"I'm sorry. Being imprisoned by Dom'rel, the bad angel, for so long has probably taken a subtle toll on my character," the celestial added.

"I'm sure you were an absolute gem, to begin with," Yana replied sarcastically.

"Your wife, Phoenicia, must be the utter symbol of patience," she added in an utter.

"Oh, that reminds me," Dehza stated.

"Hmm?" the summoner replied curiously.

"We need to go to the tree," the celestial answered.

The Firebird's Shade, Phoenicia, the Phoenix guardian's parting gift to humanity.

"There will be a handful of fruits and flowers that are unidentifiable with modern records," Dehza continued.

"I will have to…" Before allowing Dehza to continue, the summoner replied with an unimpressed glance.

"No one will think, 'O, look at Yana, carrying a basket full of all the things we don't know anything about'."

"We'll simply mark the locations," Dehza assured. "Our envoy can gather them at night."

"Envoy?" Yana asked.

"The darkdancer that remained in Shiro," Dehza answered. "I'm sure she's in some proximity to Lady Aki'rah, so get dressed."

The two eventually entered Rime's streets, catching transport to what would eventually be called "The Raven's Nest." Yana had only been to the beautiful complex a few times, and she was astonished by the progress made on the mansion. Even Dehza was surprised. Overall, the complex covered a 20-acre clearing on the cliffs overlooking Rime. Six column-lined paths diverged from the mansion, and the four-leveled exterior was gently lit by arcane lanterns…a fine touch against the dark stone of which the structure was made.

Delia was quick to meet the summoner outside. The two embraced and exchanged greetings. Yana explained the reason for their visit, after which Yana introduced Delia to Dehza. "I'll certainly relay your request to Enysa when she returns," Delia graciously agreed.

"Has she found any suitable candidates?" Dehza inquired. Delia shook her head.

"No one yet. Unfortunately, I don't think she can focus. She's worried about her friends in Ramm."

"Onyx, another destroyer celestial, shares your observation," Dehza stated.

"Enysa is young and inexperienced; however, The Melancholy intervened to stay her nightmare. I've only known him to do such a thing on four other occasions while mingling with humanity. Clearly, The Melancholy has interests in the young shadow."

"Come with us to the Firebird's Shade," Yana suggested happily.

"It'll be good for both of us to just be out and about." Delia agreed, sighing, "I suppose I've been a bit of a hermit lately, BUT I've had something made for you. Come inside for a minute," she added. She motioned for the summoner to follow her. The three went inside the mansion, walking down several hallways and eventually entering a cluttered parlor.

"It took a bit longer than we expected. Some of the materials are fairly new or flat-out rare," Delia remarked, opening a large chest.

Yana waited eagerly for her surprise. Delia laid out a shadowcraft regalia, fashioned quite accurately after what darkdancers once wore to royal courts and proceedings. The coat and battle robes were predominantly jet black and adorned with heightened accents of scarlet to pay tribute to the summoner's maiden name.

"We can alter the left glove. It wasn't tailored with your companion in mind," Delia chuckled.

Yana was already undressing and putting on the shadowcraft vestments. Delia, spot-on in the summoner's personal taste of attire, remarked, "I've learned that darkdancers, on a few occasions throughout history, have been bodyguards to legendary summoners; and what Mirym did is, I guess, a tribute to a few variables." As Yana looked herself over in a mirror, she was most pleased with the outfit. The summoner tied her hair back, smiling as she said, "It's incredible, Delia. Thank you!"

"It makes you look like a badass on the town as well as being battle-ready," Delia replied in kind.

Dehza's muffled voice came from beneath the dark leather glove. "You've clearly been doing some research. I'm impressed and pleased that such information has survived." There was a knock on the parlor doorway. Yana gasped as she turned to see a well-dressed skeleton standing there.

"Ah, Jeeves," Delia kindly greeted. "This is Yana."

"An honor to finally meet you, ma'am," the butler replied with a bow.

"Finally?" Yana uttered.

Delia explained: "Jeeves was at the Shiro chapterhouse, which is where much of the material I've accumulated has been stored. This guy is a wealth of knowledge." Yana smiled and gave a slight bow.

"Forgive me for being startled. You'd think I'd be more adept to such things by now," she said, with a faint, nervous giggle.

"The Chapter spoke well of you, Yana," Jeeves replied politely. "My service was not discontinued upon their departure, so it continues here."

"We're going to step out for a while," Delia stated.

"How's the lab coming?" she asked in an afterthought.

"Eighty-eight percent efficiency, Lady Aki'rah," Jeeves humbly replied. "All our facilities are coming along on schedule, and our merchant lines have been established."

"You're a blessing, Jeeves," Delia said, high-fiving the skeletal butler as they exited the parlor. Delia, Yana, (and Dehza) left for the Firebird's Shade, which would be over an hour's drive from their current location.

Their presence among the people certainly drew attention, but the crowds never clamored or became unruly. The Firebird's Shade was now an area that covered dozens of square miles, a place flourishing with agriculture and growing residential districts. The tree itself was large and mighty enough that entire teams of experts spent hours a day among the canopy, which was nearly a thousand-foot drop to the ground below.

Needless to say, the status of the two gave them access to the more official storage and sorting areas. They used the excuse, "We just wanted to see how things are going," allowing eager guides to give the ladies a tour of the facilities. Dehza was essentially a radial scanner who subtly alerted the summoner to materials of interest. Yana managed to mark the point with an invisible ink, a tracking chemical used by darkdancers. She used a subtle dot here and there, so as to go unnoticed by their rather jovial escorts.

Dehza directed the guides by leading Yana to where he needed to go, thus leaving the questions and conversations to his capable companions.

There were 51 items of which Dehza made a note. Some were simply tasty edibles, while others held alchemical, weaponizable, or medicinal properties.

Back at the Raven's Nest, Enysa had returned in a frenzy of joy. A curious cog followed beside her. "Helloooo?" Enysa called out from the entryway.

"Hmm? I guess Delia left?" she uttered. The boy was clean-cut, coming up on his eighteenth mortal year. The cog gave an impressed whistle while his eyes, through thin-framed spectacles, were looking at the grand complex. Enysa began running down a hall, hollering, "I FOUND ONE, I FOUND ONE, I FOUND ONE!"

The darkdancer returned a few moments later, carrying Jeeves like a plank under her arm. She stood the butler before the cog, who carried a sort of noble, yet lost dog look about him. Jeeves adjusted his attire as he moved from his unorthodox mode of transportation. He conjured a pen and pad while spectacles of arcane fire from Horus, the cog and a human male darkdancer, manifested before his eye-sockets. Jeeves glanced the cog over while he scribbled down a handful of notes. "Name?" the butler kindly inquired.

"Horus," the cog replied.

"Did lady Enysa bring you here against your will?" Jeeves asked. Enysa's expression instantly changed to one of insult. Horus grinned and replied, "No."

"Have you received any instruction as to the nature of this path? Of this place?" Jeeves continued to question.

"Umm, maybe some?" Enysa chimed in.

"But I felt his thingy! THE thingy…our thingy, the tether!" she fumbled, blushing as much as a darkdancer could. There was an awkward pause after the blunder. Eventually, Jeeves returned to his inquiry.

"Family?" he asked. "Maybe somewhere in Zuhetta but deceased to the best of my knowledge," Horus replied.

"You're free to browse the premise at your leisure," Jeeves stated, finishing his notes.

"I would suggest that the lady further inform you on the more immediate proceedings of the ritual." Horus glanced at Enysa, replying, "I said I'd help, right? I'd rather not have time to overthink."

"He's so cool!" Enysa exclaimed graciously.

"My only other inquiry would be to you then, Shadow. Are you capable of handling such proceedings?" Jeeves asked.

Enysa nodded. "Ah, yes. Lady Delia did leave a task for you," Jeeves added, explaining the system in place for this particular grocery gathering.

"I suggest the ritual wait until after the request is fulfilled, since this would give master Horus some time to settle in…if, in fact, he is set in his will." The terms were agreeable to all the parties.

It was dusk when Delia and Yana returned. They went to a master's lounge where quite an impressive bar was available. Delia was pleasantly surprised to find Enysa and her prospective subject. Enysa waved the others over, introducing them to Horus. She also promised to attend to their grocery list when the sun was down. The Lady Aki'rah was excited about their new member but remained refined in her composure.

Yana looked like she had seen a ghost when she first saw Enysa. Enysa looked like she could have been Mirym's sister. "Are you okay, ma'am?" Enysa curiously asked. Yana smiled and gave a slight bow.

"Yes. You just reminded me of someone," she said kindly. Enysa gasped happily, "Of Mirym?" she asked.

"Trova had mentioned 'a Mirym,' a human female darkdancer, from his transformation. She said to tell you, 'Hi'." Yana swelled with emotion and was unable to keep a few tears from escaping her beautiful eyes.

The summoner embraced the darkdancer tightly. This was clearly something deeper for Yana than the others present seemed to recognize. Jeeves watched with intrigue, noting Enysa's human response to such a gesture. Horus had heard enough stories about the darkdancers to confirm his own assumptions. He did notice, however, that Enysa was hardly the sort of unfeeling monster her kind had been called.

"So, this is Enysa?" Dehza asked. Jeeves, Horus, and Enysa instantly turned their attention to the summoner. Yana sighed.

"Could you please start giving me a heads-up before you do this?" as she frustratedly removed her glove.

"Oh, my," Jeeves uttered respectfully. "What have you done to yourself, sire?"

Yana held out her hand to the group, looking away in protest. "I see," Dehza pondered.

"That's why they're always so similar." Enysa was clearly the object of the celestial's curiosity as he watched Enysa's glowing red eyes shifting from one person to another.

"Mirym's mortal charisma remained more intact. The celestial Onyx also intervened in her nightmare," Dehza stated.

"Yes, they've all been remarkably similar to Onyx's wife, Shynza. I especially remember Shynza's physique. She was extremely high energy and was the light that often kept Onyx more docile and reasonable."

Jeeves, keen on the rather sad plot of history, actually stepped away. The rest of the group was speechless. "Yana, I wonder if the angel Miri'el noticed when she rescued you?" Dehza continued.

"Shynza was her name. In the early wars and in many cases of dire and deadly circumstances, she was known for gifting mortal vessels with the various disciplines. That is why none of you bore heroic gifts before your transformation, which would have otherwise allowed you to carry on the shadow raven's own M.O. Together, Onyx's sorrow and his intelligence work in remarkable ways," he complimented.

"She is a fallen?" Horus asked.

"Dom'rel betrayed Onyx and killed Shynza because he knew she knew what he'd actually done," Dehza replied. "The guardian's soul will be recoverable. Nonetheless, she suffered for a long time."

"Recoverable?" Yana echoed.

"Dom'rel will be wounded for his schemes," Dehza replied plainly. The fiery eye then turned back to Horus, who straightened his posture and glasses.

"I'll be curious about the ritual's effects on you," the celestial stated. "Ancient darkdancers did retain more of their natural character by process of dilution and corruption that often led to the less feeling composition of later generations. The variables that instated this chapter are indeed unique." Looking at Enysa, he asked, "Can I see one of the blood vials?"

Enysa unnecessarily bowed and rushed out of the room. Until the darkdancer returned about 30 seconds later, a bit of an awkward silence remained. Enysa presented the vial before the eye, who inspected the concoction for a few moments. "Bol'rel must have used a significant cleansing spell," Dehza stated. "The ethereal residues left behind are magnificently well balanced."

"It seems like we could umm…kind of use you around here, Yana," Delia remarked. "What's your schedule like these days?"

"She's quite available," Dehza replied. Yana was offended by the celestial's instant override of anything she could say, but Dehza was correct.

"Can we stay for the boy's ritual, Yana?" Dehza inquired.

"No!" Yana exclaimed, putting the glove back on her hand.

"You've done enough for one day." Enysa glanced outside and saw that the sun had set enough to conduct her operation.

"If you haven't used your shadowstep that much, I would suggest that you take extra time to train it," Dehza remarked, muffled by the glove.

"Yes, sir!" Enysa replied eagerly.

The shadowstep is a trademark ability of the darkdancers that allows them to phase through shade and darkness. The rate of travel, which is known to reach levels equitable to instant teleportation, is entirely up to its user. The ability carries the darkdancer in and out of the physical world like dolphins soaring through the ocean.

Enysa was a bold one when she wanted to be. The cliffs were veiled by the night, and the darkdancer wanted to take a path straight down. She did well for about 300 yards but lost her footing on a loose stone. With a lengthy tumble and a twirl or two, Enysa slammed into a large boulder. The force was hefty enough to move the tons of stone forward, thus causing them to roll down towards the city. The darkdancer, quickly realizing she needed to act, staggered from the impact.

Opening out her hand, she leapt after the massive stone. Just before numerous projectiles of runic energy shot forth, red rings of light and glyphs surrounded her hand and wrist. Enysa watched in awe at her own abilities as the rock blew apart into harmless pebbles. "It's like the spell knew what to do," she said to herself. She smiled in relief and in joy at the spectacle. The darkdancer gathered herself and then phased back into the shadow.

Runic energy, or blood energy, is a force granted to darkdancers upon their successful transformation. This "living power" is known to a few classifications. It is versatile and very destructive. Runic spells, which are as natural as a reflex, are extensions of the host. In this case, the spell acted on Enysa's situation and senses, thus destroying the threat in the most efficient way.

Enysa avoided any other blunders en route to her destination, but she nearly vomited when she arrived. "I guess I need to start doing laps," she muttered.

"Ugh, I'm ok. I just need to find the markers." The darkdancer walked through the facilities, gathering one of each tagged item. With her shadowstepping, the tighter quarters caused her to knock over several things along the way. She felt obligated to leave a note at one of the scenes.

"Sorry," it read, with a smiley-face drawn in a corner.

It was midnight by the time Yana made it back to her residence. Exhausted, she plopped down, face-first, on a couch. "Want anything?" Bael casually asked, while drawing at a desk.

"No, thank you," Yana replied, her voice muffled by pillows.

"You good?" he continued.

"I'm good," she answered. There was a brief pause as Bael considered something.

"Can I ask you a question?" he politely inquired. Yana sat up and turned to him, nodding, remembering Thulo's suggestion. Bael came and sat next to her, rather bluntly asking, "Had you ever tried to kill yourself before summoning Raey?" Yana was not offended by any means, but she also wasn't sure how to really begin. Bael held her hands, saying, "You knew what the cost was, and you didn't hesitate for an instant."

Yana embraced Bael as a few gentle tears began to fill her eyes. "By the way, I'm liking the black," Bael added, remarking on the shadowcraft regalia. The summoner sniffled and smiled, wiping her eyes. Yana nodded, softly saying, "Twice. Rayne saved me once. I was about to jump, and she pulled me back. I suppose the Light spared me on the other occasion. Both were in Gol some years back. I always had so many questions, and I guess I wanted answers sooner rather than later." Bael rested his forehead against hers, gently replying, "I'm happy that you're here."

"I am, too," Yana replied in kind. "I'm glad to have you."

"Ditto," Bael said with a grin. The two kissed for a moment or two before Bael said in an uplifting manner, "You don't talk about Rayne as much as you should. I know that you two were close."

Yana smiled, comfortably lying against Bael. "She was my hero. She always had my protection in mind." Yana's eyes were stoically overrun with tears. Bael would do his best to keep her dry as she continued.

"She threw herself in harm's way for me more than once. I still remember how I felt after one occasion when we found her lying on the side of the street. I don't want to go into detail about her condition. What they'd done to her--the *depravity* of humanity has no limits."

Bael saw a sudden and very subtle shift in Yana's eyes. She became colder in her own way but nonetheless smiled lovingly at him. "We ended up with Skarg because of her, and it proved to be a safe place to be," Yana continued. "I gave up trying to figure out who his connections were a long time ago. I'm pretty sure that Rayne knows."

"You could go ask her," Bael suggested, lightly stroking Yana's hair.

"Rayne is asleep," Dehza commented, certainly striking down any further mood that was to be had. Regardless, Yana and Bael laughed at the interruption.

"With the appropriate ritual, you may be able to speak with her," Dehza suggested.

"She might be able to shed light on a few matters at hand by now--even military projections."

"Do you want me to see my friend, or do you just want to go because you're curious and now you have an excuse?" Yana accused.

"Either," Dehza replied.

"Gives me a great excuse for a vacation," Bael chimed in.

"Given our current layout, Parraeysia is technically the safest location on Harth," Dehza stated. It is a Dragonkin homeland, basically an island sanctuary. "It would be illogical to refuse this trip."

"I'm glad to have your assurances, sir," Yana sarcastically replied. Bael listened with amusement at the exchange.

"You should be," Dehza plainly rebuked.

"To have such interaction with a mighty celestial is an honor," Bael laughed, "…just to hear a mighty celestial coming from that tiny voice."

"I know, right?" Yana agreed.

Hollow Places

An expansive exoskeleton of defenses was quickly being established beyond the Rammen side of the tunnel. This initial base, "The Gate," would cover over 200,000 acres. Major operations were still in waiting as vehicles and personnel continued to accumulate. A handful of smaller assault groups had cleared several towns near the parameter, yet they were finding little excitement in the snowy remains. A few shots here and there rang out, mostly from startled soldiers coming across a frozen swarm corpse.

King Amon was alone. As he looked over a model of Ramm, his mind raced between grief, anger, and tactics. Some minutes passed, and the king's anger finally prevailed. He flipped the heavy table, scattering the contents. Amon's personal guards, who were outside his tent, took several steps away in their respective directions. One of the guards had already borne a scar from trying to intervene during one of their king's outbursts.

Battle always brings uncertainty. Amon was as prepared as any commander could be in such a situation, but every strategy he had devised was now being rethought. The world viper was a new enemy, and the concept of the underworld's expanses made Amon question everything he thought he knew about his homeland-- about what was truly beneath it.

A'mi, Kasslow, and Trova were situated in the northern hangars. A'mi, the resident alchemist, was the only one who panicked by the larger artillery that sounded intermittently. "Calm down, good lord," the darkdancer casually uttered. His boots were propped up on supplies to be loaded on to their airship. A'mi was certainly embarrassed but still felt justified in her fear.

"Have you always been so jumpy?" Kasslow inquired.

"Some people are still somewhat normal, and I've been through some shit," A'mi spitefully defended.

Glancing up from a scavenged tome, Trova added, "We can't have you shouting like that on our outings."

"Yes, sir," A'mi pouted. The darkdancer grinned and put down the book.

"How's your work coming along?" he asked. The alchemist smiled and went for her stash, eagerly returning with various items cradled in her arms. The darkdancer sat forward, attentively looking over the haul.

"I've got all the basic remedies and stabilizers good to go," A'mi happily explained, as she carefully set the items down individually. "Your various powders, antidotes, etcetera…"

Getting on all fours to sniff the cache, Kasslow joined the two. "The pocket-portal?" Trova inquired. The alchemist scratched her head. "Um…I mean the equation is there, but I'm missing components," A'mi timidly replied.

"What components?" the darkdancer asked. A'mi felt odd about the request she had to make. "The blood of a living summoner," she said quietly.

"How much?" Trova, amused by the notion, asked.

"A pint should make two," A'mi replied.

"A pint?" Trova echoed, almost laughing out loud.

"You could just kill her and make ten," Kasslow joked. Then the wolvyn's ears perked up as he heard someone approaching the hangar door. Sapphira, bundled in a thick coat, turned the corner. Trova could not have asked for better timing as Sapphira was among those already assigned a void collar. Sapphira barely greeted the group before Trova made his request.

Sapphira's expression was priceless. "A pint?" she exclaimed. "All at once?"

"I know. It's kind of a morbid request," A'mi said. Sapphira sighed, putting in her earpiece.

"Give them whatever they need," she uttered to herself. The other three simply waited while Sapphira spoke with several people over various frequencies. With each individual, she had to explain and give them their clearances for this odd request. Sapphira began to look pouty as a handful of those she spoke with mocked her--thinking it was a joke.

The call began to drag on, and boredom developed to the point that Trova asked if Kasslow could fit A'mi's head in his mouth. Surprisingly, A'mi agreed to the exercise. Observation soon showed that the wolvyn would be able to decapitate the girl with a bite, albeit Kasslow still had to strain a tad to open his jaws that wide. Eventually, Sapphira rejoined the conversation, saying, "I guess it's doable. They'll pass on the request to Delia." Trova recognized the name and was intrigued that this sort of request would be funneled to her.

"Is Delia a friend of yours?" he asked.

"Oh, Yeah! We're both friends of Yana," Sapphira replied happily. Trova lit a dragonskunk cigar, smirking at Mirym's request going through his head.

The mortals could feel Ramm buzzing. The swarm huddled into every corner of every town and city. Dwarven bones littered those desecrated places. The very walls and ceilings pulsed with their movements while toppled buildings served as a shelter for the larger ones. Dom'rel, the bad angel (satan), had placed his pieces; now our allies would calculate theirs.

Baaltha, in earlier times, had killed his father, the king of Gol. Since then, he had maintained his dominion over almost two-thirds of Malene. His orders were carried out by all manner and ranks of monsters. Even Elo'ell, the fallen angel of death, had recently been gifted to Baaltha's regiments.

Deep Wounds

Os'rel's decimation of Vcil'Tasha was a true blow to the terrani race. It left a hemorrhage among the broader alliance that realistically could not be plugged. Overgrowth had already been identified in the former Veil, leaving little time to execute any sort of a plan. Veil'Liia, another terrani elf city, was now at a particular disadvantage since it had to share a massive highway with Veil'Tasha. Veil'Liia was certainly to be doomed at the hands of an underworld onslaught.

The instantaneous loss of one Veil prompted the evacuation of Veil'Liia to the remaining two, Veil'Umbra and Veil'Xaari. They would be the last points of resistance, or maybe future insertion. Ultimately, if need be, Veil'Liia's citizens would be torn from their homes. The evacuation was bitter and woeful, as it was a strike against the very pride of the terrani elves. Many spirits were broken in the process.

Thousands of terrani would eventually go to Dan-hali. Some had already been sent, simply to spread out chances for the survival of the elven people. There was an understandable frustration in the alliance regarding Mol'do, as to why they were still seemingly cut off. Swae had answered the questions as best she could, but her honesty struck fear into those she told. "There are two pylons assigned to Mol'do: one is here at Dan-hali, and the other is northeast of Tristen," she had explained. "For any consideration to be given, the pylon at Tristen would need to be cleansed, regardless of whatever evil stays there. There is at least one presence that I can feel glancing at me every now and then."

The very nether around the continent of Mol'do was unstable at best. A large enough portal in the atmosphere could become a catalyst to a very destructive reaction, thus negating such methods of reinforcements. Sheth'rel, a female archangel, was correct in her statements regarding the pylon at Tristen. Activating the system would corrupt access to the void rails across Harth. Swae's solemn preponderance of the variables quickly halted the previous zealous voices of mobilization.

One night, Swae slipped away from the evening crowds in Dan-hali. She was overwhelmed and had concluded this was her problem to handle. She soared through Mol'do's darkness and onward into Tristen. The archangel's fears were realized as she passed through a barrier around the province, which caused her to lose her flight and come to a skidding halt. It was a hurricane of nether, raw power, void disturbances, and temporal pressures. This place had been wired to obliterate half the world or more and was detonable at the source's will. Spreading her scarlet wings, the archangel shouted defiantly. Light and lightning burst from her person.

"BASTAAARD!" Swae yelled, once again soaring through the storm like a bullet. As she pierced through Tristen towards the old temple, the weight of the storm grew stronger against her. Her radiancy always increased to match the pressure for which she was under. She was now furiously charging onward. The archangel came to a swift halt outside the desecrated site, with electricity striking the ground as it pulsed from her body.

"HEROD!" she called out, her eyes fixed on the doors to the cathedral above.

The door slowly opened. A lumbering being—a primordial dragonkin-omega with four wings folded like a shroud around him--stepped out atop the steps. The guardian, calm and confident, called back. "Third-born, you're not stupid enough to come here for a fight. Your petty alliance would do well to stay clear of my affairs." The archangel drew her saber and flew at the guardian; but Herod, the dragonkin omega, met her just as swiftly in mid-air. Their very momentum created a shockwave as they met. Swae was not even allowed to miss her mark before the guardian's elbow landed square on the side of her head.

Landing over her, the primordial sent the archangel to the ground with earth-shattering force. "That was a mistake, Swae. Perhaps your reckless actions are deserving of some consequences." Even if Swae twitched to make a move, the guardian's fist landed squarely in her face, this time knocking her down. The ground behind her head cracked from the impact. In that blow, Swae was too disoriented to think about continuing. Herod, spreading his four wings wide, lifted the archangel into the air by her vestments. "Arrogance is unbefitting of you, Sheth'rel," he grumbled.

Swae's ears were still ringing from the blow, and a bit of blood dripped from the relatively small cut. "If you yield now and recognize your mistake in coming here, I'll let you leave with what injuries you currently bear," Herod calmly declared, as he held the archangel in the air. Swae could only agree. Her legs were weak after Herod released her. Grumbling, the guardian turned away towards the steps.

"The devil is foolish to think that what he started is entitled to him, alone, so begone." Swae spat her blood on the ground and shouted after Herod, "Vengeance has regained nothing for you! As of now, NOTHING you do could rewrite your name."

"Then why are you still wondering about the divine energies I've retained?" Herod replied over his shoulder. "Dom'rel stole from me, so I've stolen from him. Bol'rel took the head of my wife, so I will take his."

"She betrayed you in the same way she betrayed the Light!" Swae responded. Herod's body and wings became like steel as he turned back towards the archangel, roaring, "SHE WAS EXECUTED WITHOUT ANY DEFENSE! I do not need a lecture from one of your kind about mercy."

"AND YOU CAN LECTURE ABOUT JUSTICE? HONOR?" Swae rebuked him with all the strength she could muster.

"I have not directly shed mortal blood. The only one of your kin that I put down had engaged me in direct combat. Their dispatch was well within the bounds of war," Herod answered. "Your kind started all of this. How any of you can still be counted as trusted among eternity is beyond comprehension?"

"You've become so blind," Swae uttered, as she wiped the blood running down from her forehead. "You're a madman who has stood by while countless have been slaughtered."

"Just as you stood by while an innocent life was taken?" Herod shouted.

"She was your friend, Sheth'rel. She held you in the highest regard, and you did NOTHING." Swae fought back the tears. She began to speak but refrained from responding.

With that, Herod continued up to the doors and out of sight. Swae could say or do nothing further. She soon took a flight out of Tristen and met far less resistance than she had when entering. Swae could instantly tell when she was outside of this powerful torrent, but even so, she came to a rather messy landing. The archangel swelled with emotion. The throbbing and ringing in her head only fed the utter defeat she felt. She silently wept at seeing the desolation. At some point, however, she felt her crying was freeing in its own way.

Littlefeather, a messenger angel, appeared with a medical kit. "Come on, sit up for me," he said kindly. Swae sniffled and wiped her golden eyes, sitting so that her brother could tend to her injuries.

"We cannot have you going back looking like that. The people there deserve that much," Littlefeather stated plainly.

"This kind of bullshit can't happen again, Swae. What the hell did you think would happen?" he asked as he applied a healing agent to the cuts and the likely bruising.

"Sorry," Swae uttered. Littlefeather sighed, motioning for his sister to stand.

"Just ask…the next time you're so damn curious," he politely scolded.

"You think something so obvious hasn't been under observation? Herod made a clean getaway with unbelievable gains to his own strength by courtesy of Dom'rel's own doings. The dude is doing what he does at his own level; that is, at least as far as the current conflict is concerned." Sheth'rel remained quiet as she brushed herself off and adjusted her attire.

"Honestly, obtaining this area, without fighting him for it, would be ideal," Littlefeather said candidly.

"You can't be serious?" Swae respectfully protested.

"I don't think even Herod really knows what he wants, much less how to go about getting whatever it might be," her brother explained.

"He made it pretty obvious," Swae mumbled.

"You know, that lost your brother a spot on the council," Littlefeather replied.

"He lost a few things after the Father was done with him," Swae chuckled.

"Yeah, crazy times," Littlefeather sighed before continuing on topic.

"Look, we're aware of the situation, sis. Your place is currently in Dan-hali, and that's not a friendly request," he added, brandishing a note. Swae read over the letter and, for various reasons, was unhappy with its content.

"You insist to stay, but we can't have you continually going out and literally being in the hands of the enemy," Littlefeather declared.

"Twice now, rules more than anything else have spared your physical body, and the timing has been in relatively close succession…so, you remain a conduit among Dan'hali or you come home." The archangel understood it was best to agree to the terms. Littlefeather conjured a portal to the beaches of Dan-hali, saying, "We'll be in touch, sis." Swae stepped through the portal and on to Dan-hali's sands. She popped the top off a small vial, drinking the shot of medicine to help with her pain. There was still a faint ringing in her ears, unfortunately reminding her of those terrifying few moments that sickened her in the afterthought.

Summoner

On a cool and sunny morning, Yana was set to send a fleet of airships to Zuhetta. Crowds had already amassed in designated civilian areas as colors and cheers made the occasion a celebration. There was an uproar as propellers hummed to life and began to turn. The grand ships began to rise from the ground with their formation perfectly maintained. Yana, getting chills of her own, was a mile away as she watched their ascension.

While the summoner began the ritualistic form, Dehza provided the summoner with a vision of Dema. Onlookers gasped as a portion of the clear sky was enhanced by a fantastically beautiful glyph. The area of the sky hardened as the symbol glowed with prismatic radiance before it shattered and sent a wave through the atmosphere. Bolts of lightning fell away, revealing a reflection of Dema's pastures.

Shiro may not have been able to spare much at the moment, but what the city sent had every bell and whistle that could be attached.

The anomaly--the crafts themselves--were simply jaw-dropping to those in Zuhetta. Each airship headed to a designated color of smoke for its respective landing zones. The current outline of the Bonfire City was not equipped with formal space for such weapons. Even Kush'hera, the Celestial of Storms, sunned herself on the plains of Dema, prissily scoffing at the gunships that were as large as she was. The crews of each airship felt like celebrated heroes as cheers and lights greeted the mighty vessels overhead.

The last of the dozen ships sailed through the portal. The summoner released the spell, and the sky resumed its natural state. Yana's hands still trembled after such a feat. Immediately, she felt a quickly fleeting weakness in her stance. After the summoner paid her respects to the soldiers and heroes present at her location, one of the officers relayed a request for Yana's presence at Delia's residence.

The summoner changed from her ceremonial regalia into her civilian fatigues. The nature of Delia's inquisition never was fully disclosed. When Yana eventually arrived, Delia was quick to meet her outside with a warm greeting. Putting small talk aside, Yana could tell there was something peculiar about Delia's motives. "What's up?" the summoner asked with a curious smile.

"We received a certain request from our people in Ramm," Delia began.

"I figured it was best to wait until after your sending." Yana returned the comment with her usual peaceful glance.

Delia stopped in front of a doorway, smiling as she asked. "Could we get a pint of your blood?" The summoner paused for a second as this request genuinely caught her off guard.

"Are they trying to make pocket portals?" Dehza inquired, muffled by the wrap around Yana's hand. Delia, still nervously smiling, replied, "That's what they said."

"Jeeves would handle the proceedings."

"I...I guess it's ok," Yana replied. Delia escorted her friend through the compound, eventually guiding Yana through the door of a well-furnished bedroom. Jeeves was casually sitting by the bed, knowing that the equipment was already in place for the procedure.

The skeletal butler gave a tip of his top hat, patting the bed with his boney hand. "We always operate with your comfort in mind," he said. Yana climbed onto the large bed, positioning herself so that her left arm's veins were accessible. No one said much as the procedure began. Jeeves soon spoke up. "A lot of the volume is lost in the process. Do forgive the necessity for such quantity."

"I know that I'm in good hands," Yana replied kindly.

"Exactly, what volume do you mean?" she added.

"Essentially, it's the energy that flows through and with your blood. Removing the blood from the body weakens any anomalies therein," Jeeves replied. He then left to retrieve several trays of snacks from which Yana could choose.

Yana plucked a couple of cookies from one of the trays as she began to feel the effects of the loss of blood. "Oh, how is Horus?" Delia inquired of Jeeves.

"Master Horus is recovering quite successfully," Jeeves assured. "It's been ages since I've seen a cog among the shadow. They seem to only come when there is a necessity for substantial weaponry. It's never a coincidence."

"I wonder what they were like," Yana mumbled.

"The shadows that saved you, Delia?" Delia smiled a bit, glancing at Jeeves, saying, "I've heard that they were very impressive." Jeeves nodded subtly.

That evening, Enysa took the vials of blood to the border and began shouting at a rather mellow soldier at the outpost. Because he had orders not to allow her into Ramm, he responded. "Miss, I assure you, the package will arrive safely."

"Do you know who I am?" Enysa asked furiously, keeping the supplies tightly pressed against her body. The soldier motioned to a notification poster bearing a cute photo of the darkdancer, which read "Banned."

"BANNED?" Enysa yelled. The soldier gently took the materials from the defeated darkdancer and handed the contents to a comrade behind a counter. "Who's your supervisor?" Enysa inquired with a leer. The soldier rolled his eyes. "I'm a major with communique command, milady. Frankly, our orders come from anyone who outranks us in such matters. Should you ever decide to ignore this little poster, it would be grounds for an arrest," he explained.

"I'd like to see you try," Enysa spitefully uttered.

"Would you like a receipt?" the major asked with a sly grin.

"Yes, sir," Enysa begrudgingly agreed.

In Zuhetta, the summoner's feat would remain a hot topic. Truly, it was a miraculous sight; but it was also a symbol of the alliance's power.

"To have allies that can do such things," heroes and families would say, "maybe we CAN actually reunite the kingdoms. Could we really see such a thing?" Even among the growing darkness at Zuhetta's fronts, the summoner's feat was a source of inspiration that she would never realize.

Heroes

Gizmo, thc wolvyn cog, was finally keeping true to his bet with Twitch by enlisting a promising ghostdancer for this particularly curious task. The ghostdancer went by "Z." She resembled an arid lioness and was one of the students who worked closely with Radagast, the wolvyn priest. When the time came, the ghostdancer would be tapped for a position among the Majim'ati.

The sun would soon be rising over the waves as the cog and the ghostdancer made their way to the western coast of Parraeysia. The ghostdancer's gift had not been seen among Gizmo's people since their transformation so many years ago, and so he was unsure of this process in general.

"I was thinking…water," the girl stated, pointing towards the sea. Gizmo shrugged.

"OH! Z asked excitedly, "May I try something?"

"Try what?" the cog replied, somewhat hesitantly. "Here, close your eyes," Z said, gently laying her hands over the wolvyn's eyes.

"O…ok, that's fine, I guess. Wasn't expecting to be touched, but ok," the wolvyn mumbled. The two stood there for a couple of awkward seconds as Z channeled her newfound energies. She lifted her claws from the wolvyn's eyes.

"Can you see them?" she asked happily.

The girl stopped for a moment as she hurried to the water. She carefully stepped onto the sea. Gizmo's ears perked up at the sight. He quickly scribbled "Hover-boots" into a small notepad. Z went about a hundred yards and sat on the water like it was solid ground. Gizmo's spell faded. But, after a few minutes, he could see a bright lantern and the girl glowing. Z stood back on the shore and saw a pale blue glow coming from the container at her side. Smiling, she handed the device to Gizmo and said, "She was certainly an eager one."

"She won't be a chatterbox, right?" Gizmo inquired. "And, are we sure it's a she?" Z winked at the wolvyn.

"Alright, let's get you into your shell," the wolvyn said, heading back towards the volcano.

"How did you come by such an idea?" Z asked.

"The original body was still a prototype as far as I was concerned. It was designed to operate with elemental energies, but I never had the idea of a conscious driver," Gizmo replied.

"Twitch pretty much snuck into it, but it worked out to benefit everyone. The communication took a while."

"I think it's incredible," Z remarked.

"You just walked on water like it was nothing. Quit acting all humble," Gizmo answered.

Z laughed, happily replying, "Other than some weird dreams growing up, I could never have imagined harboring a heroic gift."

"Go practice with Zeit, your alpha warrior," Gizmo suggested with a smirk. The Ma'ji lassie halted.

"I...I've heard ghostdancers aren't really designed for battle," she responded somewhat timidly.

"All heroes are designed for battle, kid. You just gotta' find your niche," Gizmo stated reassuringly. "As excited as you kitties are about your powers, your people will need some time to acclimate and learn from each other."

The two entered a lift, taking it to the second drop-off. Gizmo shouted instructions to various groups of workers in passing as they continued to a portion of the volcano called "The Shop." This was the largest of several posts from which Gizmo ran his engineering operations. There were dozens of various crafters and workers still afoot. Z followed the runt to his office, where she saw a clutter of parts and materials. Gizmo set the lantern down next to a six-legged device--not so different from Twitch's current design.

The azure light of the lantern pulsed brightly as the spirit within bounced back and forth. Gizmo opened the lantern, and the spirit quickly entered the mechanical spider. The glyphs that decorated the suit lit up with a turquoise glow as the tiny bot came to life. Gizmo knelt in front of the elemental. "Hey, you good? Move each of the legs," he said, motioning with his claws respectfully. It took a moment, but one-by-one the legs moved. Excited to have such access to the physical plane, the elemental stumbled a bit.

"Easy there, newbie," Gizmo said, inspecting various components of the vessel.

"How did you name the first one?" Z asked.

"Twitch…cuz' the prototype twitched a lot," Gizmo answered plainly.

"It was actually really funny sometimes," he added with a chuckle.

"Well, this one doesn't seem to have a malfunction by which to go off," Z noted playfully. Gizmo looked back at the spider.

"You got a name?" he inquired. The elemental seemed to ponder but did not know how to respond.

"You caught her, right? You name her," Gizmo suggested. Z smiled, saying, "Zero, because she has no flaws." Zero chirped happily at her new name.

"Alright," Gizmo stated, "move around, but not too fast yet." Zero walked a few small circles, quickly understanding the suit's controls.

"Okay, try not to trip anyone," Gizmo said, motioning that Zero could freely explore her new home. The spirit saluted the two and eagerly scurried away, only tripping over herself twice before she was out the door.

"You're sure that was safe? Just...that easy, huh?" Z asked curiously.

"I figure the Ma'ji have quick enough reflexes to avoid any serious mishaps," the cog casually replied. "We're going to the training grounds anyway. That way, I can show more teaching time, which makes me look good."

"Yes, sir," Z said with a gracious bow. So the two departed for the northern claw of the islands, a location in Parraeysia long designated for combat training and the exercise of heroic gifts. The current hours were more laxed. A few blossoming heroes were practicing while others were socializing.

A handful of Z's friends were among the numbers here. Z began meditating by the shore while Gizmo went ahead. "Zeit!" Gizmo hollered as he came up on the tranquil dragonkin. Zeit stood and turned to greet the runt, exchanging a fist bump.

"I'm having a teacher moment; you want in?" Gizmo inquired. Zeit nodded.

"Come on," Gizmo said, beckoning the dragonkin to follow.

The students stood at attention at Zeit's presence. "As you were," Gizmo said casually. Zeit pointed to a pyromancer among the pupils who hurried to stand by the dragonkin's side.

"Stand here," Gizmo said to Z, who hesitantly moved to where Gizmo gestured. There was nothing but the ocean behind her--a safe backdrop. Zeit instructed Maari, the pyromancer, to position himself about 50 yards from Z while the other passersby and heroes curiously gathered.

"What…what's going on exactly?" Z asked.

"You're gonna' dodge an attack without moving," Gizmo stated plainly.

"What?" Zeit shouted.

"Put some oomph in it!" Gizmo shouted to the pyromancer.

"Aye, sir!" Maari hollered back. "What am I supposed to do?" Z frantically asked.

"You have access to another plane, right?" Gizmo hinted. Z's eyes went back to the pyromancer as he saw a swirl of embers quickly becoming a relative sun in the Ma'ji's claws. The panther-like caster bore a rather wicked grin as he charged the spell…a fierce ally indeed!

The pyromancer roared as the massive fireball shot from his claws, barreling towards the ghostdancer. The flames tore through Z's location and out over the sea. The ghostdancer seemed to have vanished. Onlookers were gasping and guessing about what had happened. After a couple of moments, Z reappeared, inhaling, after holding her breath from the pressure of the ethereal plane. There were whistles and cheers from the other heroes. Nicely done, indeed. Z looked like her life flashed before her, but she was able to shake it off.

"See?" Gizmo stated happily. "Instincts."

"Right," Z uttered shakily as her claws grasped the sands. She looked at Gizmo like he was insane.

"You may be doing some good work with Radagast, the wolvyn priest, but you're not learning to be creative," Gizmo explained.

"Examine your own gift and abilities. Then think about how to make everything work together." Z agreed with her comrade, nodding.

"We kept telling you to come out here," a young bladedancer playfully remarked.

"There ya go, come out and play with your friends more," Gizmo added. Z nodded stoically as she folded her arms.

Maari, a pyromancer, was standing close by and laughing as he embraced and easily lifted Z off the ground. "I had no doubt. You were always a quick thinker." If a cat can blush, Z would be blushing, even though she is still shaking a bit. Other present heroes and friends of hers added their praises and jokes.

"We'll fix you up with some armor," Gizmo said. "It should also help with your overall endurance."

"Armor?" Z curiously muttered.

The wolvyn was correct in his prescription. It is rare to find ghostdancers who wear armor akin to a warrior. Their ability to phase through the planes and capture the healing residue in their hands makes them tremendous comrades in close quarters.

"Heroes don't 'hafta' like fighting, but it definitely helps to be at least comfortable with it," Gizmo said.

"Dragons grow quickly," Zeit added. Gizmo pointed to his large friend, who nodded in agreement. "When Rayne comes out of stasis--and those eggs hatch from the broodmother--the next steps will be combat, kid," he said candidly. One of the heroes raised his claw quickly. "Ideally, the brood will be battle-ready within three years," he declared proudly.

"Bingo," Gizmo replied, "and trust me, we need the time between then and now. Pray that it won't go by any quicker than it will. Trust me."

"YES, SIR!" the heroes answered in unison.

Some of Z's friends were already crowding her, asking the ghostdancer to practice with their respective groups. Z, a bit overwhelmed, glanced around. She knew that even with the influx of Ma'ji's heroic gifts, healing energies and disciplines are always rarer to come across. "I…I need to ask Radagast about a couple of things," Z said with a smile.

"I've already done so much work in the archives," she added in afterthought.

"I'm sure he's got plenty of sages to fill your increased absence," Sosa, a bladedancer, remarked.

"I'd like to see this magical residue," Maari jovially exclaimed. Maari held out his arm towards Sosa.

"Sosa, gimme a little cut," he added.

Sosa spun a dagger in and out of its sheath and drew some blood from Maari's forearm in the blink of an eye. Z gasped, quickly focusing her energy to enter the ethereal plane. She swept her claw through the nether, drawing multicolored particles to her grip. She quickly reappeared before the group, displaying a verdant light pulsing in her right claw. She held her hand to Maari's wound, watching the flesh binding itself back together. "Feels a bit tight but relatively painless," Maari remarked.

"That's so cool, Z," Sosa added happily. "Don't act like you haven't practiced on your own."

"I mean, I've studied texts more than anything," Z, who was not keen to be the center of attention, replied.

Elsewhere, Radagast, the wolvyn priest, was transcribing a census of the current Ma'ji population on Parraeysi. To say the least, the ratio of Ma'ji heroic gifts was astounding. "It's the reality of why there is such an influx that is concerning," he said to himself.

"Between the brood and the Ma'ji, we'll easily have tens of thousands of heroes--truly a force with which to be reckoned, a force that will surely be put to its purpose," he sighed. There was a clattering behind Radagast. He turned to see Zero curiously going about the priest's office. Radagast chuckled.

"Can I help you?" he politely asked.

Zero stopped in her tracks, chirping an inquiry back at the priest. "Twitch must be in the outer construction sites if you haven't come across him," Radagast guessed. He was not well versed in the elemental mechanical code. Zero, almost pondering to herself, chirped as she returned to climbing about the desks and dressers. She seemed to recognize what she was reading with regard to the priest's work. Radagast shrugged, returning to his transcribing.

"I'm sure you can manage. Just be careful, please," he uttered.

Zero found a map of Parraeysia and took a moment to study it. Waving with her front legs, she tweeted for the priest's attention. Radagast came over, and Zero pointed to an emblem of a dragon on the map.

"That's where the Lady Rayne currently is," Radagast said as if to answer a pupil's question.

"Are you from around here?" he added curiously. Zero chirped in confirmation.

"Fascinating!" Radagast uttered.

"Do you know how to write?" he asked, motioning with his claws as if describing a pad and pen. After pondering the question,

Zero went for a paintbrush sitting in an ink vial. She fumbled a bit but was able to sloppily write a rather old glyph on the table.

"Where's Gizmo when I actually need him?" the priest sighed.

"I'd like to converse beyond a simple yes and no. Twitch provided a great deal of help in Chelsea. Perhaps you'll do the same for Parraeysia," he thought aloud. Zero scurried over to a tattered tapestry hanging on the wall and pointed to a specific location on the sea--a few hundred miles north of the island.

"Azkelon?" Radagast uttered.

"You were a spirit in Azkelon before that cataclysm." Zero chirped in affirmation.

"Oh my," the priest replied. "You certainly have been around a while. How an elemental survived such tumultuous times and events is quite the story I'm sure."

Zero chirped happily. Being able to communicate at this level was marvelous to such a being. "I trust that Z was professional?" Radagast inquired. Zero made a heart shape in the air with her front legs.

"Outstanding," the priest said warmly. There was a fairly long pause in the exchange; the two simply stared at each other. Then a young sage, startled for an instant at the unexpected sight of the spider-like suit, entered the office.

"I…I wasn't aware we had another one," he stuttered.

"Oh, yes," Radagast replied. "I don't suppose you've seen Twitch lately. "I think these two have yet to meet; and, by the way, I'm dreadfully near to being finished with these numbers," he added with a relieved smile. The sage bowed and motioned for the spirit to follow him, who energetically did so. She chirped a farewell to Radagast, tripping over herself on the way out.

It was quite a sight when the two elementals were introduced. They played like young pups of any sort, bouncing and rolling about, accompanied by a flurry of delighted chirps and clanking metal.

As a whole, Harth would see a spike in heroic gifts among its new generation of heroes. I suppose it is an unfortunate necessity in replenishing our ranks.

"Raised alongside He that will pierce the dark" – L:V:Ni

Several long-range cannons periodically shelled locations that the scouting parties had marked. The distant booms of the artillery were the only abnormalities to be heard among the chilled air of Ramm. The morale at The Gate was relatively high as some comforts and normalcies settled inside the base. Supplies and various personnel constantly streamed through the tunnel that connected Ramm and Shiro, and void-comms were still being handed out as they were produced. Families were able to communicate with their loved ones, and field operations were always in contact with the forward troops.

One day, Amon, the dwarven king, came to Trova, the human darkdancer, with a favor. "You'd be great for the young ones to learn from. Just look at how edgy you are!" the king jovially exclaimed.

"Dammit," Trova sighed. "I knew this would happen with it being so slow around here."

"Oh, come on. You're a pro at putting the fear of the almighty into people," Amon pried.

"Yup," Ami concurred, as she fumbled through a botany manual.

"We could take them out at night. It is scarier that way," Kasslow added, as he enthusiastically punched a massive bag. Trova raised an eyebrow at the wolvyn's thought.

"Exactly!" Amon agreed, noticing Trova's spark of interest. "Like a team-building exercise."

"Those poor kids," A'mi muttered.

"Fine," Trova casually declared. "I suppose it could be fun."

But, just to be clear, the point is to make it feel like they're fighting a demon." Amon nodded. Trova grinned, replying, "It's a deal."

Late that night, a group of five young heroes had been selected for the exercise and flown to its designated location. There were two warriors, a bladedancer, an arcanist, and a skycaller. The two human warriors, Juut and Marduk, were brothers from Shiro. The bladedancer, Wey'lu, was a troll from the Anoshi mainland. The arcanist, Isabel, was a girl from Vae'yir. The skycaller, Boris, was a native to Ramm. While these up-and-comers had certainly seen the conflict firsthand, the younger heroes were kept from the thick of the more recent but greater battles.

The heroes stopped in their tracks when they saw that Trova's gauntlets and reaves were like those of a lich. At the end of the darkdancer's coat, even a spine became a boney tail. Honestly, Trova took the opportunity to play a theatrical role.

"Amon said this person was an instructor, right?" Isabel inquired concernedly. Both warriors readied their shields and weapons in unison, thus prompting the rest of the group to take a readied posture and channel their respective energies. The skycaller conjured a powerful ring of wind around the group while the arcanist applied a protective dome to their location.

"YOU TEMPT SUCH AN ENEMY TO CHARGE?" Trova roared, "THEN LET YOUR LESSON BEGIN!"

The lights from the airship overhead shut off, and in an instant, Trova shattered through the spells and past both warriors. The heroes barely got a glance of the darkdancer before he was out of sight again, leaving a strange cloud of spores in his wake. Wey'lu recognized the agent, a mild hallucinogenic found among certain Zuhettan brambles. The heroes came closer together as shadows took nightmarish shapes around them and their senses blurred. Even the ground and environment seemed to shift.

"Stay calm," Wey'lu said. "He's just making us panic, making us feel trapped."

"How is this legal?" Boris hollered in fright. Juut gasped as Trova came towards him from the shadows, but he quickly blocked one blow and parried another before the darkdancer left.

Isabel and Boris reinstated their defensive spells by readying themselves to repel any ominous number of attacks. Trova phased back into the groups' formation, and he directed a flurry of strikes at the bladedancer within the blink of an eye. Wey'lu deflected each one, barely able to stay in step. Isabel tried to take advantage of what she thought was an opportunity. She conjured several dozen arcane orbs and unleashed them like a machine gun. Trova vanished to evade the attack, but the projectiles continued straight at Juut.

The warrior, crouching behind his shield, was quick enough to react to the luminous threat, although he took quite a battering from his comrade's magic. "HEY, GET AHOLD OF YOURSELF!" the warrior shouted. Marduck gave a sharp whistle to his brother, signaling for a weapon swap. Marduck tossed Juut his shield while Juut tossed Marduck his sword. Juut went back-to-back with Isabel and Boris while Marduck and Wey'lu stood back-to-back to the front of Juut's shields.

"I'm sorry," Isabel said tearfully.

"Just focus on my flank. We have yours," Juut replied reassuringly.

Boris and Isabel could hear blades meeting on the other side of the shield-bearer as the darkdancer had reengaged Wey'lu and Marduck in an impressive melee. Trova, using his own body and armor as his weapons, certainly put on a grand performance of a shadow's martial combat. Juut seemed to have an idea, something the darkdancer would not be expecting. "Boris, can you shoot us forward?" he asked.

"Isabel, do you know weapon enchantments?" Both comrades curiously affirmed.

"Alright," Juut said, putting his shields up. "On my mark, give it everything you can. Boris…Isabel, collapse the dome and redirect the energy into a shield glyph."

Juut watched the melee carefully while he waited for a window in which his comrades would both be clear. Meanwhile, a concentrated gale gently lifted the three an inch off of the ground. Juut saw the gap for which he was waiting.

"Now," he uttered. In an instant, the arcane dome vanished and was replaced by a bright glyph on the warriors' shields; and a powerful burst of air shot the three forward. They whizzed by Wey'lu and Marduck like a cannonball, leaving the two wide-eyed among the backdraft. A subtle "Oof" from the darkdancer was heard upon impact.

The spectators of the session, who were well on their way out of the base, were shocked to see the projectile soar from the swirling darkness. "Bold!" Trova muttered, planting his shadowsteel greaves in the snowy ground. The very earth was upheaved as Trova applied a counter to their momentum. The arcane glyph was shattered, and the powerful winds blew the heroes apart. The darkdancer chuckled as he brushed his claw-like gauntlets together. Windswept and disoriented, Isabel quickly sat up and looked around.

"Did we win?" she asked.

"I don't think winning was ever part of the equation," Boris moaned. Juut, breathing a sigh of relief, was on his back. The shields were steaming against the cold on either side of him.

The airship approached, and its lights shone on the location as it came to a gentle hover just over the ground. A'mi helped a couple of the participants aboard while the rest climbed in. Trova removed pieces of his costume, tossing them aside. The heroes tried to get a good look at their instructor; but when Trova peered over his shoulder from the copilot seat, they attempted to hide their stares. Other than mumblings and whispers from the young heroes, there was not much said on the short ride back to the internal compounds of the base.

Amon was among a handful of others waiting for the ship's return. Trova stepped from the vehicle. "This is a fair representation of the younger ones we have, yeah?" he asked in his relaxed tone. Amon affirmed, "Aye."

"If they're all this comfortable around each other, then they need to run exercises with the soldiers," the darkdancer stated.

"To say the least, I don't know if that arcanist understands the concept of friendly fire as well as she should." Amon agreed and motioned for Trova to follow.

"Yer'self," he said.

The heroes stood at attention when the darkdancer and king came from behind the ship's gun. They were clearly impressed with Trova's overall presence. There was a hush while the darkdancer lit the stub of a dragonskunk cigar. "You did alright," Trova said, "and I'd venture to guess that the lot of you are keen enough to understand the purpose of such an exercise." A'mi's jaw practically dropped at Trova's compliment as she gathered the gear from the airship. Truly, it had a positive ring within the young heroes as well.

Trova looked at Wey'lu; and, in a trollish-tongue, said, "The troll bladedancers, the Anoshi Quickblades, would be proud." Wey'lu graciously bowed and then returned to attention. Trova looked to Juut, saying, "You may want to formulate more of an endgame for those sorts of stunts in the future. You went from protecting the youngest and more inexperienced on your team to taking them towards the threat and away from other skilled defenders."

"Yes, sir," Juut replied respectfully. Trova motioned for the shield that took the hits from Isabel's bolts to be tossed to him. A few spots of the high-quality shield had nearly been penetrated, a sight by which Isabel was clearly disheartened.

"You've got potency, kid," Trova remarked. "Standard body armor wouldn't hold up very well against that." Trying to keep herself together, Isabel sniffled and wiped her eyes.

"Hey, no tears," Trova stated.

"Yes, sir," the arcanist replied. Then, Trova's eyes met with Boris' eyes. Even now, Boris, the young dwarf, was visibly intimidated by the darkdancer.

"Hmm." Trova noticed how shaky the boy was. "The spores may not have worn off yet." Trova slowly waved his hand in front of the lad, who slightly flinched.

"I'll fix him up," A'mi kindly said, taking the dwarf aside. Trova cleared his throat, saying, "He'll be fine."

Marduck quickly raised his hand. "Hmm? Oh, you."

The darkdancer responded, "Individually, I noticed that Wey'lu kept more distance than a bladedancer should because it was causing you to overexert on a strict offensive. A warrior should always think of himself as a shield, no matter what weapons they're holding." Wey'lu subtly bumped Marduck with his elbow.

"Realistically, you each died a number of times," the darkdancer pointed out. "I could have had this base under my heel."

"See? You're a natural," the king happily boasted.

"Ugh," the darkdancer sighed. "I know that you've been sneakin' off at night and killing demons," Amon slyly added.

"Don't act like you're not gettin' yer fill." Trova's eye twitched a little as he tried to hide his outburst to rebuke the revelation. The shift in the darkdancer's expression was quite more noticeable than he could know as Amon continued laying his cards on the table.

"Legally, I could reprimand you for disobeying orders…," the king continued, "not to mention drugging minors." Trova looked down at the dwarf with as much shock as a man like he was capable of showing.

"You wouldn't," he replied.

"Oh, I have quite a few colorful ways to handle the situation," Amon stated.

"You're blackmailing me?" the darkdancer uttered. A'mi could be heard laughing in the background.

"How many monsters have ya killed?" Amon inquired.

"Three thousand, two hundred seven," Trova grumbled.

The statement clearly struck a chord with the young heroes. "It's not just me that's been askin', lad," Amon said with a humble smile. Trova took a drag of the cigar and tossed it into the snow. His fangs briefly showed a defeated grin.

"I get to continue my outings?" he inquired.

"You'll at least take a collar, but yes," Amon answered.

"And now you can share some of the notes I'm sure you have," he added.

"Nothing outstanding yet," Trova sighed.

"Either way," Amon happily replied.

It was a beautiful morning in Shiro when Enysa eagerly woke Yana and Bael in their bed. She had essentially broken into their home. Enysa was excited about a new ritual they had apparently rediscovered, and she came to the summoner like a happy puppy. Bael wrapped a pillow around his head, trying to muffle the darkdancer's antsy inquiries. "I really thought Horus would keep her calm," Yana mumbled, her tired eyes staring at the ceiling. Horus shouted from outside a window, "I didn't want to enter your home in such a manner."

"I'm sure Dehza would have something to say," Enysa said slyly.

"No," Yana replied, quickly sitting up. "No, no, no! Too early for him to care. Just give us a sec."

After it was clear that Enysa had no intention of leaving the room, Yana and Bael dressed into casual wear and eventually shuffled out of the door behind the darkdancer. Horus saluted the two. Bael and Yana looked about, seeing that their comrades had not brought a mode of transportation. So, Bael re-entered the home to get his void collar, asking for a line to Delia, the Aki'rah. It took a moment before an equally groggy-sounding Delia answered into Bael's ear. It was clear by his expression that Enysa really had not thought this through in any way. After a very brief exchange, Bael removed the earpiece and said, "Thirty minutes."

Eventually, a vehicle arrived, and the group was on their way. "Sorry," Enysa said innocently. Bael pulled his hood over his eyes, replying in a sigh.

"A home invasion and no proper escape car! You guys are awful at this."

"Not to mention an utter lack of respect for privacy," Yana added, grinning through a puff of smoke.

"True," Horus added. Enysa leered at Horus for his betrayal in this situation.

"Oh, that reminds me," Yana said. "How did the uh…things go with you two?"

"Enysa's excitement during the initial phase was concerning at points," Horus replied plainly.

"He made Jeeves stay cuz' he didn't trust me," Enysa rebuked. "Who gave me a passing grade, by the way?"

"Your dream?" Yana asked Horus.

"Boring," Enysa mumbled. Horus shrugged in agreeance with Enysa's explanation.

"Essentially, a lesson in making and improving our gear. The old man didn't speak to any other matters," the darkdancer said.

"Well, I'm glad that you guys have got your footing here," Yana replied kindly, lying across the seats with her legs across Bael's lap.

Horus pulled a bound file from a satchel, clearing his throat before saying, "I looked into the official rosters regarding allied command and ranks. Does the Firebourne family control every matter…not to mention you, lightmarshall?" Not being entirely up to par with such matters, Yana quickly turned her eyes to Bael, who grinned and replied.

"Alliance rank is essentially a network of councils and representatives. Everyone, including royalty, answers to someone. Yana's more of a celebrity than a military tactician; she answers to a council of our best and brightest. Amon is still technically the king of Ramm, so he has been given the authority to represent the people of Ramm. The Firebourne bloodline is out of the ruling business, although Bree Firebourne, the mother of the Christ child, has been kept aware of everything.”

“She doesn’t think that will change,” Yana chimed in, “even after the baby. I do know that much.”

“So, it really is just like a patchwork,” Horus mumbled in a curious understanding.

“Don’t ask how long it’ll last,” Bael added in a yawn.

“It’s not like there’s been much to disagree on lately.” Yana nodded in agreement. Horus glanced back at the pages, uttering, “I used to think legendary hero status was corny but seeing this many among our forces is quite remarkable.” Yana blushed, “Yeah, I’m not a fan.”

Bael chuckled, “I give her hell over it.” Yana may have blushed a bit more as she looked at Bael, hoping he would not go any further. Bael winked at his wife.

“Ninety-nine percent of them actually earned it,” Yana said with a nervous smile, redirecting the conversation.

“Some others and I just sort of have it all dropped in our laps.” Enysa looked at Horus, asking, “Are we legendary?” Horus simply shrugged.

Legendary hero status is applied to individuals who have reached an ascended function of their heroic gift; that is, mastering every aspect and discipline. While some paths may require a level of divine intervention, others are made with time and heroic feats. Yana, a summoner, and Stella, a voidkeeper, serve as prime examples of the first example, while Azotus, the wolvyn warrior chief, and Diisu, the female troll elementalist, serve as the other. Horus could achieve such a status through divine intervention, but Enysa cannot.

Enysa sighed heavily, saying with exasperation, "I feel like I've made my rounds through Shiro enough by now. All I've found is Horus. I'm gonna' have to go back to Zuhetta."

"She still has to ask permission from Trova," Horus added.

"Do not," Enysa replied confidently. Horus looked at Enysa with skepticism.

"I have to take some equipment to him later. I could pass your request along," Horus offered.

"What? YOU get to go over there?" Enysa exclaimed in disbelief.

"To take some equipment, yes," Horus affirmed plainly.

"Fine," Enysa agreed in a pout.

The group eventually arrived at Delia's estate, where Delia insisted Bael and Yana have breakfast of some manner while she informed her friends of their discovery. "Jeeves brought a spell to our attention," Delia explained, "something that hasn't been used in an exceptionally long time--a battle ritual that intertwines summoner and darkdancer energy signatures." Yana listened as she enjoyed the food that was provided.

"Sounds intense," Bael remarked. Delia nodded, saying, "It's not dangerous to practice, but Jeeves hasn't been entirely clear in explaining the effects."

Enysa watched and waited impatiently while Horus tinkered with a scope. "I was going to properly send for you," Delia continued with a smile, glancing over at Enysa, "but she's something of a free spirit."

"How did Jeeves explain it?" Yana asked through a mouthful of eggs. Delia thought for a moment, blushing as she whispered into Yana's ear. The summoner blushed as well, grinning as she looked over at the two shadows.

Yana nodded, saying, "I'm down." Bael sipped some coffee while he acquired a cigarette from Yana. Soon enough, the group went to a beautiful training area on the premises. The otherwise rocky terrain had been outfitted with greenery and decorative pools as an area reserved for less destructive practices.

"So?" Enysa asked excitedly. "What do we do?"

"Nothing, for the time being, dear," Jeeves replied. "I believe these first steps will be all too natural for this group." Motioning with his boney hand, Jeeves asked Yana to take a seat on the ground. The summoner complied, curiously staring up at the skeleton.

"This is more about meditation," Jeeves explained. "It's about the spirits of the hosts connecting and empowering each other at the soul's level."

"Holy shit, this sounds like fun," Enysa remarked, nudging Horus with her shoulder. Horus remained quiet, hiding his reservations.

"So I just…sit here?" Yana asked.

"The shadow's runic signature beats through the nether with their veins," Jeeves replied.

"In this case, you'll feel them before they feel you." Yana tried not to look at the two darkdancers, as she was unable to do so without blushing a little.

"Why does he make this sound so easy?" Bael asked. Delia shrugged, replying, "He told me it was about kindred spirits…that it was a simple equation as long as you had the right materials."

"It's something about Enysa and Yana?" Bael pondered.

"I suppose," Delia replied curiously.

"That connection to Mirym, Yana's friend and darkdancer, must be it." Bael subtly nodded in accord. Delia smiled, commenting, "You're a good match for her too."

"I know; I got lucky," Bael replied with a wink. Jeeves strolled over to the two, saying, "I'm sure we'll have results momentarily."

The summoner took a deep breath as she closed her eyes and placed her palms on the ground. The darkdancers, waiting for some sensation, remained as they were. As the summoner's mind cleared, she began to feel the very nether around her like gentle breezes striking her from every direction. Each current pulsed with different signatures and frequencies quite distinguishable to those who know how to look. The summoner soon found the shadows' beats, opening her own energies to meet theirs.

A gentle red aura manifested from Yana as dozens of ethereal runes flashed on the ground around her. The energy snaked through the ground and air as the nether mixed between the heroes. The optics were one thing, but what soon followed was quite different. As the ethereal signatures intertwined, Enysa and Horus seemed immediately struck by something. Enysa practically collapsed while Horus managed to stay on one knee.

Delia and Bael hurried over while Jeeves maintained his slow stroll. Yana, unaware of her comrades' seeming incapacitation, was still in an initial trance. When Bael and Delia got to the darkdancers, they were…well, certainly not worried anymore. Enysa was practically purring and moaning sensually as she rubbed her scarf on her cheek. Horus simply seemed a little awkward to whatever was happening. "Mmmmm, this feeeels soooo gooood," Enysa groaned, the red glow of her eyes brighter than ever. Horus finally slumped over and fell to the ground, still trying to fight against the sensation.

Jeeves had made it to the rest of the bunch, saying, "No matter the individuals. It's quite a repetitive process, a simple side effect that is removed with tolerance."

"You, you said, repetitive?" Horus uttered.

"Awesome," Enysa sighed, while hugging herself tightly. "I loooooove you, Yana."

"It would be preferable to have the entire formation present for these exercises, but I wanted to gauge an initial attempt," Jeeves stated.

"Yana doesn't seem affected," Delia noted.

"It's just the shadows that have to adapt to this ritual, ma'am," Jeeves replied. "Yana is practically asleep."

"Should we go ahead and turn it off?" Bael asked.

"Noooo, don't turn it off," Enysa moaned.

"Pleasure is a rarity after the transformation. You'll have to excuse the lady," Jeeves remarked, nodding at Enysa.

"A simple poke will bring Yana out of her state. Judging by the seeming intensity, Yana must be a very loving woman," he added politely. Bael could not help but blush a little, knowing at what Jeeves was hinting.

"She always was," Delia said with subtle awe.

"Her nature simply amplifies her gift," Jeeves nodded. "Our world's greatest heroes have always had such traits." Bael smiled and gently laid his hand on Yana's shoulder.

The summoner awakened, and the spell ceased. "Aww," Enysa sighed. Horus was taking deep breaths, as he slowly rolled over to stand.

"Are they okay?" Yana curiously asked. Bael chuckled some and said, "I think you made them feel more than okay." Yana could only smile as she remembered what Delia had told her. Horus had made it to his feet, still supporting himself on a nearby post. Enysa had yet to bother trying.

"It'll be fun seeing the whole lot of em' at once," Bael joked, helping Yana to her feet.

"I'm a little worried about that one," Yana remarked, looking at Enysa.

"She will find her pace and place soon enough, lightmarshall," Jeeves replied. "Believe it or not, she's an excellent shadow for you."

As dusk fell that day, Horus was headed out of the compound with the pieces of gear he had augmented for Trova. Enysa, uncharacteristically quiet, had kept in close step for some time as she followed. "I'll be back in a couple of hours," Horus kindly said.

"You better be," Enysa mumbled, her arms folded.

"I'm sure there's a reason that they keep you here," Horus replied. Enysa glanced away, giving a downhearted sigh.

"Anything you want me to tell them?" her comrade asked. Enysa smirked, replying, "I'm sure that they can guess."

Horus drew more attention than to what he was accustomed to as he arrived at the Gate that night. The young darkdancer was directed to his comrades' whereabouts and eventually came to the small hangar that served as quarters to Kasslow, A'mi, and Trova. A'mi joyfully smiled and shouted when she saw Horus enter. "TROVA! HE'S HERE!" The alchemist rushed to hug their newest member.

"I'm A'mi, your resident mixer and fixer. That's Kasslow, our furry pilot," she added, motioning respectfully to the large wolvyn. Kasslow nodded but kept eating and drinking in the kitchen.

As the sound of footsteps came down the stairs, leading to an upper loft, Horus quickly laid out two items on a table—a long coat and a large rifle. Kasslow's ears perked up at the sight of the awesome weapon. Horus saluted Trova, who casually returned the gesture. Trova came to stand on the opposite side of the table, and he motioned for Horus to resume a normal posture. Trova said, "Well?" Horus cleared his throat.

"The coat itself was made by artisans in Shiro," Horus explained. "I reinforced it with ebonfiber lining and runic insulators that line the sleeves with down. It is designed to help with the immediate energy circulation—and, ultimately, better directional application."

Horus turned his attention to the rifle and motioned Trova that he could freely handle the weapon. "There's no ammunition," Horus said. "It charges from the radiation of its user. It is made with all of our components, so there's no real worry about the weapon being damaged or malfunctioning. Unimpeded, I believe the resulting projectile could travel upwards of three miles."

"Unimpeded," Trova subtly echoed.

"You'll see some bullets drop if you choose to shoot through stone or metal," Horus replied plainly. Trova grinned.

"The scope contains a nether refractor," Horus continued.

"Essentially, it works like infrared works on humans. It has a zooming function appropriate for the weapon's effective distance." Trova was clearly pleased with the order.

"Impressive would be an understatement," he said.

"Thank you, sir!" Horus replied. "Enysa certainly did some good work in finding you," Trova stated.

"Speaking of Enysa, sir," Horus said respectfully.

"Hmm?" Trova uttered.

"She wishes to return to Zuhetta in hopes of expanding the chapter." Trova gave little thought to the matter, replying, "Tell her to go to Zufa'zuf. If the rainbow bridge is offline, I doubt Stella would decline the request. You'll hold down the fort in Shiro?" he asked, as warmly as his character permitted.

Stella, the voidkeeper, was quickly made aware and agreed to the notion of meeting Horus on his way back into Rime that night. When Enysa found out about her sanctioned expedition, her level of shock suppressed her characteristic outburst. While Stella was certainly genuine in her agreement with the idea, she saw this as a unique opportunity of her own. There were no real preparations to be made, so the two soon left for the rainbow bridge's waypoint in the Shiroan cliffs. Stella's glass-like scars shone with a pinkish hue, feeding the network that soon brought the two into the Anoshi isles.

Allied territories ran from the Anoshi isles in the northwest to the south along the coastlines. From the southern corner, Anoshi isles ran east along the coasts, with Dema being the only portion of inland territory controlled. Asheya, a central area of Zuhetta, was an exception. Allies here were amassing naval capacities that would echo into ages to come. Their seafaring transportation networks ran like a well-oiled machine. By courtesy of Tal'Traxxi, the Celestial of Tides, there was never a day of rough water. The voidkeeper and darkdancer would board a vessel and arrive at the southwestern edge of Zuhetta in a few short hours. Their conversations and the surroundings certainly helped to pass the time. They both came from the same slaughter that took place in Uhr'Erra, and only now did they learn about it.

"YOU'RE FROM CHESIL!?" Enysa shouted in marvel. "I GREW UP IN TARIP!"

Tarip was a town only 20 miles south of the capital fortress, Chesil. No matter their level of defense or stature, entire territories were lost in a matter of hours or days. Some areas would never be recovered from this cataclysm.

Stella shared the darkdancer's level of shock and merriment, replying, "MY MOTHER WAS FROM TARIP!" The two embraced each other, both sharing in the *common obliteration* of their homeland. Then they just looked at each other in awe.

"You became a darkdancer?" Stella gasped.

"You became a voidkeeper?" Enysa replied in kind. Each told the other their journey--how they had survived.

They arrived in the ports of Zufa'zuf, an area that was bustling with all kinds of activity. The grand temple was easily seen in the distance of the relatively small city, now known as a vacation home for a certain angel. It was a joyful reunion for Enysa and Miri'el, as the darkdancer explained her cause. Miri'el agreed with Enysa's plan, so long as Enysa stayed well within allied areas. Then Stella eased her own desire into the equation by asking the angel.

"Can I go to Dan-hali?" The question obviously caught Miri'el a bit off guard; but, honestly, Miri'el could not say no to Stella's request to go to this alliance stronghold in Moldo.

"ONLY to Dan-hali," Miri'el answered sternly.

"Let me just check ahead with Swae, so give us some time to talk," she added with a sigh. The voidkeeper and darkdancer agreed to wait for Miriel to talk to Swae, the archangel. While Miri'el was gone, Stella stayed in the temple while Enysa explored the growing city. By now, the story of Trova and the darkdancers, in general, had spread. Enysa was greeted and saluted as an invaluable ally of Harth. Her looks and personality would end up making her a personal favorite of many.

I digress...

Zufa'zuf, a small coastal town and slang for "Water's water," is about as close a translation as one could get. The name is slang itself; but the idea is, "Water has a source like everything else." Most of the roads and walkways were still dirt paths. Construction was being focused on the harbors and less foliaged areas. The tallest buildings were only three stories high and were in few numbers. Trees often stood above the homes and businesses, and exotic plants and flowers lined a number of the prominent roads.

Enysa had walked to the southern harbor of the peninsula, which further confirmed a theory she and Stella had formulated as they sailed from Anoshi—that is, that new islands and shallows had appeared.

Indeed, they were appearing. Tal'Traxxi, the Celestial of Tides, had been heaving the very sands of the ocean to aid our allies. Some would be large and sturdy enough for entire bases or towns, while others were meant to simply expand coastal territory held by the alliance. Tal'Traxxi went out of his way not to affect the major maritime routes already known and used by humanity, thus resulting in some creative layouts of newly formed land.

Enysa found herself struck by the magnitude of the overall situation. Her life-long home was gone. She lamented that had she not been there at that moment, she might never have been able to see the emptiness where it once stood. Having been to Shiro and soon to Mol'do, the darkdancer was finally developing a deeper sense of the world around her. Enysa, feeling invigorated by the sensation, smiled as she leaned against the wooden railings of a pier. Ultimately, her time in Zufa'zuf would be short and relatively uneventful. There was to be a rendezvous, however, behind the temple that afternoon where Miri'el would provide a portal for Stella and Enysa.

The two heroes appeared in Dan-hali. They stood before Swae and Xavus at a palace. Xavus was the king of Dan-hali. Stella bowed respectfully, and Enysa followed her lead. "Damn!" the archangel uttered, looking at Enysa.

"The few times I've bumped into one of you, I've felt like I was seeing a ghost." The darkdancer became distracted because she was already feeling a pulse in the tether.

"I'll escort her through Dan-hali. We wouldn't want anyone mistaking her for an enemy," Xavus said happily.

"You had some words for the voidkeeper, right?" Swae nodded. Stella looked at Swae with some level of surprise.

Xavus and Enysa would head out of the palace while Swae and Stella remained. The king found amusement from the odd and curious stares they received along their way. He jokingly commented, "Anything with glowing red eyes in Mol'do is usually someone trying to kill someone. I've heard darkdancers haven't been among these territories in a millennium."

"I wouldn't really know, sir," Enysa uttered in awe, as she looked at the city streets of Dan-hali.

"Well, if you're here looking for candidates, I know a good place to start," the king remarked, "unless you already have a heading?"

"I can't really tell," the darkdancer replied. Xavus beckoned the darkdancer to follow, taking her to a section of the city that housed a number of soldiers and heroes.

Enysa soon pulled ahead of the king as though she were a dog chasing a scent. A number of groups and exercises would briefly halt as the two passed by them. The king was in a full run as he closely tailed the darkdancer. People simply shrugged their shoulders and curiously raised their brows at the sight. Eventually, Enysa came to a sudden stop outside one of the barracks. Xavus quickly followed. There were a few individuals out front carrying on with conversations that stopped quickly when the two arrived.

The handful of persons saluted the king. "Can we go inside?" Enysa asked the king. Xavus motioned for Enysa to freely enter.

The three-floored building was plain and somewhat flimsy, but it was serving its purpose while repairs went on throughout Danhali. Each floor had two dozen rooms and a common area. Enysa, looking up at the central stairwell, leapt almost directly to the third floor. Xavus sighed and ran up the stairs after the darkdancer. Enysa was standing outside one of the rooms. "I'm pretty sure it's coming from in here," she said. Music could be heard from the room, and there was a white light flashing from beneath the door.

"I doubt they'd hear you knock," the king remarked.

Enysa opened the door, revealing a terrani woman whose naked body was bathed in electricity. The elf, sitting with her back to the doorway a couple of yards away, appeared to be meditating. The king quickly turned his eyes away and closed the door behind him. Some curious residents of the building had come up the stairs by now and were assured by the king that there was nothing to worry about. Inside the room, Enysa watched with a curious smile but kept some distance between herself and the terrani.

"Most of my clothes would be vaporized by this," the elf remarked, still not turning any attention to the darkdancer.

"My attuned robes are just so bulky," she added, as the lightning dancing about her began to subside gently. Truthfully, Enysa was at a loss for words. Aside from the obvious abilities of the terrani, Enysa had never seen one of the elven races before. The woman stood before she took a few relaxed steps to grab a nearby cover.

"Are all elven women like you?" the darkdancer asked.

"Like what?" the terrani replied.

"Fuckin' perfect," Enysa uttered. The terrani laughed a little, replying, "Is it conceited to say yes?"

The darkdancer approached and extended her hand in greeting. "I'm Enysa." The terrani elf darkdancer shook Enysa's hand, replying, "Lua." A couple of moments went by as the two just stared at each other.

"Did you come here for something?" Lua asked with an awkward smile. "Surely a shadow hasn't come to Mol'do and into my little nook just to see an elf."

"You know?" Enysa asked with rising hopes.

"I'm 116 years old, kid," Lua replied with a mild chuckle. "Even though bloodlions kept you guys out of Mol'do, the terrani have managed to maintain some level of awareness of darkdancers over the ages. Physical giveaways aside, any hero worth his salt would have felt that unique energy signature," she explained.

"My concern was with our more inexperienced lot," Xavus added from the other side of the door. The nature of the darkdancer's visit was all too obvious to Lua. Enysa smiled, nodding in agreement to the unspoken request. Of the five eavesdroppers pressed against the door, Xavus was the only one keen enough to jump away, quickly enough to avoid the excited Enysa bursting through. The very door was practically obliterated, which sent the other four individuals to their backs some feet away.

"Slap a bow on that pretty ass and get her to Shiro!" she declared happily.

"Easy does it. You and whoever else you may find will be returning together," Xavus said.

Enysa sighed because she was unsure that she would be able to distinguish between the pulses she had already identified and any others within range. Without much hesitation or warning, the darkdancer dashed off, leaping back down the stairwell. "Dammit," the king uttered, quickly taking off after her, bypassing the stairs in a more direct way. A couple of residents nodded in the direction Enysa had gone; and, soon enough, Xavus was closely tailing the darkddancer. The pursuit was similar to before. Enysa often came to sudden and brief stops, paying little mind to the warrior king that was rather enjoying the exercise.

Enysa decided to take to the rooftops, jumping back and forth from the sides of two buildings to make her ascension. "To hell with that...maybe if they were closer," the king panted. The darkdancer was soon on her way, jumping from roof to roof, as the king tracked her from the streets below. The man did quite well, only plowing into a handful of his fellow citizens along the way.

The two would continue northwest beyond the walls of Dan-hali into a more agricultural portion of the island nation. By the time the two were on a level again, Xavus was completely winded.

The king rested against the side of a barn. A perplexed farmhand passed by Enysa and Xavus as they waved to him. "Yeah, there's definitely one around here," Enysa said with a grin. "I think I'm getting the hang of this."

"May I ask that we commandeer a vehicle or perhaps a large four-legged animal?" the king rhetorically requested.

"Hmm? Oh, sure thing, majesty!" Enysa replied happily.

"I bet that guy's not far away, she added, as she sprinted off in the direction the farmhand had strolled.

Just as the king began to drink from his water, he heard a man's high-pitched shriek. Enysa's voice followed, as she tried to calm the man. The man was shouting, "TAKE ANYTHING YOU WANT." There was a hush followed by the man screaming again and then another hush. The king grunted as he stood up and made his way to where the commotion occurred. The darkdancer was on top of the farmhand and had wrapped her scarf over the man's mouth. The man became much calmer when he saw Xavus. The darkdancer let the man get up. He said to Xavus, "I wasn't totally sure it was you, sire, but when I saw this one in some light…." Enysa quickly responded, "He started thinking I'd killed you."

The king explained the situation. Although still a bit wary of the red-eyed comrade, the farmhand chauffeured the two on a tractor. The trip was only a couple miles due north, but the king provided the farmhand with a generous payment for his services and the overall encounter. The farmhand left the two to their business and returned to his. Enysa and Xavus found themselves at the perimeter of a cheering crowd. Enysa was convinced whoever was at the center of the crowd was the origin of the growing vibration along the tether.

As people noticed the king and his unique companion, a hush from the back began to make its way inwardly through the crowd. The two made their way to the front and found the gathering was to be for a show of strength. It was apparent that even the king was unaware of the particular individual before them now; that is, a towering Fo'hemut elf, who was apparently as equally unaware as to who the two strangers were.

"I wasn't aware we already had Fo'hemut here," Xavus remarked.

"Fo'hemut?" Enysa echoed.

The elf's complexion was dark grey. This mountain of a person was covered in bright red tattoos. Clearly, the Fo'hemut had been exerting himself but had noticed the crowds' hush before these two strangers appeared. He gave a brief bow of his head. Enysa and Xavus continued towards the Fo'hemut, both having to look up at the man.

"Have a name?" the king asked.

"Sij, short for SUIRASTE-AKU'BOVANORII," the darkdancer elf replied in a heroic voice as he flexed his arms.

"Is that just your first name?" Enysa inquired.

"Yes!" the elf replied hardily.

"Sij is good," Enysa concluded.

"I'm Xavus; this is Enysa," the king said.

"Xavus?" the Fo'hemut gasped.

"The king? Forgive my ignorance of your person, sir," he pleaded, as he bowed low before the two.

"I suppose I'm not really sporting a regal look today," Xavus replied with a chuckle, as he motioned for the elf to stand. "Did you come with the earlier arrivals from Veil'Liia?" the king asked.

"Yes, sir. I was taken into custody some time ago, and I was thankful to the hosts of Eternity that I was as far from Emi-Shet, the capital of Mol'do, as I was when everything happened. Our terrani kin grew weary of me some time ago because I'm mostly an entertainer. There's good money and fun to be had for someone with such strength."

"Wanna' arm-wrestle?" Enysa inquired with a grin. Sij looked curiously and confidently at the darkdancer. "I'll try not to crush your hand," he agreed in kind. The crowd, unsure of what to think about this "pair up," remained in a hush. Indeed, at least two of Enysa's hands could fit into one of the Fo'hemut's. When the event started, there was not a tilt in either direction; but Enysa's expression changed to show a hint of surprise. She had not expected her own newfound power to meet such resistance. As she put more strength into the simple competition, Sij could only smile. His forearm remained upright. "You're certainly stronger than you look, little one," Sij complimented.

"I do believe my arm is trembling a bit." Runic energy became like an aura around the darkdancer, as she grunted and strained to get the elf's arm to budge. Sij found joy in meeting the darkdancer's strength and was visibly working to match and overcome the girl. Enysa could not believe how easily the elf seemed to be able to summon such power. As she helplessly saw herself losing, she decided to use both arms. Even that would not prove to be enough. The darkdancer's actions were disqualifying, but it was never of any consequence.

"I don't think we should make you any stronger; you may just pop or something," Enysa remarked.

"Stronger?" Sij replied with immediate intrigue.

"Have you ever heard of darkdancers?" Enysa asked.

"History is time-consuming and often boring. I prefer to stay in the present," Sij replied happily. "That is where the most can be done."

Enysa understood the Fo'hemut's overall capabilities, and she gave him a proposal. If he joined them, she would guarantee him an increase in his strength. Sij agreed and rendezvoused with the group that night.

Meanwhile, Swae and Stella were discussing their circumstances. "Your concern for the people here is outstanding, Voidkeeper," Swae stated; "but the truth be told, the path here will remain closed for the foreseeable future. I've recently been made aware of a complication regarding such matters."

"I see," Stella replied with a downhearted tone. Swae conjured her pipe and began to puff, humbly continuing.

"I didn't think Herod could get much scarier than he already was, but he certainly has. Even after being away all this time, it would seem that his constitution has kept him from being completely compromised. As if we needed an obstacle," Swae sighed, while smoke gently escaped her nostrils.

"Herod? I'm sorry to say that I haven't heard of him. Can he not be eliminated or reasoned with?" Stella asked.

"It's complicated," the archangel quietly affirmed.

"He's a guardian dragonkin omega. I've not been aware of anything that can be done with him." Stella's lilac eyes looked away.

"Then, please, can you at least help me with my dreams? With the sounds, the voices?" she pleaded as her voice began to break.

"I see death every night. I can hear people screaming." The archangel embraced the voidkeeper like a mother to a daughter.

"I fear that I'm not strong enough…that I'll let everyone down," Stella said. Her voice was muffled by the archangel's coat that she was pressed against.

"The void runs through the universe, child," Swae explained with empathy.

"It runs through the very fabric of existence and through the breath of the living and dying, encompassing this world and every realm in between. Unfortunately, as long as Dom'rel is alive, the void will always contain pain and death. Do not underestimate yourself, Stella. We would not have placed you in such a position if we had the slightest doubt about your resolve. You've only had this energy for a few months, and you have carried it remarkably well."

Stella nodded her head ever so slightly. The archangel held out her left hand, where a small beautiful crystal vial manifested. A starry clear liquid formed within the vial, and the archangel handed the item to Stella.

"Hopefully, I won't get in trouble for this, but it will help with the dreams. It is called mana. Angels need rest, too, ya' know," she added with a grin.

"Use it as needed. The vial will refill itself." The voidkeeper kindly bowed as she put the vial away.

"Have faith in the alliance and pray for them, voidkeeper," the archangel continued.

"I'm glad to have seen you, but this is the last time you will set foot in Mol'do for some time. Shiro, the alliance capital, is where you can do the most good. Continue your work, child. You are a gift to humanity."

"How is Herod known?" Stella inquired for her own interests. "The Steel Dragon," Swae answered reminiscently, "and guardian of the shield. His wife was the Celestial of the Blade."

"Was?" the voidkeeper echoed. It was apparent that the archangel's tone indicated the memory was not the fondest.

"Her title alone makes her out to be every bit as dangerous as she was, but the way her life ended was of poor taste and judgment. The irony at that point was that she hadn't even killed anyone. It was a conspiracy charge. There were a number of my kin that concluded she was simply too much of a threat, and for that reason, she needed to serve as an example."

"Did she?" Stella asked. Swae subtly shook her head.

"Was the celestial's soul destroyed?" the voidkeeper continued to ask.

"If she's adrift somewhere, the Light will have known her whereabouts before Bol'rel's blade was about to meet her neck. Dom'rel, on the other hand, could attest to the celestial's soul not being among the pit, a fact that he wasn't too happy with," Swae answered. "There is a handful of safe places among the planes of existence. For all we know, she could be relatively comfortable."

"Such interactions among the ancient beings so long ago is hard to fathom," Stella remarked.

"I try not to spend much time in such memories. It makes our history seem so dreary in hindsight," Swae replied in kind. The archangel began to walk away, but she stopped to beckon the voidkeeper to follow her.

"Come on," she said. "I've arranged for some introductions before you leave."

So the voidkeeper went on with the archangel, inquiring, "What sort of introductions?"

"You'll see," Swae replied. Indeed, the voidkeeper had spent some time with the people and heroes that were among Dan-hali, but she had not been made aware of a planned sendoff that involved a speech and military formations. It was to Stella's relief that only Swae would be speaking at the event. It would be even more of a shock to Enysa and her recent additions when they arrived at the rendezvous with crowds already lining sunset-painted streets.

Since their introduction, both elves had been in a "back and forth" over matters of which Enysa had absolutely no clue. The darkdancer was able to put a halt to the two elves bickering at each other by telling them, "You'll have plenty of time to have at each other's throats AFTER we look good here!" Lua had a particular distaste for the Fo'hemut race, and she saw Sij as being particularly belligerent.

There was not anything especially flashy about the procession, but the turnout as a whole was impressive. Sheth'rel's words were to the point as she addressed the masses. She spoke about the realities of the present situation and the hope that needed to remain among the alliance. She introduced the darkdancer and voidkeeper as a representation of Shiro, and she also reminded the soldiers and peoples of The Birth in Rime. She maintained her charm as she gave an abridged history of the darkdancers. She paid particular attention to this blossoming chapter and how one of the darkdancers remained engaged in a neighboring country to Shiro.

Swae *did not feel the need to go into detail about the nature of every enemy they had faced. The people in Dan-hali were well aware from their own first-hand experiences, as well as they saw the scar that Os'rel, the fallen archangel, had left on Swae's face. Stella was the first mortal to hear Herod's name even mentioned by the archangel, but she was unaware that Swae's presence there had been spared by the being at the old cathedral in Tristen. The end of the speech led to the crowds cheering, and the archangel personally exchanged farewells with the group. Swae opened a portal around the departing party, which was a rare sight for such a gathering of people. Stella wanted to convey her own sort of message with the spectacle.*

With that, Enysa, Sij, Lua, and Stella found themselves back in Zufa'zuf. As Lua took a breath to continue her accusations against her Fo'hemut comrade, Enysa shushed her before even taking a step. "We're gonna' have to figure this out before we get back to Shiro. I need this to look really good," Enysa said. Sij confidently nodded at Lua with his arms folded.

"She started it. It must be a miracle that she wasn't assigned as one of the jailers in Veil'Liia."

"Don't act like our people haven't still been at war. AND ANY Fo'hemut prime your size would HAVE to come STRAIGHT from a family in the Old Blood Terrace!" Lua accused.

"Woman, I told you. I had no investment in Emi-Shet!" Sij rebuked. "Bullshit!" Lua immediately replied.

While Stella had been relatively amused with the back and forth, she decided to interject her suggestion. "We'll be reporting to Miri'el before heading to the Anoshi pylon; perhaps she can help you in your disputes."

"At least…I don't know; try to bond over going to beaches like this or something," Enysa added.

"Aye, Mol'do's coasts were rarely this pleasant," Sij replied with his usual charisma. Lua silently and respectfully agreed.

It was roughly midday, so there were plenty of people who would see the elves in passing. While Sij smiled and greeted a number of individuals along the way, Lua eventually put a hood over her head.

"You didn't seem so modest when I first met you," Enysa remarked playfully.

"There are different kinds of attention," Lua replied. "Whatever sort this is, is just awkward."

"Just a couple of local heroes with a couple of elves in tow," Enysa happily affirmed, putting her arm around her comrade.

The party would soon arrive at the temple. Miri'el was already waiting outside the massive ornate arch that served as the main entrance. The angel smiled and gave a slight bow of her head to acknowledge the group.

As Miri'el got a better look at the two prospective shadows, it was apparent that she was personally impressed. "This is too perfect!" she remarked. "The Light must certainly have plans for this 'handful of you'."

Enysa sighed, replying, "Two to spare. I don't know if that's good or bad."

"Time will tell," Miri'el answered assuredly. "You can remove the hood, Lua. You'd think with everything people have seen, they wouldn't be so awestruck by an elf," she kindly added. Keeping her eyes low, Lua removed the hood and remained quiet. The angel grinned.

"Sij has been as truthful as he can be about his family and ties to the Old Blood Terrace, Lua. I know why you have a disdain for his people, but you cannot project those atrocities onto him," she said softly.

Miri'el then turned her eyes to Sij, adding, "That doesn't excuse any number of your crude actions over the years. You're one of roughly 3,000 Fo'hemut elves remaining in this world. Please try to be respectful of such knowledge."

"Wow, she was totally ready for it," Enysa remarked.

"I'm a custodian of Eternity's archives, Shadow," Miri'el replied with a laugh. "Anything else I need to know is usually being spoken through the nether."

"You've been on the offensive against an endangered race, Lua. Shaaaame," Stella added jokingly. The terrani rolled her eyes. Sij held his hand out to Lua, bearing his usual smile and saying with his usual bolster, "Never any hard feelings, comrade."

Lua glanced at Sij with her arms folded, although she never totally uncrossed them as she returned the handshake. A spiteful jolt of electricity shortly followed the grasp, causing the Fo'hemut to yelp and withdraw his hand. Lua resumed her previous stance, casually uttering, "I'm good now."

"Close enough," Enysa excitedly declared at the truce. The angel beckoned the party to follow her inside, commenting as she walked.

"We'll be sending you back from here with our own representative for Shiro. The nature of his assignment is truly a blessing for him for a handful of reasons. We haven't seen Bol'rel without his armor for a few thousand years. He suffered a consequence for an unfortunate disciplinary action, which perhaps has ended?" she concluded in a reminiscent tone.

Among Eternity's ranks, Bol'rel, the second-born archangel, holds a unique level of renown. He has taken the burden of war from a number of our kin and saved thousands more from tragedy. He intervened on behalf of humanity when it was too weak to stand against Dom'rel's titans. He is mentioned in such regard within the scriptures of their history. After the fall, Bol'rel was placed as second in command of Eternity's armies. He was given access to powers that even the celestials respect, yet he is also the only one of us to directly endure a moment of The Light's wrath.

A man stood in front of the altar. He was a weathered and stoic fellow. The irises of his eyes were like golden bands, and he had platinum hair and a tapered platinum beard. A strange and miraculously restored burn scar went across his eyes and into the archangel's hairline.

Truly, one would not be able to recognize the handprint that it is...

The archangel was well dressed. He had a ring on his right hand and one on his left. "I have your luggage," Miri'el said, smiling as she addressed the group. Bol'rel grinned at the jest, replying, "Then I suppose we're ready to go." The archangel barely waved his hand, conjuring a portal to Shiro. Miri'el bid farewell to her brother and the heroes. She took a couple of steps back as the portal enveloped the other five.

Celestial Hunter

Dom'rel sat upon his throne. Vil'el, a fallen angel, was sitting with the babies before him. Hosts of silent demons stood like statues along the walls, with hardly an echo from down the surrounding hallways. Vil'el was laughing and playing like any mother would with her own children while Dom'rel watched in amusement. A strange break in the nether began to occur in the center of the throne room, and the demons began to stir. Vil'el's expression quickly changed. Dom'rel was shocked and confused at such a sensation. However, he was the only one to remain unphased by the rapidly growing phenomenon, as he watched with interest.

Lightning and fire began to manifest in the spot as the air cracked and began to shatter like a beast charging a pane of glass. The nether was whipped into a variable storm as it began to suck almost everything in the room towards the center. The flames and bolts intensified as gales of wild energy blew in every direction. Dom'rel shielded the babies with his wings just before there was a massive explosion.

Every manner of the demon was obliterated or incinerated by the reaction. Vil'el shielded herself just in time, although her wings bore signs of charring from the blast. A fiery portal was revealed from the aftermath; and Yojun'Sha, a fallen rogue guardian of fire, casually stepped through the portal from the other side. The fallen guardian pulsed with newfound energies. His elemental armor and appearance had even changed in response to his fusion with Deth's wife and Phoenix guardian, Phoenicia. Yojun had quickly mastered the power he had taken from his kin. Flares of celestial fire had already begun to materialize from his inferno.

Vil'el could not comprehend what was happening. She looked to Dom'rel for solace but found none. Three fallen archangels appeared. Quiet and calm, they showed no kind of hostility towards the intruder. Each fallen archangel gently took one of the babies into his arms. Afterwards, they disappeared back into the dark as easily as they came. "Dominus," Yojun'Sha said cordially, although his voice sounded like a bellowing fire.

"Yojun," Dom'rel replied in kind. Remaining speechless, Vil'el hurried to Dom'rel's side.

"You didn't use all of it, did you?" Dom'rel inquired as he grinned. Yojun opened his gauntlet and conjured a raindrop of pearlescent liquid. The bead floated towards Dom'rel as it passed through a tiny portal that the devil conjured at the tip of his finger.

"Dom?" Vil'el asked, with a clear sense of dread growing within her.

"Certain things truly are priceless, dear," Dom'rel replied plainly.

"You were right to accept my offer, Dominus," Yojun stated.

"Offer?" Vil'el quietly echoed.

"Now, for your end of our little bargain," the fallen demi-celestial added. Vil'el then realized what was happening and clung to the devil's arm, crying, "DOM?" Dom'rel smiled as he glanced back at Vil'el. Yojun'Sha held out his blazing hand towards the fallen angel, saying, "Come, child. You have been chosen for a greater purpose." Vil'el refused.

Dom'rel took her by the throat, throwing her down the steps. She landed before Yojun's molten greaves. Dom'rel laughed, saying, "Let's see this, Yojun." Yojun'Sha chuckled as he conjured a "sun of a sword" in his hand and drove its blade into the fallen angel's back. Vil'el's screams were agonizing. Her body writhed from a kind of pain for which she had never known. Her skin slowly became like charred stone with vein-like cracks glowing with flames. Her sullied wings became like solar flares, and her eyes glowed like stars. As the process came to its end, Vil'el began to calm down, and her screams became distorted.

Dom'rel clapped, as he was genuinely pleased with what he had witnessed. Yojun'Sha helped Vil'el to her feet, saying, "My firebird, together we will strike at the very elements and bring down false ancient idols."

"Aye, sir," Vil'el answered in a monotone. She was robotic in her overall demeanor, and her eyes looked downward. Dom'rel had approached. Waving his hand in front of the firebird's face, he received no response. "She responds only to me and my consciousness," Yojun stated. "She even shares my energy signature…fed by my power."

"Marvelous," Dom'rel complimented.

"How about a demonstration?" Yojun'Sha chuckled, nodding in accord. Waving his arm, Dom'rel bore a sinisterly excited smile, changing the very reality of the circumstances.

The three beings were moved to a sublevel of the pit (The Bestiary), where every breed of demon could be readily found.

Monsters of every magnitude roared and howled, and some of them were already charging the two intruders. "Go, spread your wings," Yojun uttered. In that instant, the otherwise dormant firebird violently snapped to life. Two blades of flame manifested in each of the firebird's hands as she soared to meet the endless hordes. Her blades cut through pit-forged armor like bloody grass.

Smaller demons were entirely incinerated as Vil'el zipped through the hordes. She was like a shooting star among the merciless masses that continued to come from every side and endlessly in every direction. Miles were covered in seconds by the firebird, breaking other worldly sound barriers.

"You may need to resupply if you allow her to continue too long," Yojun remarked, as swirls of demonic ashes poured past the two spectators. Dom'rel held up his hand, and the earthquake of stampeding monsters halted.

"Cheap to manufacture," he scoffed. Far in the distance, the yellow tracer could be seen going straight up into the sky before circling to come back.

The firebird came to a swift and graceful landing as she returned to Yojun'Sha's side.

As ash rained around them, I had not seen such an excited expression on Dom'rel's face in ages.

"How soon?" Dom'rel inquired. Yojun'Sha conjured a portal beside himself and Vil'el.

"No time better than the present," he happily grumbled. The devil gave a tip of his brow as fire, lightning, and stone churned about. The portal consumed Yojun and Vil'el and brought them from the realms of the pit into the plains of Asheya. Thick smoke quickly covered a massive area, obscuring everything below the ancient peak. The sea of smoke filled with embers and areas of spontaneous combustion and spread like a tidal wave in every direction--at least two miles high.

Kush'hera, the Celestial of Storms and her drakes, sensed Yojun instantly and were dive-bombing from the perch above. When the dragons were at a certain altitude, the firebirds shot from the ground and soared through their formation without resistance. Kush'hera gasped. "When could he fly?" Then a projectile pierced through one of her drake's wings. Shot from the smoke below, its head was coated in an angelic element. The stormdrake was roaring in pain. The fire was slowly spreading from the wound to the rest of its body. Before Kush'hera could react, an arrow went through her wing.

The celestial barely had time to respond to her own problem, much less help her drakes. Instead, she had to watch as the firebirds decimated her stormdrakes with the bolts and flames in the sky. One drake was falling at least every minute. Kush'hera was horrified as more arrows found their mark in her wings. Her feathers and webbing caught fire before her eyes, and she quickly lost her ability to maintain flight. In its own way, the spectacle of that celestial catching fire as she fell was astonishingly beautiful. She hit the azure grounds of Asheya with an earth-shaking thud, rolling and flailing, while arrows continued to puncture her beautiful scales. By the time the arrows had ceased firing, Kush'hera's insides were starting to boil; and she was in no condition to fight.

Yojun'Sha came through the smoke, conjuring his blade as he approached the celestial. Kush'hera was in some disbelief as she gasped for breath. She was crying. The skies are no longer yours, Kush'hera, Yojun'sha stated, as he began slicing open a portion of the celestial's throat. However, just as he began reaching into the wound for what he was truly after, his gauntlet was blocked by a phantasmal shield.

Dozens of archangels and angels had manifested around Yojun'Sha. The firebird soon returned to his side. There were no words or blows exchanged between any of them. Several burning drakes were still falling to the ground...their shrieks echoing through the skies. Yojun'Sha looked about as he considered his odds.

"Are you ready to finally risk destruction, Yojun?" an archangel taunted.

"Frankly, there are a few of us who are eager for a piece of you." Another archangel shot a bolt of light through the celestial's head, ceasing her pain.

"If the time of such beings as Kush'hera is ending, what logic is there to such ascension in your power?" an angel inquired of the fallen guardian. "You've only proven how foolish your scheme is. You're a monster that will be put down accordingly."

"Then try," Yojun grumbled. Two arrows lodged in the firebird next to him--one in her brow and one where her heart would have been. The body collapsed, and the fires went out. Yojun did not flinch as he replied, "A life for a life…a repeatable process."

"It won't be one of us that gets to end you, Firelord," and the archangel responded, "You will be destroyed by the hands of darkness."

Yojun conjured a fiery portal, simply scoffing as the elements closed around him. He vanished back into the smoldering pyre lands of Dak, a country destroyed by Deth.

Wars

One after another--war after war--be it between spiritual principalities or humanity at each other's throats. Be it between all of us--everything in existence. How many bodies? How much blood has truly been spilt upon Harth's grounds? Hmph…unfortunately not enough at times. Ever since the *First Rebellion*, this has been the way of life. Peace tends to come in short spurts and is often squandered.

Like many children over many years, Yana was one to be orphaned at an incredibly young age. Like many others, her parents were lost during a conflict. Is everyday murder not an act of war, comrades?

That's a rhetorical question.

What comes with war?

Defilement, hate, fear, sorrow, insanity, loss, and the list goes on.

But war becomes a necessity in and of itself after so long.

*It **forces** alliances and understanding, weaving itself in as an element of **balance**.*

In such an imperfect and fallen place, war becomes a source of justice, separating wicked fools from righteous souls.

As it stands, Harth can never be a peaceful world.

*Lies and the **nature** of the fall will endlessly perpetuate war upon this world.*

*Ultimate **correction** is a tricky topic, comrades.*

*Jealousy started all of this...jealousy for affection, worship, and **love**.*

Love is as easy to corrupt as the next thing, and it is one of the most dangerous elements in the world when it is corrupted.

*How many have **bled** and died for love alone, comrades?*

How many have bled and died because they have not felt it?

How many have gone to war because they did not want others to feel it?

*How many have gone to war because they **hate** it?*

***Over**, and **over**, and **over** again.*

*The drums of war have steadily beaten...**millennia** after **millennia.***

***Heroes** are a response to conflict, whatever the sort.*

Some are far more tangible than others; some come and go quickly.

*Some will be remembered forever; others will be recognized only after they return **home**.*

Words

Spoken** into the **dark,

*They **ignited** life.*

*Time still **bends** to them.*

*They **wound** and **mend**…fostering **peace** or **rage**.*

*They **are** incantations, curses, blessings, truths, deceptions.*

*They are written in the **sands** of the shores; they are written in **ink** and in **blood**.*

*Carried through the nether by angels and forces that even we **await**.*

*Spoken in various **tongues**.*

*Carried by glistening **feathers**.*

*Passing through malicious **fangs**.*

***Weaving** between the in-between.*

*Giving the **heart** a voice.*

*Giving the **heart** a set of **lungs**.*

*To **cry**.*

*To **scream**.*

*To **beg**.*

*To **howl**.*

*To **gnash**.*

*To **mourn**.*

*To **praise**.*

*To **be**.*

*To **laugh**.*

*To **breathe**.*

*They are a **poison** and the **anti-venom**.*

*They are the **embers** that engulf a forest **and** the **rain** that soothes the aftermath.*

*Must words **escape** the lips?*

*How many have been spoken by the **mind**?*

*How many have been spoken by the **heart**?*

*The **soul** has so much more to say than the **mortal** tongue ever can.*

Onlookers within the Bonfire City's borders gasped as a severely wounded stormdrake came crashing to the ground. It hit almost dead center in the construction project. The last of Kush'hera's nest was roaring in sorrow as the fire still ate at its flesh. Heroes and civilians rushed to extinguish the smoldering embers, doing their best to stay the flailing beast's pain. Spellflingers cast soothing mists to douse the flames while others applied cooling frosts to numb portions of the dragon's body. Several lightcallers laid their hands on the stormdrake, sending pulses of healing energy throughout the beast's system. Eventually, the stormdrake was able to sleep. Dozens of individuals remained, however, to tend to the majestic creation's injuries.

Fear was palpable as the reality of the situation struck those who witnessed the crash landing. In recent history, a stormdrake had never been seen in such a condition. In a moment of historical significance, the dragon had fled and was now the last of its kind. Asheya's glow had gone dark with the otherworldly smoke that remained there.

"Wildfire will speak into the depths" – R:09:C

Wards

Shiro, Dan-hali, Parraeysia, and the Broken Bow of Zuhetta-- all are places of safe harbor and a refuge for humanity. Each has been consecrated by life and death...by blood and symbols.

*There is **power** in the word **Shelter.***

***Protection** is sought by **all** things.*

*By **all** people.*

All** mortal entities become **weary.

*Is the **soul** not mortal amongst this **reality**?*

*Does it not **beg** for **rest**?*

*For **solace**?*

*In **total** darkness, the pillars of Light are **readily** seen.*

*But the **journey** to those pillars is too far for some to make in **time**.*

*For **darkness** has its **own** wards.*

*It has its **homes** and **bastions**.*

*A **beautiful** and tragic **system**,*

Bol'rel had come into Rime with Stella, Enysa, Lua, and Sij. The archangel kept a low profile, and his stay would be brief--a quick stop and a few words to fewer people. It was a relatively clear and starry night over Shiro as the people went about their lives as best they could. They seemed happy enough as music was played, and laughs could be heard.

The removal of Kush'hera from the battlefield had resounded through the expected channels, thus prompting humanities to hasten their work with void energy. The continent of Zuhetta was more on her own than ever. The cities would have to rely on their alliance and faith. Kush'hera's corpses and those of the dead stormdrakes were salvaged for certain materials that would benefit humanity. Otherwise, the control of the sky over those lands was theirs.

Finally, the *Skysword Project--the development of fighter jet technology--had truly opened the doorways between two eras.*

Melancholy

Yana and Bael made the mistake of stopping by the Raven's Nest to see Delia before their departure. Enysa had just wrestled their luggage away and was now in a desperate battle to keep the summoner where she was. Delia, Jeeves, Horus, Lua, and Sij had been casually watching the exchange. Lua and Sij had only met the summoner some minutes ago and were amused that their comrades had such spirits in Malene. Bael was as eager as his wife to take this leave and was working with her to corner the darkdancer who clung to the bags.

"All I have to do is ask for our other friends to intervene, Enysa," Yana huffed.

"It's over." Bael held out his hand, motioning for the bags. Enysa looked at the two with puppy-dog eyes, sadly replying, "But we just learned that ritual spell. We were supposed to do this together."

"You can all play together when we get back," Bael said as he readied himself to make a move for the luggage.

"They still have to go through their transformation, Enysa. The timing will work out fine," Yana added. Enysa surrendered the bags and slumped down to the floor.

"Good girl," Yana smiled.

"How long?" Enysa uttered defiantly, shifting her red eyes away.

"Maybe five days?" Yana replied. "Fine," Enysa mumbled. Yana and Bael rejoined the group and breathed a sigh of relief at the resolution. Enysa slowly shuffled behind them. Horus just shook his head as Enysa passed by him.

"Enjoy your time, both of you," Delia said with a kind smile.

"We'll always handle matters here," Jeeves added, tipping his top hat as he spoke. Yana gave a gracious bow to the group and then turned her attention to the elves. She softly said, "It was wonderful to meet you. I can't believe I now know elves." Sij smiled and gave a thumbs up.

"It's gonna' be fun," Lua replied.

With Dehza's insight, Yana knew she could conjure a portal to Parraeysia. Seeing the bluest skies anywhere left in the world, the group watched as a beautiful image of the island came through the curious anomaly. Yana and Bael stepped through as they came onto the sandy shores.

That same night, Bol'rel had an audience with his sisters atop the Shiroan cliffs. He had seen the Child and mother and had left them a letter.

"I heard about what happened between you, Herod, and Swae," Bol'rel remarked. "I should have stepped in sooner."

"You weren't meant to," Swae replied plainly, as she puffed her pipe. Miri'el was worried about the matter at hand and stayed relatively quiet during the conversation.

"What are the actual odds of him not deciding to kill you?" Swae inquired.

"There's no way to tell," Bol'rel scoffed. "You know how bold that will make the darkness in the planes outside of this one."

"Herod will be given his choice."

"Swae, if your physical body is slain, it will take thousands more of our kin to report to the battlefield," Miri'el uttered.

"Our kin still suffer enough beyond here." Bol'rel's armor began to manifest on him. He grinned, saying, "Have a little faith." Then lightning and void began to swirl around the archangel. His feathers became like blades. The powers hummed and made the earth tremble. Then, BOL'REL TOOK OFF LIKE A BULLET. A thunderclap pierced the skies over Malene. Lightening and void surrounded him and trailed him as he soared across the world. Conjuring two swords, he approached Mol'do's coast.

THE STEEL DRAGON WAS READY FOR HIM, FULLY MEETING THE FORCE. The community of Tristen was obliterated from the map by the resulting impact. The two engaged in a melee duel that would take place in history books. Their very speeds caused the dark clouds to flee around them.

"You dare not bring a shield, archangel?" Herod roared.

"I don't need a shield for you," Bol'rel calmly replied as he parried every strike the demi-celestial made. Other than the ringing of their steel, it was eerily quiet for miles in every direction around the two. The stars were their only audience, which was their delight; because, once more, they were able to see the world below. The archangel and demi-celestial's wings met like weapons in and of themselves as sparks, and stray energies lashed about over rushing seas.

Neither combatant tired during the endless strikes. Going back and forth, both were utterly unyielding in their focus. SUCH INTENSITY HAD NOT BEEN SEEN IN A DUEL SINCE THE FIRST WAR. As seconds turned into minutes, Bol'rel began to kite Herod back over the Mol'doan mainland. The two created an anomaly in the skies. When they clashed, a powerful supernova appeared. Nether storms were whipped up in several places as energies in the atmosphere were quickly jostled about, thus obliterating demons and monsters of the underworld that now inhabited the lands.

Dan-hali was safely out of range, though the spectacle created by the two beings was becoming easier to see on the horizon. To those in the terrani Veils beneath the surface, the storms could be felt above them.

Bol'rel, with his furious pursuer at his heels, soon landed in the dreary aftermath of Mera. The archangel took a deep breath. As his armor left him, he braced for the hit of his life. Truly, the move halted the demi-celestial in his tracks as torrents of wind blew by from the ceasing momentum. Bol'rel, relieved to have been spared at least that time, laughed out loud. Herod was momentarily in awe of the gesture, but that did not quell his malice. Herod approached the archangel, grumbling, "So, this was your play," as he punched Bol'rel in the jaw. The archangel barely kept his footing and readied himself for more. Blow after blow landed as the steel dragon laid into the archangel.

Bol'rel's bones broke from Herod's punches and kicks, and the archangel's innards were receiving substantial damage.

"FIGHT BACK!" Herod demanded as he slammed the archangel to the ground, shattering the very earth. Bol'rel coughed blood as he gasped for air. The steel dragon took him by the throat and lifted him into the air.

"This is what you want, right?" Bol'rel said, his eyes barely able to open. Herod threw the archangel some yards away, shouting, "YOU TOOK HER AWAY. SHE WEPT AS YOUR SWORD CAME DOWN!" Herod glided over to the archangel and put the edge of his sharpened wing to Bol'rel's neck.

"She isn't lost," Bol'rel uttered.

"LIAR!" Herod yelled and kneed the archangel in the face. Bol'rel grunted, spitting his blood aside and saying, "Kill me and have your vengeance or take a path of redemption." Herod roared and pierced the ground, wrapping his wings around the archangel.

"I was wrong," Bol'rel grunted, "but the Light was well ahead of my mistake." Herod was tormented by the situation and took some steps away from the battered archangel. Bol'rel, groaning from the pain of his beaten body, tried to support himself. He said, "Release the energy around the pylon at Tristen. Allow humanity to connect to their brethren across the world."

Herod's knuckles cracked as he clenched his fists. "There is more to your scheme, second-born," he grumbled.

"You're no fool, Herod," Bol'rel replied.

"There is light left in you, but to see her again, atonement is required." The steel dragon scoffed.

"Yojun'Sha must be destroyed," the archangel stated.

"Send him to oblivion, and you will see Eternity again. You will see your wife again." Herod was silent and conflicted. He slowly stepped away from the archangel and took flight into the darkness. Relieved, Bol'rel laid back but was still in excruciating pain.

It was a beautiful dusk when Yana and Bael came through the portal onto Parraeysian sands. A handful of awe-struck Ma'ji citizens were present at the location. The Ma'ji greeted the two strangers, and Yana and Bael returned the gesture. The two were subsequently escorted to Radagast, the wolvyn priest, who happened to be fishing off the eastern shorelines. He was struggling to reel in a large catch. Shocked at the sight of his two visitors, he let go of his rod.

"Oh! My, my, my!" Radagast happily exclaimed as he embraced each guest. "What brings the two of you to our quiet sanctuary?

Bael was busy taking in the scenic sands and palm trees, waving at several Ma'ji that passed by. Yana cleared her throat, somewhat quietly replying, "I was hoping to see Rayne." Radagast pondered a moment before saying, "Hmm…yes, I think that is doable. We'll simply need to enlist one of our pupils for assistance."

"Pupils?" Yana curiously echoed.

"Indeed," the wolvyn priest replied with a grin.

"Physically, Rayne is a slumbering dragon. Any encounter with the girl, as you know, would have to be metaphysical in nature. Z, the ghostdancer, should be able to handle this task." Yana glanced and smiled at Bael, saying, "I'm sure you can manage without me for a bit?" Bael winked and smiled in return. Yana and Bael kissed before Yana accompanied Radagast in search of Z.

"I don't think I've met a ghostdancer before," Yana commented.

"A ghostdancer having a heroic gift tends to be a rarity," Radagast replied. "Not as rare as a summoner by any means--or as powerful--but their abilities make them a commodity when they do appear among the ranks. Of the 33 ghostdancers confirmed in Parraeysia, Z has stood out in her mastery of the gift."

"Only 33?" Yana asked.

"Relatively speaking, that's an astonishing number," Radagast answered. "I'm expecting that count to increase and especially in the dragonkin brood that will eventually rejoin Harth's population."

"By design," the summoner uttered. Radagast nodded, saying, Radagast nodded, saying, "Parraeysia will have its army, milady, to be gifted to the world by your dear friend, Rayne."

"This may be a stupid question but an army for what? Would they join the forces in Malene? Zuhetta? Mol'do?" Yana inquired.

"Not a stupid question at all, milady," Radagast kindly replied.

"While there will certainly be a time that dragonkin and Ma'ji will walk upon the foreign continents, their initial purpose lies within the shattered lands of Azkelon." Yana blushed, not being keen to such historical references. Radagast chuckled, "Don't worry, Yana. Much of Azkelon's history has been lost for a reason."

"Was it really such a terrible place?" Yana inquired, curiously. "Was it meant to be forgotten?"

"When Harth was formed, there was essentially one massive continent, Zan'kar," Radagast explained. "It was the *First Kingdom,* a place where humanity and heavenly principalities comingled freely. But then, *The First Rebellion* introduced an enormous amount of corruption among the pious people. They began to worship celestials and angels. *Sin* found harbor in the hearts of humanity. Consequently, Azkelon was carved from Zan'kar in an attempt for humanity to regain its bearings." Yana listened intently as the two continued to stroll.

"The bloodlines that you know today ruled in Azkelon together," Radagast said.

"Similar to the setup in Shiro?" Yana asked.

"I would imagine so," Radagast affirmed. "For a time, they did well to maintain the Light's ways; but, as time went on, darkness only intensified among the astral and physical planes. Treachery has a dreadful way of repeating itself."

"How was Azkelon destroyed? How was an entire continent obliterated?" Yana asked. Radagast answered, "Zan'kar, or what remained of it, was scattered into the three continents we know today. Many celestials took part in dispersing Zan'kar. It is also said that the Light's own wrath annihilated Azkelon, leaving only the anomaly that exists there today."

"What could possibly be left?" Yana remarked.

"There are only theories," Radagast replied, "but such an action would have created a rift between the planes of existence."

The two came to the training grounds where Z was sitting with some of her friends who were participating in the ongoing exercises. There was a halt to the activity at the sight of Radagast and the summoner. Yana smiled and waved to the Ma'ji. Radagast motioned for Z to come over, and she eagerly responded. Meanwhile, Zeit had come from behind Yana. He hugged her and lifted her into the air. The summoner gave a somewhat startled laugh, saying, "Hey, big guy." Zeit nodded happily and put her back down.

Z introduced herself to Yana. "How may I be of service?" she asked politely.

"The summoner wishes to converse with Rayne," Radagast said with a smile.

"You'll need to project her soul into the stasis chambers." Z clapped her claws together, jovially replying, "That would be wonderful! I'm honored to be chosen for such a task." Yana gently hugged Z, and he returned the gesture. Z escorted Yana to the stasis chambers, where the summoner could not believe the sight she was beholding. Yana laid her hand on the massive and stunning dragon, awestruck that this was Rayne.

"Please, lie down here," Z said kindly, as she motioned to a plot on the ground in front of her.

Yana complied, lying on her back as the Ma'ji knelt by her head.

"Close your eyes," Z softly requested. "Take deep breaths." Yana did as the Ma'ji instructed and came into a relaxed state. Z held her hands over the summoner, with her palms facing up, as she whispered in her native language. Yana could feel a peaceful sensation like a drug entering her veins. When Yana opened her eyes, the world was a different shade…almost foggy in nature. Seeing Rayne standing not far from her, the summoner sat up, gasping, as tears immediately made her eyes misty. Rayne's arms were open as she smiled and also began to weep.

Yana rushed over, and the two souls embraced tightly. "I can't believe this," Yana uttered in a whisper.

"I've missed you, girl," Rayne said quietly.

"I've missed you," Yana replied in kind. The two briefly looked each other over. Tears began to flow as they remembered how they were before the cataclysm. As they embraced again, Yana could not help but glance about the room…

Which, in all reality, is a two square mile plot of time and space?

"Definitely spacious," Yana commented.

"Yeah," Rayne sighed. "Stuff just kind of appears as I need it." Yana looked around and saw various things still just lying about on the ground.

"Why are you still messy in the spirit realm?" she asked with a laugh. Rayne blushed, replying, "Aron Skybourne said the same thing." Yana knelt down to examine some of the numerous tomes scattered around them.

"You were never a reader either," she said, with some level of awe.

"There's not much to do," Rayne shrugged. "I can turn on music, so that helps. It's like living in a netherbox."

"I wanna' see," Yana said curiously.

Rayne snapped her fingers once, and music began playing all around them. It was a dreamy and rhythmic tune. Yana was quite impressed. "I also muted your little friend when you came in here," Rayne added with a wink.

"Awesome," Yana happily replied. "He's probably so pissed."

"I imagine that relationship has been interesting," Rayne remarked. "You know, that's a historical first…for the destroyer of worlds to pair himself with a mortal."

"I still think he's up to something," Yana uttered.

"Probably," Rayne chuckled.

Yana smiled as she looked around the otherworldly place and then back at where her body would have been. "I wonder how long she can keep this up?" Yana asked.

"The ghostdancer?" Rayne replied. "She's just as peaceful as you are. Your energies are cycling back and forth, which keeps both of you in a state of suspension. She can maintain such a spell for at least a couple of hours at a time."

"So, you're like a hero expert now?" Yana asked with a grin. Rayne shrugged and answered confidently, "I'm practically a celestial, babe. I have to know things now."

"Practically?" Yana echoed, clearly impressed by the notion.

"A celestial lens, he called it," Rayne stated. "Essentially, I'll get to be an actual celestial for a minute or two, but a still one."

"So, a minute or two makes you practically a celestial?" Yana asked slyly.

Rayne smiled as she stuck her tongue out at her friend. "So...pop quiz, Miss Celestial?" Yana continued. "Tell me a little about heroes. Tell me something new."

"A number of Harth's heroic gifts are evolutionary," Rayne began.

"Each one, including yours, has a different pinnacle. A ritualist becomes a summoner as the gift becomes naturalized in the host's body--and through the exercise of sheer power. I don't suppose you've noticed that you don't really need a staff anymore?" Yana agreed, realizing that she had never given much thought to her own advancement. She looked at her hands, remembering as she did, that she had not recently used a staff to cast a portal for the airships.

162

"You weren't a ritualist for long," Rayne said kindly.

"The ritualist phase is more of an initial test of the subject. Only once in humanity's history has a ritualist been cut off from her gift's ascendance." Yana looked at Rayne as if she wanted to hear more.

"Other gifts, like the warrior, are more complicated," Rayne continued. "There are multiple disciplines to master, and the ascendance to paladin is extremely rare. It can only be unlocked through direct angelic intervention. Some gifts, such as the gunslinger or bladedancer, don't even have an ascended state. Gunslingers are linked to firearms and can enter a gunpowder trance that induces a hallucinogenic targeting system that works directly with the mind and body. Bladedancers maintain something of magnetization to blades within a certain weight class that becomes an extension to the host's body and energy. Is any of this new to you?" she asked with a smile.

Yana nodded. "Spellflinger is an umbrella term," Rayne stated, "which is something that encompasses any wielder of magical potency--arcane, fire, water, wind, ice, lightning, stone, or any elemental power that can be manipulated. Some heroes seek to master all of the branches while others specialize in a core discipline."

"I feel embarrassed," Yana said with a mild blush. Rayne laughed, asking, "Why?"

"You'd think a summoner would know these things, right?" Yana answered.

"You just don't talk to people," Rayne said. "You've always kept your circle pretty small."

"Maybe I should read more," Yana uttered.

"You used to say that all the time," Rayne joked, "but you never did. You are a good listener. I always liked that about you."

"I wish you could see how things are in Shiro," Yana remarked. "It's changed so much since all of this began."

"I've heard whispers here and there," Rayne said.

"I'm hoping that I have time to stop by at some point. How are the others?" Yana grinned and responded, "Delia hosts the darkdancers in Rime, and Sapph is kind of an officer. I am not too sure what her role is. She is married to a lead captain and is friends with us, so she's kind of like the military's pet. Skarg is a siege engine operator. I think he's having the time of his life."

Rayne chuckled, replying, "Not bad, considering where the lot of us started." Yana smiled and agreed.

Powershift

There had been a snag as work was progressing on the skysword aircraft. Stella, the voidkeeper, had attempted to charge one of the prototype engine apparatuses. Upon releasing her void currents, Stella had caused the engine apparatus, as well as most of the vessel, to melt.

Her face was priceless.

A number of engineers, cogs, military personnel, and workers were somewhat upset, even though the sight of such power was a sight in and of itself. Kira, Bael's sister, and To'to, the troll, were still laughing at the voidkeeper's expression, imitating it and cracking jokes back and forth. Ma'ji, Vega, and Morgan, the necromancer, were doing their best to console Stella, who was pouting by now. "It was just a hiccup," Morgan would say.

"You haven't used your energy in such controlled capacities before," Vega added. "Perhaps some practice would help."

"Yeah, an aircraft isn't the same as a pylon," Morgan agreed.

Continuing to hear the ongoing commotion from the various individuals involved with the project, Stella huffed and shifted her eyes away.

"At least it was just the one," Kira commented. Morgan quickly smacked her companion on the back of her head.

"OW!" Kira exclaimed. "What the hell was that for?"

"You damn well know," Morgan said with a leer. As To'to began to open his mouth to speak, Vega smacked him on the back of his head. "Hey 'mon? What gives?"

"You damn well know what," Vega scorned.

Stella stuck her tongue out at her mockers. One of the cogs working on the project cautiously approached the group. Stella's eyes immediately glanced at her. The cog smiled and waved, saying, "A minor setback, ma'am. At least we now know, right?"

"Won't happen again," Stella mumbled, shifting her gaze to other crews that were looking at the group with disapproving postures.

"We're gonna' give the crews a day or two to decompress while we figure out a more effective way to move the process forward," the cog cheerfully stated. Stella sighed as she began making her way out of the hangar, which also had a gaping hole melted through one of its sides.

As Stella shuffled along, Kira came alongside, happily saying, "Let's go see Delia. I haven't had a chance to meet the new darkdancers. They're elves, yeah?" Stella downheartedly nodded. The group made their way to the Raven's Nest, and Jeeves greeted them at the entryway. They briefly toured the complex. Eventually, they came to one of the training grounds where they saw quite the spectacle.

Lua and Sij, who had both successfully undergone the transformation, were engaged in a sparring match. With the exception of To'to, the visitors were rather shocked at the intensity with which the two elves were fighting. The very ground shattered with Sij's movements, and torrents of lightning shot from Lua's hands. The martial combat was utterly impressive when the two were within close range. Neither was able to land a definitive blow on the other. Sij was wearing a full set of shadowcraft plate armor, which allowed him to take some hits from Lua's bolts. Lua was sporting shadowcraft mage garments. Both of their gear had been modified by Horus, the darkdancer, to amplify their natural strengths, and those strengths were indeed being exercised.

"Dis be awesome, 'mon!" To'to cheered. Enysa smiled confidently.

"Unfortunately, this is something of a counseling session as well," Delia giggled.

"The large one doesn't use a weapon?" Vega noted.

"He insisted against it," Horus replied, "so I focused a lot of attention on his gauntlets." Just then, several bolts of lightning were deflected by Sij's gauntlets; and, unfortunately, some came dangerously close to the group of spectators. Kira was one of the ones who took cover. As she did, she shouted, "OYE! Situational awareness!"

"Sorry!" Lua shouted back but continued in her duel.

"I suppose they've been at it for long enough," Jeeves calmly declared, holding up his hand for the session to cease. Lua and Sij bowed to one another before coming to join the rest of the group. The visitors were taken aback by the sheer size of the Fo'hemut elf, as well as the beauty of his terrani counterpart. Morgan, Vega, To'to, and Kira introduced themselves. Lua and Sij did so as well.

"Elven darkdancers," To'to remarked.

"Dem gonna' be around a while, assuming dey y'know, don't get killed." Sij laughed, replying, "Jeeves has told us as much. Personally, I'm excited!"

Lua smiled, saying, "I'm still coming to terms with such a notion."

"Meaning what, exactly?" Morgan asked.

"The elven races are already gifted with extended lifespans among Harth's mortal kin," Jeeves said. "The darkdancer's transformation only further benefits such an aspect."

"We have two vials left for the infusion," Enysa added. "Assuming we don't come across any more candidates, they could be used to further extend my life or Horus' life."

"Only time will tell," Vega kindly remarked.

"Miri'el said the exact same thing," Enysa commented curiously.

"What's with the glum look, Stella?" Sij inquired.

"Did you NOT just witness that awesomeness?" he added, as he triumphantly flexed his biceps.

"A mishap at the airfields," Stella mumbled.

"Pffft...she was trying to charge a void engine and instead nearly vaporized a squad in the process," Kira spiritedly remarked. Once more, Morgan swiftly smacked the reaper on the back of her head.

"OW!" Kira exclaimed. "Why ya bein' so rough today?"

"Because you're just being an ass now," Morgan replied, as she casually glanced at her nails.

"I thought that was one of the things you loved about me?" Kira answered slyly. Morgan rolled her eyes.

"How many voidmancers does it take to screw in a lightbulb?" Enysa remarked with a grin. To'to high-fived the darkdancer by her comment and was met with a return gesture.

"Enysa!" Delia gasped. "I can't produce the amount of energy required without death magic," Morgan grumbled, leering at the darkdancer.

"It requires a very controlled flow," Stella grumbled, leering back at Enysa.

"So Morgan can work well with the collars, and Stella can activate the global pylons. Our problem is that there's no middle ground yet," Kira noted with a wink.

"An interesting conundrum," Jeeves said. "I have no doubt that you will surmount the obstacle, voidkeeper."

"Thank you, Jeeves," Stella graciously replied and bowed.

"How are things coming along here?" Vega inquired. Nodding at the two elves, Horus answered, "They've been interesting. It's certainly become a lively place since the addition of these two."

"Hey, they're getting along," Enysa remarked. "I'd say that we have an awesome team."

"I'm pretty curious about this tether ritual that has sparked Enysa's attention," Lua said.

"Oh, I can't wait," Enysa uttered.

"I'm sure she'll be back in a couple of days," Delia sighed with exasperation. "She and Bael needed their time together."

"I have no doubt that they're taking full advantage of their getaway," Kira added hintingly. "That girl is gonna' be feelin' good when they come back."

"Only to be ambushed by this one?" Sij laughed as he nodded at Enysa.

"I don't ambush her," Enysa defended.

"You broke into their home," Horus rebuked.

"I was just excited," Enysa replied, "and that was only one time."

"She's just a free spirit, 'mon," To'to commented. Enysa smiled.

"Thank you, To'to. See? He gets me." To'to gave her a thumbs up.

"Don't encourage him," Vega sighed.

In the smoldering remnants of Dak, Yojun'Sha sat upon a molten throne while he contemplated his next move. The skies were dark as eternal pillars of smoke still ascended into the thick clouds. Since Deth's departure, the environment had become tolerable to certain beings but still intolerable to mere mortals. Suddenly, a being soared through the darkness, coming to an earthshattering landing not far from Yojun. "Herod," the Firelord uttered. The steel dragon's flesh was that of eternal metal and bore something of a tempered glow from the heat of their surroundings.

"Yojun!" Herod roared. "You are an abomination to our kind. It has fallen upon me to end you!"

"You're a fool, Herod!" Yojun, the fallen Firelord, scoffed.

"Whatever the angels offered you is a lie. They're weak by having you come to do their dirty work. Together, we could ascend to levels beyond equal. We could shape this world and the universe by our power. It would be wise to accept my hand in partnership."

"Only a coward would make such a plea!" Herod rebuked. "I can smell your fear from here."

"THEN, SO BE IT!" Yojun yelled as he conjured his sword. THE TWO DEMI-CELESTIALS CHARGED EACH OTHER, CLASHING IN A BLAST OF ELEMENTAL POWER. The solar energy of Yojun'Sha's blade was met by Herod's steel claws. With lightning flowing wildly with each parry and riposte, fire and void swirled violently around the duel.

The elemental storm could be seen flashing against the dark skies from Shiro as citizens and soldiers clamored in concern. Strike after strike, the demi-celestials fought with eternal strength and speed. Inferno poured from the firelord's body while void energy coursed through Herod's veins. Magnetic fields lifted stones from around them for miles while dark clouds were incinerated above the two. The martial skill displayed was astonishing…such discipline and utter focus! As the fight continued, tornadoes of fire spawned around them as lightning began to strike along the Shiroan border. Dozens of strikes were exchanged in each minute as the duel continued. The elemental storm also continued to grow in intensity.

"How do you intend to finish me?" Yojun mocked.

"Clearly, you won't be able to do it on your own. This land will perish before I fall to the likes of you…as if the Light would allow you to live on?" Herod and Yojun'Sha clenched.

"I never said that I intended to walk away," Herod replied.

"What?" Yojun uttered, noticing the increasing glow of void energy radiating from Herod. "You're insane! You would waste such power?"

"Only a fool such as yourself would see this as a waste," Herod replied. As Herod allowed Yojun's blade to pierce his abdomen, he wrapped himself around the firelord.

"RELEASE ME, HEROD!" Yojun yelled.

"Our time has ended, brother…unfortunately, yours more than mine," Herod stated. Then Herod detonated the energy within himself. THERE WAS A BRIGHT FLASH OF VIOLET LIGHT, WHICH SENT A BLAST RADIUS IN EVERY DIRECTION FOR MILES. Everything in the immediate vicinity was obliterated as the winds of the explosion blew down the trees in Shiro. The streets of Rime shook while the spectacle could be seen throughout the land.

The aftermath in Dak was eerie as nothing remained of either combatant. Only the sounds of stones falling back to the ground were breaking the silence. A hole had been punctured in the dark skies above. A crater remained in the wake of the blast that covered a quarter of Dak's decimated lands. The mighty elemental storm slowly ceased as the void radiation actually began to stabilize the countries' climate. The scent of rain would soon fill the air in Dak as drops slowly began to trickle down from the remaining clouds.

Meanwhile, in the depths of the pit, Dom'rel summoned one of his companions from the frontlines of the shattered lands. Before her fall, Vox'rel was once a revered legionnaire among archangels. Her ferocity matched her beauty. For now, she was still caked in the blood spatter of the battlefield from which she had recently been called. She bowed low before the devil, saying, "I have heard the nature of my summons. My body and my services are at your disposal."

"I know, dear," Dom'rel said with a smirk.

"I expect you to exceed Vil'el's duties in every way. She did well to lay a foundation for us. Her sacrifice has ensured a secure future for my children."

"You wish me to oversee the titan project in Mol'do, sire?" Vox'rel asked, still bowed low.

"Indeed," Dom'rel answered. "But, first, the services of your body are required."

Vox'rel's armor phased away, revealing her flesh. Dom'rel stood and approached his selected consort. He pinned her to the ground with his foot. As he looked over her body, he said, "All that fighting and not a scratch on you." His right hand became a wicked claw. He knelt and dragged it slowly down Vox'rel's back, cutting into her skin. Feeling the blood run down her sides, the fallen archangel groaned. Dom'rel licked the blood along the wounds and said, "I'll have you screaming by the end of this."

That Sinking Feeling

In Ramm, several towns and cities were being bombarded by allied airships and tanks, leveling the infested places by shear firestorms of artillery. Machine guns rattled, cannons boomed, and railguns flashed. Spell casters hurled powerful elements, and marksmen picked off their targets. The shrieks of the fiends were inaudible beneath the hail of destruction they faced. They were incinerated, crushed, and blown to pieces.

Knowing there was nothing left of his former kingdom to mourn, King Amon watched from the deck of one of the lead destroyer ships. He had made his decision and had given the go-ahead signal for such operations. Void communications were buzzing with chatter between troops on the ground and in the darkened skies as their operations were finally taking shape in the swarmlands. Honestly, alliance forces were having a bit of fun with this strategy and were rather enjoying the spectacle.

Amon, joining Eli, the pilot, and the handful of present crew, went to the helm of the airship. "How are you, sir?" Eli asked.

"I'm good, lad," Amon sighed. "I'm as much at peace with this sight as I could ever be. We will rebuild our kingdom. First, we have to send all these putrid monstrosities back to the pit."

"Aye," Eli affirmed. Then Skarg came over the void comms, saying, *"The town of Hensloft appears to be docile; permission to roll onward?"*

"How are the munitions?" Amon asked.

"More than enough, sir!" Skarg laughed.

"Aye, proceed," Amon stated.

Eli chuckled. "What's funny?" Amon asked with a grin.

"I still remember when Skarg and the gals rolled up to the Al'var airbase in Vae'yir," Eli replied. "They were in this old mining junker, and they certainly didn't look like much."

"You know your comms are on, babe?" Sapphira said over the network. Eli blushed.

"Too bad we ended up rocking shit," Sapphira continued.

"Yana saved that sexy ass of yours. Have you ever thanked her?" Glancing about at the crew members that were staring at him in amusement, Eli replied, "Uh, maybe more of a collective thank you."

"And what'd you mean, 'didn't look like much'?" Sapphire persisted. *"We were the hottest thing in that desert. Don't act like I didn't take you to school."*

"That's not what I meant!" Eli defended. "Are we really doing this? I kind of need to focus."

"Oh, please…like you're having to do sooo much maneuvering right now," Sapphira laughed. Eli finally disabled his comm device, clearing his throat as he ignored the amused onlookers. Amon chuckled, patting the Captain on his back.

At the base, Sapphira was in the hangar that served as Trova's company quarters. "That totally made my day!" she said with a smile. Kasslow was priming their gunship as A'mi finalized her checklist of materials. Trova was sitting with his boots propped up, shaking his head at the exchange between Sapphira and Eli.

"So, you're good in bed and are besties with a summoner…amazing to be in your presence," he said slyly.

"I can do other stuff," Sapphira rebuked. A'mi giggled as she put several potions in her backpack. After Kasslow got the airship ready for their departure, he joined the group.

"What did I miss?" he asked.

"Terribly important conversation," Trova uttered. Sapphira leered at the darkdancer.

"Aw, sorry I missed that," Kasslow remarked.

"All good, big guy," A'mi said with a smile. Kasslow shrugged.

"Well, the ship is ready to go. Let me piss; then we'll take off." Trova stood and sighed with satisfaction as he cracked his back.

Then…

Rumbling and quaking with increasing intensity, the very world began to tremble.

Void comms lit up with chatter as those on the ground clamored with confusion. *"A bloody earthquake!"* Skarg, the dwarf, exclaimed.

"There's never been an earthquake in Ramm!"

"All units hold positions," Amon declared. *"What is the status on the ground?"*

"Really fuckin' shaky!" one commander replied. *"Shit's falling off the walls, but the structural integrity of the base seems to be holding,"* an officer at the Gate answered.

Yarimheim, the central mountain in Ramm, was the epicenter of the phenomenon. Dust and dirt shot out from its base. The mountain could be seen crumbling, cracking, and even sinking. *"Is anyone else seeing this!"* Eli exclaimed. His question was met with a number of affirmations. There was a violent jolt, and the massive mountain sank even more. Dust and debris went in all directions as the mighty tower of the earth continued to fall. Thuds and booms were echoing throughout the chilled air. The mountain continued to sink in stages, and a massive hole kept widening. All at once, the last of the mountain collapsed into the abyss.

The tremors began to become lighter as the terrain slowly stabilized. *"All units, check in!"* Amon demanded. There were no apparent casualties from the anomaly, and damage to the alliance base was relatively minimal. However, enormous legs began to emerge slowly from the gaping hole. The creature was similar to a monstrous spider barbed and lined with spikes.

"All units! Fire! Fire! Fire! Don't let that thing come up. I don't want to see any more of it!" Amon shouted in a frenzy.

Each leg was as tall as some of the smaller surrounding mountains. A monster of this size had never been seen in recent history. Airships moved as close as they could and unloaded every ounce of ammunition they had. Artillery and tanks, firing at the massive targets, adjusted their heading. The beast roared and hissed as explosions tore into its appendages. Dozens of airships focused on one of the legs. After nearly emptying their ammunition reserve, they finally severed a piece of it.

"GOOD! KEEP HITTING ONE LEG AT A TIME! DON'T LET THAT THING CRAWL OUT!" Amon ordered. Bullets, shells, bombs, and elemental blasts continued to pummel each leg that became available as a target. The sky lightened the darkened lands. The monster continued to howl and screech as the alliance forces displayed their power and superiority. After another leg was practically severed, the beast slid back into the hole. Despite their gains, they saw another leg begin to rise...and so the cycle continued.

Eventually, the monster receded, and its nightmarish roars faded into the abyss of the fissure. There was a sigh of relief amid expressions of sheer horror. *"Status report,"* Amon uttered. His eyes were still fixed on where Yarimheim once stood. The order was given to return to base because their munitions, across the board, were empty. Clearly, everyone needed to regroup after such an event. Sapphira was more pale than usual as she relayed what had happened to her counterparts in Shiro. To be sure, those in Shiro had felt tremors as well.

Trova was furious and was shouting obscenities because their mission was now cancelled. "Let me guess," A'mi smiled and mocked. "You could've soloed that thing?"

"DAMN RIGHT!" Trova shouted.

"We appreciate your confidence, sir," A'mi answered kindly. As Kasslow rejoined the group, he said, "That was the most difficult piss of my life…things falling off the wall and everything shaking. It was madness!"

"Mission is cancelled, Kass," A'mi said, as she began to puff her pipe.

"Cancelled?" Kasslow replied curiously. "I miss something?" Still shaking, Sapphira said, "I'm gonna' go to the strip; you guys just hang out, okay?"

"This is bullshit!" Trova yelled from across the room.

In the forsaken city of Evermore, King Baaltha walked along the ramparts of the Citadel, observing the defenses and fortifications that were still being constructed. The dead king's lead scientist, Nojum, accompanied him. Elo'el, the fallen angel of death, also walked alongside Baaltha. Demons cowered at his presence. "Everything will be in working order when the time comes, your majesty," Nojum said. "My focus has been on defenses against their air power and, in particular, shield generators that will hold off explosive ordinance--as well as any magical attacks. It will deplete much of their munitions to break through that barrier alone."

"How else can this barrier of yours be disabled?" Baaltha asked plainly.

"Only by direct sabotage," Nojum answered. "But the paths from the ground are too narrow for their armors to climb. They will have no choice but to proceed on foot from below. Our hordes will be more than prepared at the choke points. I have also outfitted many of our dragons and airborne beasts with detonable devices, rail cannons, and turrets. Their losses will be great, your majesty."

"The explosives are in place?" Baaltha inquired.

"Indeed," Nojum chuckled. "Any of their forces that set foot in the city will find their escape routes quite closed."

"Good," Baaltha declared. "I have left my mark on this world, and I will see the Light's alliance scarred forever. They will come, and I will be ready to meet them."

"Dom'rel applauds your loyalty," Elo'el uttered in a deep and distorted voice.

"My service is not yet finished," Baaltha smirked.

"Why not unleash Elo'el on them at the onset, sire?" Nojum inquired. "He would stop them in their tracks before the first shot is fired."

"His kin would come for him," Baaltha replied. "His strike will be swift and at their very heart."

The Midnight Prophecy

In Parraeysia, stars dotted the clear sky as Yana and Bael laid together in their accommodations. The two held one another with a tender and loving embrace, feeling as if time itself had halted for them.

"How are you feeling?" Bael asked as he looked into Yana's eyes. Yana smiled, kissed him, and then rolled over to grab a skunkweed cigarette. Bael kissed her along her back and neck. Yana moaned and smiled as she conjured a runic flame to light the cigarette. "I could definitely live here," she said.

"I know, right?" Bael concurred.

Yana took a deep inhale of the smoke and handed the cigarette to Bael. She exhaled, softly saying, "You know that I love you." Bael kissed her again.

"I love you too."

"This was so nice," Yana said.

"It was such a trip seeing Rayne again and listening to all the things she told me. It's almost crazy that she's leading an army of dragons and cats into some long-forgotten battlefield," Bael said with a smile.

"Exactly." Yana laughed.

"The Ma'ji are definitely some well-mannered folk," Bael remarked through a puff of smoke. "Watching them train was pretty cool. They're in good hands here."

"Everyone's where they need to be," Yana said contently.

"Exactly," Bael agreed with a wink.

"You think everyone's held up without us around?" Yana asked playfully.

"I'm sure that you've been missed," Bael chuckled. "You're everyone's favorite summoner."

"Pfft...I'm the only summoner," Yana giggled, puffing her cigarette. "I better be your favorite."

"You're definitely my favorite," Bael replied, kissing her breast.

"Good," Yana said with a kind smile.

On the shores of Dan-hali, Swae was meeting with Bol'rel, who still bore injuries from his fight with Herod. It was a cloudy afternoon, but the seas were gentle in their motions as a gentle breeze occasionally wisped around them. "The air feels wonderful," Bol'rel remarked.

"I can't imagine how it must feel to you," Swae said, "but I imagine you'll return to the battlefields soon?"

"Indeed," Bol'rel stated.

"The chaos of the other realms of existence never ceases. However, something beautiful about this world is that there are periods of rest." Swae nodded in agreement as she puffed her pipe.

"Tal'Traxxi, the Celestial of Tides, will need to raise the pylon at Tristen," Bol'rel stated, "but that will only come when the time is right."

"It has not been revealed?" Swae asked. Bol'rel shook his head. Swae sighed, "Brother, humanity is vastly outnumbered here. Between the forces of Anri'Vex, the underworld guardian, and those of the pit, how can they even begin to reclaim this land?"

"Humanity is outnumbered everywhere, sister," Bol'rel replied.

"Their resources cannot be spread too thin, and their time must be their own." Swae sat on the sands, pondering. "The terrani may have no choice but to go on the offensive; but, to go into the underworld, they would be going in practically blind."

"The faithful are never blind, sister," Bol'rel replied. "Though the shroud of darkness will be dense, the Light will guide them. As much as the Anri'Vex are focusing on the surface of this world, they would probably meet less resistance if they traversed those depths."

"Regardless, he'll see us coming," Swae sighed.

"But he won't know their strategy," Bol'rel replied.

"Humanity has always been clever. They'll figure something out." Swae laughed out loud.

"They'll figure something out? I've never heard such a laxed statement from you about such matters." Bol'rel shrugged. "Everything is in place, sister. Take some solace in that."

"What of the people in Dan-hali?" Swae inquired. "Some of them may actually get restless without a fight to be had."

"More battles will surely come," Bol'rel answered. "For now, they should enjoy the repose. The world needs fighters and non-combatants." Swae nodded as smoke escaped her nostrils. Bol'rel's armor began to manifest upon him, and he conjured a portal to another domain, saying, "Littlefeather delivered our orders to you. As tempting as it may be, please do not step out of line again."

"You mean Vox'rel, the fallen angel?" Swae chuckled confidently. "I can take her."

"I'm serious, Sheth'rel," Bol'rel declared. Swae grunted, saying, "I hate it when you use my name like that."

"That scar on your face should be enough of a reminder that you aren't untouchable," Bol'rel replied.

"You are unique among our kin and a cherished asset of the Light. The Father will still see to the protection of his children, even those as powerful as you." Swae smiled, blushing ever so slightly. The portal closed around Bol'rel, and he once again disappeared, re-engaging elsewhere among the ongoing ethereal conflicts.

Tal'Traxxi, Celestial of the Tides, and Anri'Vex, the World Viper, were the only two beings of such status remaining on Harth. With the departure of Deth, Josun, Ilsoluum, Kush'hera, Yojun'Sha, Phoenicia, and Herod, there was a palpable shift in how this war would continue. Humanity, assisted by only a few of our kin, was regaining its strength. While Sahja and Fiaria were honorary guardians, their reach would remain limited to that of conduits of the Light in Zuhetta and a defense mechanism for the growing forces there.

"The time of ancient powers upon the world must surely end, as the treasured people find their song among the nether, singing their battle hymns amongst darkened skies" – M:A:E:II

In Rime, a meeting of various counsels had just concluded regarding the recent anomaly in Ramm. Thalis was walking in the halls of Blackwolf Keep with Thulo, an owl, perched on his shoulder. Azotus and Kora accompanied them. "This must be the underworld incursion we've been hearing about," Thulo stated. "To think that there was a monster of such size…it could be likened to a titan of the pit."

"Sounded like we had the firepower to handle it," Thalis casually replied. "Besides, there haven't been any further reports of new monsters breaching the area. Frankly, what happened may have saved us a lot of lives. The battle for Yarimheim wasn't going to be easy."

"How can you be so calm, Thalis?" Thulo asked concernedly.

"Probably because I've just gone somewhat crazy," Thalis chuckled.

"But why now?" Azotus pondered. "And in such a display? From what I understood, Thalis is right. There would have been hundreds of thousands of those bugs in Yarimheim."

"You think it was actually meant to benefit us?" Kora inquired of her husband. Azotus shrugged.

"Do we have any actual experts regarding this underworld?" Thalis asked.

"Indeed," Thulo concurred.

"Most of what we have is second-hand at best." Kora snapped her fingers as she had an epiphany. "Weren't there elves that came in recently?"

"Aye," Thalis affirmed. "I believe they came in with one of the darkdancers."

"I'll go speak with them," Kora stated. "Perhaps they can shed more light on this matter."

"Sounds good, love," Azotus said. So Kora departed from the group and caught transport to the Raven's Nest within the cliffs that overlooked the city. Delia greeted the wolvyn with a loving embrace, asking, "How are you? I hear you wanted to speak with our newest members?" Kora affirmed her question.

"I'm not sure how much you've heard of what happened in Ramm, but I'm hoping our elven comrades may be able to shed some light on the occurrence."

"I'm not as keen as others are. Sapphira contacted me and was quite shaken by whatever it was they saw," Delia replied.

"Come, I'll introduce you," she added, beckoning for Kora to follow.

They came to Lua's room and found her playing a stringed instrument. The sound was distorted and amplified by the electricity that flowed from her person. The melodic tune ceased when Lua caught a glimpse of the snow-white wolvyn standing in the doorway, and the arcing bolts subsided. Kora and Lua just sort of looked at each other for a moment, neither having been exposed to the other's kind before. The two approached and exchanged respectful greetings.

"A gifted hero and musician," Kora kindly remarked, as she noted the elf's talents.

"I almost thought my eyes were playing tricks on me," Lua said. "I saw a few of your people when we arrived. It's incredible seeing one like you up so close."

"I was hoping to ask you about something?" Kora inquired.

"Surely you felt some of the tremors yesterday?" Lua nodded and asked, "What can I help you with?"

"Well, for obvious reasons, certain histories aren't well known in this part of Harth," Kora began.

"It's only been recently that our forces have begun to discuss the underworld." Lua's ears lowered, and her expression notably shifted to one of concern.

"Indeed." Kora continued. "You see, the tremors we felt in Shiro were apparently caused by a monster of unspeakable size--a massive spider by all accounts. It sank the largest mountain in Ramm before attempting to crawl from the fissure that now remains in the wake of the event."

"Were they able to kill it?" Lua emphatically asked.

"Our forces were able to wound the creature enough so that it retreated into the abyss," Kora replied. Lua sighed with some relief, asking, "How big is big regarding what they saw?"

"By all accounts, it took every ounce of firepower that our forces could throw at it to even damage it as badly as they did," Kora answered.

"It is sort of a monstrosity none of us are familiar with." Lua was clearly concerned, pondering as she spoke. "Could it have come from *The Web*?"

"The Web?" Kora echoed curiously.

"Yes, a place of elven legend and hypotheses," Lua uttered, "…a home of such beasts that are of cataclysmic scale."

"Oh, dear!" Kora gasped. Lua nodded as she continued. "It's thought to be the last level of the underworld before coming into Anri's coil, but it is almost inconceivable that one of those things could breach the surface. It hasn't happened to my knowledge since the primordial wars."

The primordial wars, also called "The Wars of the Elements," occurred when humanity was young...when celestials, eternal principalities, and demons fought against one another on the world's surface. Gigantic titans of the pit and cataclysmic monsters were common upon Harth.

"Were there reports of any other monsters appearing?" Lua asked.

"Living vines?" Kora shook her head.

"No further engagements were discussed." Lua seemed baffled at this notion.

"Could he have been testing the waters?" she wondered. "Anri'Vex will not encounter such military weapons like the ones you have here. Even the imperials in Mol'do didn't have the sort of expertise or devices that Malene seems to have."

"There is a consensus among commanders that the sinking of Yarimheim actually aided in their overall objective in clearing

Ramm of the swarm," Kora remarked. "Would Anri'Vex have deliberately provided such assistance?"

"Honestly, it's hard to say," Lua said.

"How many of those creatures would have been in that mountain?" she asked.

"Our best estimates put their numbers close to a million," Kora answered.

"That certainly will serve as a substantial food source for Anri's beasts," Lua stated, "and the world viper is known for providing some amount of mutual benefits in the past. However, nothing can be certain."

"I see," Kora replied, pondering the situation.

"The underworld is definitely expansive, but the network was never thought to be entirely global," Lua explained. "It's possible that a pathway of this magnitude to Malene has only recently been made. For such a monster to have survived the aftermath of the attack, it might well be that the Anri beasts are at a depth that even the terrani have not mapped."

"You're very knowledgeable on this matter, Lua!" Kora remarked.

"Not nearly enough to provide suggestions about moving forward," Lua replied.

"This information would need to be relayed to my people in Mol'do to even begin a real process of understanding. My advice is to tell your troops to remain vigilant and to keep their distance from the fissure." Kora bowed her head, responding, "I'll relay what you've shared with me, darkdancer, unless you'd like to speak with our commanders and council yourself." Lua smiled and shook her head. "I'd rather not for now. I'm enjoying the space I have."

"As you wish," Kora replied.

Let's Try This Again

Yana and Bael were set to leave Parraeysia as a rather large crowd of Ma'ji' gathered to bid the visitors farewell. Before Yana even began to conjure a portal back to Shiro, Gizmo's voice was heard coming from the rear of the crowds, shouting, "Hold up! Wait, wait, wait!" Yana and Bael watched as the crowd parted to let the wolvyn (running on all fours) pass through where they were standing. Gizmo made it to the epicenter where he approached the two…panting.

"What's up?" Bael asked.

"I'm goin' with you two lovebirds," Gizmo declared.

"I need some supplies." Yana looked at the runt with a straight face.

"What?" Gizmo asked. "It's not out of your way, is it?"

"Everyone just uses me," Yana uttered with some level of amusement.

"Well, yeah, you're like the only being that can make portals other than angels, right?" Gizmo answered, "And there aren't any of them hangin' around here, so, you're it, doll. Besides, I kinda need a break from the whole beach scene."

"The Ma'ji can continue their work without your endless amounts of wisdom?" Yana slighted.

"I'm gonna' choose to take that as a compliment," Gizmo replied. The summoner rolled her eyes.

Yana conjured the portal. As onlookers gasped in awe and waved, she reflected the likeness of Rime. The three bid the citizens of Parraeysia farewell as the portal closed around them. Once again, Yana, Bael, and Gizmo appeared within the city limits, thereby startling a few people near the point of ingress.

"Thanks a bunch," Gizmo said, beginning on his way. "I'll send for you when I'm ready."

"You'll send for me?" Yana replied, with some amount of insult. Gizmo laughed as he walked away. Yana sighed and glanced at Bael, who seemed to have his attention turned in the other direction.

"What?" Yana asked as she turned. But before she even saw it coming, Enysa practically had the summoner pinned to the ground.

"You're back!" Enysa exclaimed happily.

"How on Harth are you already here?" Yana asked with some amount of surprise.

"I could feel you. It's like you're one of us," Enysa replied with glee. Yana looked up at Bael, who was gathering their bags.

"Where are you going?" she asked helplessly.

"I'm gonna' put this stuff away and then go check in with my people," Bael replied with a chuckle.

"You're all mine," Enysa said slyly.

"Would you mind letting me up?" Yana kindly asked.

So, Enysa helped the summoner to her feet, smiling all the while. Yana brushed herself off and was able to grin at her friend's spirited nature. "You ready to go?" Enysa asked.

"Would you accept anything other than yes?" Yana replied.

"Nope," Enysa said with a wink. So the two began their trek to Delia's estate.

Elsewhere, in the airfields of the city's parameter, Stella was attempting to charge another of the void engines. Though the first mishap had claimed one of the aircraft, there were still three skyswords ready for this final touch. Two of the aircraft were designed for a single pilot…Katana, they were called. The other was a larger model called Broadsword. Stella approached one of the Katanas while the spectators kept their distance. She took a deep breath as her crystal scars began to glow, and she opened her palms towards the apparatus. Void currents slowly snaked from her person into the receptor devices. Her energy output increased steadily but stayed well within the limits required.

Surely enough, the engine began to hum and glow with a similar radiance to that of the voidkeeper. Stella ceased the flow of power as the void engine came to life. There was an uproar of cheers and whistles, and Stella herself was greatly relieved. The voidkeeper then went on to charge the remaining two aircraft in the same way. Both were successful. Some of the cogs, engineers, and crews, anxious to see their skyswords in action, were brought to tears to see their masterpieces come to fruition. General Nix approached Stella and gave her a congratulatory pat on the back. "This is a glorious day for our forces and a major step in taking the fight to those demonic cunts."

Stella, still knowing the duality that came with the production of these weapons, gave a half-smile and replied, "It is my privilege to be of such service, sir."

"Hang around for a bit," Nix stated. "We'll get our pilots here shortly. They've been eager to test these marvels." Stella bowed graciously, doing well to hide the two gentle tears that escaped her eyes. Within the hour, a vehicle arrived with those that had been selected to undertake the maiden mission of these aircraft.

These individuals had been tested to the ultimate, undergoing exercises with watercraft similar to the instance that had taken some of our friends to Chelsea. While the amount of force generated by these engines would be substantially greater, these pilots and crew were as adapted to such force as any mortal body could be. These individuals were Rufus, a Shiroan native, selected as one of the Katana pilots; Ada, a Vae'yiri, selected as the other Katana pilot; and Micah, also a Vae'yiri, selected as the Broadsword pilot.

The crew of the Broadsword included Jethro, a dwarf from Ramm; Bartholomew, also a dwarf from Ramm; Asher, originally from Dak; and Chloe, a Shiroan native. All of the pilots and crew had served in their respective militaries and arrived with accommodations from across the board. The airmen saluted those present and then boarded their respective vessels. Did you intend to list the crew of the Katana?

At the Raven's Nest, Yana and the darkdancers were about to undergo the tether ritual. Enysa was already lying on her back, eagerly awaiting the process to begin. As Yana took her place, something in the distance caught the eyes of some of her comrades. The summoner turned to see the skyswords slowly ascending vertically as they rushed to the railings of the pavilion. "Ugh, seriously?" Enysa sighed. However, as she got up to see what had delayed the ritual, her expression changed to match the awe that her friends bore.

Then there were three loud bangs as each aircraft took off over the sea. The thunderclaps resounded for miles, startling many citizens of Shiro. The aircraft quickly fled from sight, leaving only tracers in the sky behind them. Each aircraft was outfitted with void comms, allowing the pilots to communicate with one another.

"How's everyone holdin' up?" Rufus asked.

"Green across everything," Ada said.

"We're good, baby!" Micah affirmed. Within a couple of minutes, the aircrafts were passing over the now-abandoned isle of Chelsea. The roar of their engines echoed over the chilled seas. As they swung back around, they looked down at the sparkling snow and ice that reflected the overhead sun.

The aircraft eventually came back within the eyesight of spectators in Shiro. Their seamless formation covered miles in mere seconds. The aircraft buzzed the skies of the city before swinging back out over the seas. Cheers rang throughout Rime as the sight of these new weapons brought every manner of business to a halt, giving chills to those who watched the spectacle. How marvelous it was! Soon enough, the formation hovered over the airfields before coming in for their landing. There was celebration among those that met the crews, and the airmen themselves were ecstatic to have undergone such a historical event.

General Nix motioned for his cogs and personnel. "Let's get the payloads ready. We may not know exactly what those monsters are doing in Vae'yir, but it's time to give them a big fuckin' middle finger."

"Aye, sir!" his troops replied.

"Okay, the show's over," Enysa said eagerly, pulling Yana back to her initial position. The summoner could not help but laugh a little as Enysa sprawled herself on the ground. Horus sat down, knowing what to expect. Lua shrugged and sat down as well. Sij, remaining on his feet, laughed. "Let's see you knock me off balance, Yana."

"A gold coin says he goes down," Enysa said with a grin.

"I'll take that bet," Horus agreed.

"I'll double it," Lua added. So Yana closed her eyes and put her palms to the ground beside her.

Once more, runes of ruby light spawned on the ground around the summoner as she entered her meditative state. Intertwining and snaking energies began to flow between her and her comrades. All at once, the sensation struck the four darkdancers.

"Yeeesssssssss!" Enysa moaned sensually.

"Oh, wow!" Lua uttered in kind as she slumped over a bit. Horus was attempting to take controlled breaths, trying not to vocalize. Sij's heroic posture was quickly becoming laxed. He fought as best he could as his knees gently began to buckle.

"What…what is this wonderful magic? Sij asked. "No! I must remain steadfast."

"Just give in, baby," Enysa purred and giggled in her pleasure. Sij began to stagger more and more, uttering, "So much power, so much ecstasy! This is phenomenal!" Delia and Jeeves were also present, watching the session with intrigue. "I'm honestly surprised he's still up!" Delia chuckled.

"Give it another moment, milady," Jeeves replied.

"Even a hero of his natural strength cannot fight against this attunement." Sij continued to wobble and sway as if he had quickly become blindly intoxicated. Sure enough, the mighty elf was overpowered by the sensation and collapsed.

The ritual continued for such a time that the darkdancers eventually entered a sleep-like state as the runic energies between themselves and the summoner continued to embrace. A level of peace blanketed the group. Solace and power gently flowed through their veins. Eventually, Jeeves laid his hand on Yana's shoulder, waking the summoner. One by one, the darkdancers slowly stirred from the peaceful trance. Enysa stretched and groaned with satisfaction. Horus was a bit shaky in his attempts to stand. Lua took a deep breath and smiled at how good she felt.

"In…incredible!" Sij uttered in awe, slowly getting to his feet.

Yana gave a kind smile to her comrades. "A wonderful exercise," Jeeves declared. "Eventually, while the spell is active, they will be able to retain their composure and be able to engage in combat well beyond their current potential."

"You owe everyone two gold coins, Sij," Enysa uttered happily. Bearing an awestruck and almost sad expression, Lua approached Yana. Lua embraced the summoner tightly. Somewhat surprised by the gesture, Yana nonetheless returned the hug.

"I won't pretend to know what just happened," Lua said quietly, "or to understand what all of this means, but I'm honored to be here."

That night, Sij, Lua, Horus, and Enysa were lounging together on a balcony, sipping on slayers' remedy and puffing dragonskunk from a pipe. Synthetic beats played from a nearby netherbox as lights from the city and stars provided the atmosphere. "This stuff would kill the common man," Sij jovially remarked, after taking a drink. His character had become increasingly mellow.

"Anything that brings you down to a normal speaking volume is welcome," Lua said, smirking at Sij.

"I'm not that loud," Sij answered.

"Your voice carries," Horus added.

"Why am I always being picked on?" Sij asked with a chuckle.

"Because you're the biggest and probably the strongest," Enysa said through a puff of smoke.

"Probably?" Sij echoed with a smile.

"Don't encourage him too much, Enysa," Lua remarked as she reclined. "Miri'el told him to become humbler."

"She also told you to quit agitating him," Enysa replied with a giggle.

"Lately, I've been nice," Lua sighed contently.

"Indeed, I dare say that you're warming up to me," Sij stated.

"You and I may well have been lovers under different circumstances." Lua leered at Sij.

"And just like that, the truce was shattered," Horus uttered.

"I'm going to refrain from slapping you just to prove a point," Lua said, still leering at Sij. Sij just smiled back.

"Were all darkdancer chapters so dorky?" Horus uttered to himself.

Then the group sensed a presence approaching from the cliffs before them. The presence appeared friendly but powerful. They watched as Trova, the powerful darkdancer, phased from the shadow. He looked striking and as dangerous as ever. His glowing red eyes peered at each member, but he rested his gaze on the two elves. Lua was impressed, saying, "You're the guy Enysa mentioned. You totally look the part." Sij grinned widely as he was able to recognize the power Trova carried. Enysa saluted, and the others did as well. Trova nodded his head, and the group lowered their salutes.

Enysa hurried to embrace their leader. She confidently held her arm towards the other three and said, "I think we look good."

"It's a tight group," Trova commented. His face bore a sly smirk as he glanced down at Enysa. Enysa was ecstatic at the compliment, exclaiming, "WE HAVE FREAKING ELVES!"

"I trust your trips weren't too awful?" Trova asked of the others. Horus shook his head. Lua shrugged and grinned.

"I never got a good look at the guy that protected me during my trip." Sij agreed with his comrades, saying, "A being that could part the darkness and an onyx dragon the size of a mighty city…I asked him to let the darkness pass. It was deserved, but he refused. He told me that I was too sure to be overrun."

"The lashings, beatings, and stuff with the powder still sucked," Lua added. Horus, Lua, and Sij now shared the same stare, looking at Enysa.

"Equal justice, right?" Enysa said with a wink. By now, Delia had joined them at the balcony.

"You got here early," she said.

"Wait, she called you?" Enysa remarked.

"She said they'd had some time and were ready for deployment," Trova said. The other three perked up a bit.

"The military is on with their primary objective. The swarm between where we are now and Lok'rom are just fodder. It's good to get a little wet. I want you three to help push the front," Trova explained. "So, pack a bag. We leave soon."

Enysa immediately sank to her knees, pouting. "Oh, come on!" Trova sighed. "Why can't I get wet?" Enysa huffed.

"Trova, let her go for a bit," Delia stated.

"I think it's safe enough up to a certain point, and then she comes back here." Enysa certainly agreed with Delia's offer.

"Fine," Trova uttered. "I'll pair you with Sij." Enysa jumped to her feet and ran off to pack.

"Sij and Enysa will be with an infantry-focused advance; that is, door to door, ruin to ruin, building to building," Trova said. His attention was now on the other two.

"Horus and Lua will be with an armor-focused line, closer to the eastern border of the hole. Close air support is available for both of your respective fronts, but airpower is being focused north and west of the hole. I'll be with that group, clearing out the cleaver ones that survive the rain." The squad agreed.

Delia approached Trova. She smiled and softly said, "Thanks for taking her; it really would have been hard for her not to get to go."

"I know," Trova replied. "She'll be fine, especially with that one," he added, nodding at Sij. Trova continued.

"Their military is beyond well-armed, and they are very well trained. I'm hoping she can actually get some kills," he chuckled.

"How's Sapphira?" Delia inquired.

"She deals with our lot," Trova replied, "and other hero units. She's a go-between and go-getter. She has good people skills, I guess." Delia paused as she analyzed the darkdancer.

"Sometimes, it is really hard to tell when there's sarcasm with you." Trova shrugged slightly in reply. Delia inquired, "People are doing ok outside the consecration?"

"They seem to be managing, but it's darkness. It will find its ingress to the mind and body," Trova answered. "*We*, however, are immune," he added.

As Trova walked towards the railings, Delia kept at his side and asked in an uplifting manner. "Found any cool demon heads for the mansion yet?"

"There are a few being cleaned at the Gate," Trova answered. So far, she was satisfied with his work. "They will be delivered as they arrive. The military is doing well at blowing everything back to the pit, but that leaves little to be pilfered. I have to go far ahead on my hunts."

"I trust your judgment," Delia stated. Trova leapt from the balcony as he phased into the night.

"Well then, I guess the rest will have to find their way on their own." Delia sighed, as she leaned against the rails.

Throttle Up

The alliance campaign to retake the dwarven kingdom had resumed in Ramm, though with a new level of caution in light of the recent anomaly. Entire towns and cities were being leveled by a barrage of airpower and artillery. At the same time, countless other assets remained beaded on the massive fissure that now replaced the mountain of Yarimheim. With the removal of the dwarven capital from the equation, there was a heightened focus to push to Lok'rom (a city within Ramm) before anything else might appear from the abyss that had opened in the center of the country. Other major cities, especially those that dwelled within other mountains, became secondary objectives.

The alliance forces knew they needed an outward buffer from the base in order to create a relative no man's land for countless miles. While the anticipated fight at Lok'rom was still a daunting task, it was now practically a straight shot from the Gate. Among the airships in the darkened skies, there was only one smaller vessel hovering over the gaping fissure. As Trova looked down into the hole, A'mi, the alchemist, was huddled and trembling in the corner of the cabin. "This seems like a safe altitude," Kasslow, the wolvyn, casually stated.

"We're practically inside of it!" A'mi furiously rebuked.

"How did we get tapped to investigate this?"

"I volunteered," Trova said with a smirk.

"You son of a bitch," A'mi muttered. Trova chuckled as he lit a flare and dropped it into the abyss. The light from the flare quickly faded as it fell, which indicated there was no bottom to the pit. The darkdancer gave an impressed whistle while Kasslow came to join him at the cabin door.

"That is a very deep hole," the wolvyn remarked.

"Ya think?" A'mi scolded.

"Alright," Trova stated. "I'll be back in a minute."

"Wait, what?" A'mi asked. Then Trova leapt from the aircraft, phasing into a shadow as he descended. Kasslow looked over at A'mi and smiled.

"You two are insane!" A'mi uttered. "He's probably going to piss off whatever is down there."

"He just went to look," Kasslow reassured.

"That man is incapable of just looking," A'mi sighed, as she took a hearty swig of a calming syrup. Sapphira came over the void comms asking, *"Anything to report?"*

"Trova is in the hole now; he should be back any minute," Kasslow replied.

"HE'S IN THE HOLE?" Sapphira exclaimed.

"Yes, Trova is inside the hole," Kasslow answered.

"What the hell is he thinking?" Sapphira asked.

We're told to investigate," Kasslow said, "so, he investigates." Soon after, Trova reappeared in the airship.

"Oh hey, buddy!" Kasslow greeted.

"He's back?" Sapphira inquired. *"Put him on."* Kasslow handed the collar to Trova.

"Well, there is a shit ton of rubble down there and lots of bug guts and stuff," Trova stated, "and a tunnel that you could fit more than one army through. You can't see the top from the bottom." Sapphira sighed, saying, *"Thank you. Hopefully, you didn't draw any attention."*

"Nah, whatever that thing was, is long gone," Trova replied and sarcastically added.

"You want us to board this thing up while we're here?" Sapphira cut off the line of communication.

"You're such an ass!" A'mi stated.

In Rime, the skyswords were being finalized with their extensive ordinance payloads, and the void engines were already humming in anticipation of the mission. Based on the intel gathered from a reconnaissance in Gol, the pilots and crews had been fully briefed. "Essentially, your target will make itself apparent once you're in Vae'yiri airspace," General Nix said. "We don't anticipate anything capable of countering these aircraft; but, regardless, stay aware. You'll be the first assets to enter Vae'yir since its downfall, so any additional recon will be valuable."

The skyswords were loaded and ready to go. Flying south, they quickly bypassed the Shiroan countryside and were now into Gol. The formation intentionally kept some distance from Evermore, but the demons there surely heard the roar of the void engines. Within minutes, the aircraft entered Vae'yir, and the pilots gasped in awe at the utter desolation they witnessed. However, as they came to the center of the country, their target truly presented itself. *"HOLY SHIT!"* Ada exclaimed.

"DO YOU ALL SEE THE SIZE OF THAT THING?" Rufus affirmed.

"THAT'S WHAT THEY'RE BUILDING?" Micah asked.

Truly, these soldiers were witnessing the construction of a pit titan...an abomination of a creation. This was a monster that could single-handedly lay siege on any well-defended city...a biomechanical humanoid that was the stuff of legend and nightmares.

The squadron soared over the location with lightning speed and circled back as they prepared to release their payloads.

"Focus everything on it! Don't mind the little shits!" Rufus declared.

"You got it!" Ada affirmed.

"Aye!" Micah and his crew answered. The two Katanas took the lead, releasing dozens of rockets along the titan's putrid body in a display that could flatten entire towns. The broadsword's bay doors opened, dropping dozens of cluster bombs. Glorious explosions riddled the inactive creature…a beautiful firestorm of justice.

The skyswords, preparing their second round of ordnance, turned to make another pass over the dormant monster. Once more, their rockets and bombs rained down on the titan, blowing apart its torso and limbs. They soared around, coming back for a third pass. *"Let's show 'em how big our bullets are!"* Ada stated excitedly. The chain guns of the aircraft unleashed a hail of projectiles that penetrated the monster's flesh and blew entire chunks of meat into oblivion. Clouds of dust poured into the air while craters and decimated demonic components littered the ground.

Before heading back north, the squadron circled the peninsula, briefly noting other entrenchments and points of interest. Their first mission was more successful than they had even anticipated.

In the emptiness of the Golian forests, the wolvyns--Shoshana, Jovuk, and Holen--traversed the mush and mud. Holen was a bit pouty since their route was made with their safety in mind rather than engaging with the enemy. In fact, Jovuk had ordered Holen to hand over his weapons for safekeeping. They walked along the eastern border with Dak, where mountain bases met the tree lines.

The three had heard the aircraft pass overhead but were unable to see them due to the dark cloud cover.

"Are you going to keep your arms folded the entire time?" Shoshana asked with a grin.

"Yes," Holen answered in a huff. Jovuk sighed.

"Why are we setting up markers in one of the most dangerous places on Harth?" Holen complained.

"Because those were our orders," Shoshana replied. "We're pretty much mapmakers; you should be proud."

"Being mapmakers is boring," Holen uttered.

"I'm sure there will be plenty of fighting to come, Holen," Jovuk stated. "If anything, you should be upset at your wife for appealing to Azotus to let you come with me," he added with a chuckle.

"I am," Holen mumbled.

"But he would never let his wife know that he is!" Shoshana laughed.

"I hate that the two of you are friends," Holen said.

"Oh, she's shared so many stories about you," Shoshana answered.

"If I need to laugh, I can just look at you and picture any number of incidents." Holen leered at his comrade. As Jovuk placed a small marker in the mud, there came a voice from above the three, saying in a friendly tone.

"Oye!" Shoshana and Jovuk immediately aimed, had their weapons beaded at a large raven.

"'Uhh, no need for that," the raven said. "Do I sound like one of those monsters?"

The three looked at the bird with some level of confusion. "You three from Shiro?" the raven inquired.

"Is it a spy?" Shoshana asked.

"Hah," the raven said. "A spy she says!"

"Then, who are you?" Jovuk inquired. The bird hopped down to a lower branch, now about eye level with the wolvyn, saying, "Name's Gif; thanks for not shootin' me."

"How uh…what happened to you?" Holen asked.

"Bloody witch did all sorts of things to me, including this lovely number," Gif replied, as he motioned to himself with his wings. "I was a janitor in the Citadel. I guess I'm happy enough to have made it out of that mess alive.

"Are there more survivors? Prisoners?" Jovuk asked.

"Nah, mate. By now, everyone else is dead," Gif answered.

"They kept a handful of people for a bit, to use in rituals n' stuff…really twisted shit. The last few of us were sent to their laboratories. I was the last subject on the list."

"You must have seen horrific things," Shoshana said with empathy.

"Yeah, well, when I wasn't in a cell, y'know?" Gif replied in good spirits. "This has been a nasty place. It's refreshing to see some friendly faces, even if you're massive walking wolves."

"This guy doesn't seem right," Holen uttered.

"Says the dog with no weapon!" Gif rebuked.

"Hah," Shoshana said. "I like this guy already."

"So, why hang around?" Holen grumbled. "Gol isn't exactly comfy, even for a bird as ugly as you."

"Oye…no need for that," Gif answered offendedly.

"Just so happens that I have a horrible sense of direction; been flyin' in circles since I broke away from that witch. Don't suppose I could hitch a ride with you three?" Holen and Shoshana looked at Jovuk, who just shrugged in affirmation.

"Great!" Gif exclaimed happily, as he perched on Holen's shoulder. "I can tell you that you're clear for a while. Most of those monsters stay close to home these days."

"Thanks for the heads-up," Jovuk chuckled, as the group continued on their way.

Sunset, Sunrise

Yana was by herself in the Shiroan cliffs as the sunset painted the northern seas. She took a deep drag on her skunkweed cigarette as she laid back on the grass that swayed in the gentle breeze. She soon heard someone approaching from behind her. It was Gizmo with a small cart filled with odds and ends. "Oh, hey!" the summoner said with some surprise.

"I thought you were going to send for me," she added with a grin.

"I can appreciate the need for alone time," Gizmo replied.

"Besides, I mean…come on, you're the summoner. I'm not that much of a dick!" Yana laughed and asked, "I guess that you're ready to go back?"

"Yeah, I can't leave those kitties alone for too long, ya' know?" Gizmo answered. Yana got to her feet; and, giving a slight bow of her head, conjured a portal to Parraeysia. With a kind smile, she said, "I guess I should get used to being a taxi service, huh?"

"Exactly," Gizmo replied with a wink.

"It's not like you're saving the city every day, anyway, taking trips to the beach and all. Well, swing back by when you get the chance. There may be some Ma'ji looking to see more of the world, too. I'll ask around."

"That sounds fair," Yana pondered. "I hadn't really thought about that."

"You're just selfish. It's okay," the wolvyn said as he stepped towards the portal. Yana smirked and rolled her eyes. Before entering the portal, Gizmo stopped and said, "We'll be seeing you, kid." The summoner smiled and waved as Gizmo entered, and the portal vanished.

"Yana!" Dehza remarked. Yana opened her hand, looking at the fiery dragon's eye, and replied with a simple, "Hmm?"

"I have some news," Dehza stated plainly.

"What, what kind of news?" Yana asked with a slight level of concern.

"Nothing too worrisome," Dehza replied, "or, I wouldn't think it to be troubling." Yana sighed, asking again.

"What kind of news, Dehza?"

"You're pregnant, Yana," Dehza stated. Yana's jaw dropped ever so slightly, causing the cigarette to fall from her lips.

Elsewhere in Rime, Bael was seeking out his sister, Kira, also a female warrior, to get her opinion on a gift he had purchased for Yana. He had been directed to To'to's quarters within The Keep. There he found a few familiar faces, as well as a number of items gathered from within the Firebird's Shade. Azotus, the warrior chief, was reclining near the doorway, seemingly just observing the situation. He casually fist-bumped Bael as he entered. Kora, wolf, and wife of Azotus, and Vega, Ma'ji female, were conversing between themselves and were taking notes and studying several of the items. While To'to was tinkering with vials and chemicals, he was humming to the tune that enchanted instruments were playing. Kira and Morgan, a necromancer, were reclining side by side and, from the looks of it, were practically asleep.

Bael approached Morgan and Kira, curiously waving his hand in front of them. He got very little in response. Kira barely opened one eye, smiling a bit as she quietly said, "Heeey big brother, what's uuup?" Bael sighed and turned his attention to the troll, saying, "I'm assuming they're your test subjects for something?"

"Ya, mon'," To'to replied. Bael smiled and shook his head, saying to Kora and Vega, "And you two just let it happen?" Thulo, a male troll, and the two ladies shrugged.

"Well, they volunteered," Kora replied innocently.

"Nothing harmful," Vega added, "at least in a professional setting."

"Professional setting?" Azotus chuckled.

"Oh, hush!" Kora kindly rebuked.

"So, what're they on?" Bael inquired.

"We're kind of trippin' along," Morgan contently mumbled.

"Ketamine extract," To'to stated, as he came to take the vital signs of his subjects. "It hadn't been on Harth in a long time…an ancient remedy wit' regenerative aspects for da mind."

"It's recorded to help with trauma and certain amounts of psychological damage," Kora added. "It provides a certain peace to the individual…rest. It can be used for soldiers and citizens alike."

"The mind and soul are linked," Vega chimed in. "Thus, there is a certain spiritual aspect to this medicine as well." Bael looked over at Morgan and Kira with a curious expression, saying, "They certainly seem peaceful…maybe incapacitated…but peaceful."

"It doesn't take much," Kora commented.

"But I gave em' a lot," To'to added.

"Dey gonna' be out for a bit." Bael sighed, saying, "I was hoping to get her opinion on something," as he brandished a lovely necklace. Vega and Kora, clearly impressed with the piece, came over to Bael.

"Is it for Yana?" Vega inquired. Bael nodded.

"It's very pretty," Kora added.

"It would be nice if a certain someone got me something like this," she added, as she leered at Azotus.

"You never wear jewelry," Azotus stated.

"I do, too!" Kora rebuked, motioning to several earrings she bore.

"See what you've done?" Azotus said, stretching in his chair.

"You don't think it's too much? Too little?" Bael asked.

"I think it's perfect for Yana," Kora said.

"Beautiful, but not too flashy," Vega concurred. Bael was quite satisfied with the feedback and neatly stowed the piece in a safe place. To'to approached Bael with a cup of greenish liquid.

"Have a drink, mon'," To'to replied. Bael looked at the troll with a straight face. To'to smiled back.

"It's just tea, right?" Vega remarked.

"Herbal tea," To'to replied.

"Define herbal?" Bael said.

"I had some," Azotus stated.

"It'll relax you a bit. Personally, I needed some time away from all the chatter." Bael accepted the cup and took a sip.

"There certainly are many moving parts these days," Kora said. "In relation to the world around us, Shiro is a blessed place to be."

"We at least know that the alliance has its footholds on each continent," Azotus added. "Getting details is another ordeal, especially regarding Mol'do."

"Patience and faith," Vega commented. "We've come this far even during such ongoing chaos."

"People need ta learn to chill in da meantime," To'to added, as he puffed on his pipe and continued his work.

"Da Light want em' to be happy, ya know?" Azotus nodded, saying, "The Island of Chelsea was a strain on our people. The icy undead made a good night's rest a rarity. I have no qualms being in more of an administrative role for the time being."

"I think you've put on a few pounds recently," Kora slighted. Azotus shrugged.

"You still love it," he replied.

"Awww, puppy love!" Morgan uttered contently. Her eyes barely opened as she glanced over.

"That must be some good stuff," Bael chuckled. "For Morgan to joke is almost unheard of."

"She's a softy under all that dark badassery," Kira muttered happily, as she took Morgan's hand into hers.

The sun would soon be coming up in Ramm, but the darkness that shrouded the kingdom cast a never-ending nightfall in these times. Most of the airships and ground armors were refueling and resupplying at The Gate. The darkdancers had come onto the base and were being introduced to various persons. All of their comrades warmly welcomed them. Lua, the terrani elf, and Horus, the darkdancer, headed towards their assigned regiment. Darkdancers Enysa and Sij were en route to theirs. Trova, the darkdancer, was at a hangar with A'mi, alchemist; Sapphira, military communicator; and Kasslow, a wolvyn. The general mood at the base was uplifting. Soldiers and personnel were in good spirits. Some were on the void comms with their friends and loved ones.

As Lua and Horus strolled amongst the tanks, Lua abruptly halted Horus, saying, "I have my suspicions. I wanted to wait until Enysa wasn't around to ask." Horus looked at Lua curiously, replying, "What suspicions?"

"You seem like you've always been a quiet, nice guy," Lua said. Horus shrugged but otherwise affirmed the statement.

"Are you a virgin?" Lua asked. Horus blushed as much as a darkdancer could, exclaiming,

"What kind of a question is that?"

"Just a friendly inquiry," Lua casually stated.

"It's none of your business," Horus replied combatively.

"So, yes!" Lua rebuked with a wink.

"I didn't say that!" Horus defended.

"Yeah, you pretty much did," Lua replied. "Plus, you got all defensive."

"I am not being defensive!" Horus exclaimed.

"You are being defensive," Lua echoed plainly.

"I just figure…how else does this guy have such an uneventful nightmare? No celestial intervention, no massive dragon, or no otherworldly being that protected you. Not that you're sinless, but you clearly have something different from the rest of us." Horus folded his arms as he began walking ahead of Lua.

"Oh, come on!" Lua said playfully, catching up to her comrade. "Look at us bonding and stuff. I promise I won't tell Enysa!"

Enysa and Sij were touring some of the barracks. The odd pair was drawing a number of stares. Enysa was strapped with firearms, which included an assault rifle that was practically as big as she was. And she was walking next to the towering Fo'hemut elf. Both of them had the sort of personalities that enjoyed the attention. They were high-fiving and greeting soldiers and persons along the way. The darkdancers, as a whole, were a welcomed addition to the fighting force, but these two had a knack for inspiring crowds and feeding off of each other's charisma.

Let's be honest! They had every right to strut a bit.

"You ready to play, little one?" Sij asked.

"I can't wait to get into some action," Enysa affirmed.

"I appreciate your confidence. It helps me to trust that you won't end up shooting me," Sij chuckled. Enysa stuck out her tongue in response.

"There's a good reason Trova put us together," Sij said.

"Which is?" Enysa replied. "He wants you well protected," Sij laughed, flexing his arm. "Know that I have your back. I wouldn't want to get on that man's bad side."

"And I have yours," Enysa stated. "So, Trova even strikes some fear into someone like you?" she slyly added.

"His aura is incredible!" Sij exclaimed. "He's wicked and righteous. I could sense the very air change the first time I saw him."

"He definitely fits the role," Enysa answered.

"He gives me something to strive towards," Sij stated.

"Hmm?" Enysa muttered.

"Mastery of this gift that I've been given!" Sij boasted. "I hope to hold my own against him someday. That would be an honor worth having."

"Why not have a friendly match now?" Enysa pried.

"It would be embarrassing," Sij laughed. "After all, I have an appearance to maintain."

Sapphira was walking back towards the hangar. She brought several items with her that Trova had requested. "Sapphira, do this! Sapphira, do that!" she said to herself in a mocking way. She came to a darkened corridor and simply assumed the lights had gone out. After a few steps, she slipped on something wet and cursed as she hit the floor. She brandished a luminescent orb, which revealed a blood-soaked hallway. There were several mutilated bodies lying here and there. Her eyes grew wide. She began to stumble as she attempted to activate her collar.

A blade slashed across her throat. The cut was shallow enough not to be an instantaneous death, but it was open enough to be a fatal wound. Sapph fell back as she gasped for breath. A vile hunter came into sight from the shadows. As the being came for a killing blow, its sword was deflected. Trova phased from a shadow in front of her. "A'MI," he hollered.

"Get in here now! Bring your kit." Trova engaged the vile in a flurry of strikes and clashing of blades. Sapphira began to weep as she held her hand over the gash. Trova's combinations were seamless. He soon found his opening and sliced the monster in half. Black blood flung to the ground and walls. Sapphira watched in horror as she clung to her life.

A'mi rushed to Sapphira's side. The gunfire began to ring out throughout the base, and alarms began to blare. The alchemist brandished a small glass bottle and said in a huff, "This is gonna hurt, babe." A'mi applied the regenerative tincture to the wounded area. The flesh began to slowly mend itself back together. Sapphira was filled with tears. She was unable to vocalize her pain as A'mi kept the pressure on the opening. Another vile hunter manifested behind A'mi. Trova hurled a knife at the fiend, which landed square between its eyes. Trova's expression was that of bloodlust and excitement. Another hunter came from the shadows and began slashing at Trova. The darkdancer phased in and out of the darkness as he dodged and maneuvered with utter mastery. He gave a single upward cleave with his sword and cut the fiend vertically in half.

As Sapphira's wound healed, she cried and gasped for air. Kasslow came running with his shotgun ready. "What can I do, boss?" he asked.

"Prep the ships and get them into the air," Trova declared.

"Aye, sir!" Kasslow answered. The wolvyn stowed his gun and took Sapphira in his arms. He took her to their ship and was ready to take off. Ami hurried to meet them.

"I'm going to kill every one of these bastards!" Trova uttered with a sinister smile. Once more, Kasslow took to the darkness and onward into the developing chaos.

Heroes and soldiers were engaged throughout The Gate. Projectiles and spells went back and forth. Blades were sparking and clanging. Within the first few minutes of the assault, many fell victim to these monsters. They were completely outmatched by the hunters' abilities. Void comms were lit up with exclamations and screams. The fighting had broken out everywhere, from hall to hall and room to room. Many personnel were caught unarmed and completely off guard. Entire squads would fall to a single vile hunter before anyone could fight back.

Firefights quickly became intense, and melees became brutal. Small arms were nearly useless against these fiends. They were able to absorb dozens of rounds from small-caliber weapons without staggering. Mortal weapons barely scathed the monsters. A dozen soldiers firing hundreds of collective rounds would not bring down a single hunter. The viles' agility, strength, and otherworldly capabilities were shocking and terrifying to many. Men and women were cut into pieces in what seemed to be the blink of an eye. Bones were broken and crushed, and flesh was charred. Most of the monsters used blades or their bare hands to fight. Some used firearms, and some even displayed a command over magic.

In the barracks, Enysa and Sij fought side by side with the personnel there. Sij stayed close to his comrades. He engaged in hand-to-hand combat with any hunters that breached the firing line. A mighty swing of his fist shattered the face and broke the neck of one hunter. He broke the spine of another and stomped its head. Enysa's rifle worked with her own runic energy. It hurled bolts of sheer power and ruby light through their aggressors. Six of the monsters were laid low before there was a lull. Sij and Enysa wasted no time in taking to the shadows so they could move onward to assist elsewhere.

Horus and Lua were among the engineering sector. They shadowstepped to a nearby engagement and flanked a handful of hunters that were massacring soldiers and personnel. Lua unleashed a torrent of lightning that practically incinerated four of the fiends. Horus put a large hole through one of the fiend's heads with a powerful pistol. He deployed a gadget from his armor that fired sticky runic grenades at several other monsters. Each found its mark and detonated, thus splattering the fiends. The scene before them was gruesome. Only three of fifty individuals in the area were even breathing. "Leave them!" Lua shouted.

"Neither of us has the supplies to help. We have to keep going." Horus agreed. He shot a flare into the air, hoping that aid would come. Screams, gunfire, and noise continued to echo throughout The Gate. Even the younger heroes found themselves in the skirmishes. They had to "group up" to even put up a fight. Soldiers took to using mounted machine guns while some of the smaller airships tried to provide precision aerial support. Some of the vile hunters simply laid waste to the structures. Fires had broken out everywhere. Pillars of smoke rose into the dark sky.

Sapphira felt the tender scar on her throat. She was still in a mild state of shock. A'mi kept close to her and periodically checked her vitals and physical state. Kasslow had locked in the airship's altitude and now tried to provide sniper fire from the bay door. "These things can move like a darkdancer," he calmly remarked, as he looked down the scope of a large rifle.

"Technically, they are," A'mi uttered. "I've read about them. Individuals who fail the nightmare phase come back as slaves to Dom'rel."

"That is unfortunate," Kasslow stated, as he fired a shot into the back of a hunter that blew off its head.

"Heh, I got one!" he said with a grin.

"Eli," Sapphira muttered in a weak and raspy voice as she pointed to A'mi's void comm collar. A'mi had wanted to avoid going over the comms. She knew what she would be hearing, so her hesitancy was visible.

"Please," Sapphira said, her eyes misty with tears. A'mi took a deep breath and activated the collar. Her ears immediately filled with the noises of the battles below.

"This is DARK-1 to all forces listening. Commander Darius, do you copy?" she asked.

"I love our call sign," Kasslow mumbled, as he fired another shot.

"A lot of the command hasn't checked in," a soldier replied. *"We're en route to officer quarters with a couple of yours."*

"A couple of ours?" A'mi echoed.

"Aye, the big guy and the blonde," the soldier replied. A'mi sighed, as she fought against the emotions rising from all the sounds filling her ears.

"Keep me posted," she uttered.

"You got it!" the soldier answered.

Sapphira curled up on the floor. All they could do was wait. Another voice came through the comms, shouting, *"Can someone do something about the lights? The power grid is barely hanging on, and it's not fucking helping!"* Lua answered, *"Horus is on his way. Things will soon get brighter."*

"Lua, you split up?" A'mi asked.

"We're fine," Lua replied.

"I don't think these comms things were expecting to have to deal with us. Honestly, they seem a little rusty!"

"Everyone, keep fighting!" A'mi shouted with conviction. "We will win this!"

"Aye, we will!" Amon said over the comms. *"Sorry if I had anyone worried. I just now caught a breather."*

There were many that were relieved to hear the king's voice. He rallied their spirits during the ongoing battle. Trova was quickly moving through the base. He made relatively easy work of the monsters he encountered. His blades were swift and precise, and his power, radiant. As a handful of personnel found themselves cornered by two hunters, they watched in awe as the monsters were obliterated by a wave of runic energy. They were incinerated before their eyes. Unfortunately, they never caught a glimpse of the one who saved them. They only felt an anomaly pass by them in the dark.

Trova continued to track his prey through the nether. Traces from the red glow of his eyes were all that could be seen as he phased through the shadows. He cut the fiends into halves and then into pieces within seconds. The unsuspecting monsters barely had time to react. Bright lights then appeared, which briefly stopped him in his tracks. "Dammit. Who did that?" he asked over the void comms. "Some of us are trying to work here!"

"The majority of us can't see in pitch black, you selfish bastard!" a soldier answered back.

"I said that Horus was going to restore the grid," Lua chimed in.

"I doubt he was listening," A'mi added. Trova grumbled. He took off on foot and shot out lights as he went about his way. The number of fiends he was encountering was beginning to thin to one or two. His blades cut through the fiends like paper, thus painting the areas with their putrid blood. He came upon a hunter that was heavily armored and larger than the others. It was surrounded by mutilated corpses. The monster turned to Trova and gave a bellowing hiss.

Trova smirked and charged at the fiend. He dodged a cleave of the monster's sword. The hunter met Trova in the very shadows and actually parried a number of the darkdancer's strikes. One after another, their blades met. Their martial skills dueled beautifully. "You must have been an impressive warrior while you still had a soul!" Trova laughed.

"You're going to make me use magic, huh?" The darkdancer gave off a shockwave from his aura that put distance between the two.

"Have a taste, bitch!" Trova yelled, as energy coalesced from his arm to his hand.

A massive torrent of runic energy shot forth and completely engulfed the fiend. The beam broke through the walls of the base and into the mountains behind them. It was a glorious display. Nothing was left of the monster. Trova smiled, saying to himself before he continued on, "That was fun!"

Enysa and Sij had several squads of heroes and soldiers with them as they advanced. The darkdancers cleared enemies from the front as their comrades covered the flanks of the formation. A door burst from its hinges before the darkdancers, and a mage was thrown against the wall with such force that his blood burst. A hunter immediately engaged Enysa, slashing wildly at her. Enysa parried a handful of the attacks with her rifle but was soon off balance and unable to find an opening to counter.

"Duck!" Sij exclaimed. Enysa quickly hit the floor. Sij's fist landed square in the monster's sternum, which caused the monster to be hurled towards Enysa. She put several rounds into the hunter before it could stagger back to its feet.

"I'm glad you listened, little one!" Sij chuckled. "I would've hit you had you not."

"You're kidding, right?" Enysa huffed. Sij did not reply as he continued to advance.

"Right?" Enysa hollered, chasing after him. The group behind them followed. They had melted two additional hunters with a hail of bullets and magic. A few among the tailing squads recognized the mage, but they were directed to keep moving.

Horus and Lua had reconnected. They were fighting back-to-back in a common area. Horus had deployed several spheres that were arranged in the shape of a tower shield. Runic energy passed between the devices, thus providing an energy barrier. The shield passed back and forth between the darkdancers, seemingly on its own, as it deflected strikes and projectiles. Horus was using two shadowsteel firearms, as well as a targeting system that partnered with his runic energy. Together they acted like heat-seeking missiles.

Lua had conjured a lightning whip in her right hand. She used her left hand to cast arcing bolts of powerful electricity infused with runic bolts. This was quite the light show between the two of them. A number of the monsters were constantly on the attack, and more seemed to be coming into this open space. Few of the hunters ever made it close to the darkdancers. They were vaporized or blown apart by wild spectacles of the shadow's powers. As more monsters came into view, Lua hollered, "Horus. Cloak yourself in that shield!"

"What?" Horus shouted.

"Do it!" Lua answered.

Horus recalled the shield and surrounded himself with it. Lua supercharged herself, which caused a dome of red lightning to engulf the immediate area. Entire portions of the structures around them were vaporized, along with roughly a dozen of the monsters. When the lightning subsided, Horus looked at Lua with a rather curious expression, saying, "I was trying not to damage the place too much."

"Are you serious?" Lua replied with some exasperation.

"Wait. So you were holding back?" she asked. Horus shrugged, and Lua smacked him on the back of his head.

Trova pulled his sword from the spine of a hunter and casually stepped over the corpse. He said into the void comms, "I dare say that I've run out of targets. I've lost any trace of these things."

"Things have been lightening up for us too," Enysa answered.

"Ditto," Lua added. *"We're coming up on the command quarters,"* Enysa said. *"It's really quiet through here."*

"They clearly had objectives," Trova uttered.

"Aye," Amon said. *"This was meant to be a strike at our core. First, that damn beast from the depths. Now, this!"*

"Having second thoughts?" Trova asked as he lit a dragonskunk cigarette.

"No," Amon declared.

Sij and Enysa reached a dining area first. They and everyone accompanying them paused at the sight of a total bloodbath. There were three vile corpses among dozens of fallen soldiers and personnel. Bodies were everywhere--lying on the ground, slumped over tables, and some were in pieces.

"This was probably the first place they hit," Sij said, as he walked alongside Enysa through the pools of blood. Enysa said nothing. She simply looked around with saddened eyes. Hall after hall, room after room, the scene was the same. There was not a single soul clinging to life.

"Update, Enysa?" A'mi downheartedly asked.

"There's no one," Enysa replied in kind. "It's a total slaughter."

"Thank you," A'mi answered.

The ordeal lasted only an hour. One hundred and fifty vile hunters were slain between the alliance forces. Four thousand, five hundred and nine alliance personnel were lost. In all honesty, it was impressive that our friends did not lose more.

News of the attack spread quickly through Shiro as some individuals had been in communication with loved ones and comrades when the assault started. Many had begun to clamor around outposts and The Keep, begging for information and answers. Yana had not even been able to tell Bael about her news before she heard of what happened just beyond the border. Knowing she would have more information through her channels than most, Yana made haste to Delia's estate. She caught transport up into the cliffs and to the complex. Upon arriving, she rushed through its doors to find Delia.

Yana found Delia in a central garden. Delia, with a solemn look on her face, was listening to someone speaking through her earpiece. She gave a half-smile to acknowledge Yana but said nothing. Delia motioned for Yana to wait a moment. Jeeves was there as well, and gave a respectful bow to the summoner.

"I see," Delia uttered, "thank you, Horus!" With that, Delia turned to Yana and opened her arms. Yana rushed and embraced her friend.

"What happened? Tell me that Sapph is ok? Skarg?" she asked.

"Sapph is alive; no word on Skarg," Delia replied quietly. "Two armor regiments were away from the base during the attack. It's possible Skarg is among those."

"You said Sapph is alive. Is she injured? I didn't see many forces going to assist," Yana said.

"It happened too quickly," Delia replied. "There are only a handful of injured. Many are dead. They're assessing the aftermath and not requesting much from Shiro. Sapph is catatonic. Eli is presumed among the dead."

"Oh, no!" Yana muttered. Delia nodded. Yana was at a loss for words.

"Amon is hailing the shadows as heroes," Delia added. "He said the attack would have been scored worse had they not been there when they were. They'll be staying in Ramm for future deterrence and operations."

"This wasn't some undead horde," Yana stated. Delia agreed, answering, "They're being described as our shadows' failed counterparts."

"Vile hunters," Jeeves said. "Demonic special forces--this was a specified task."

"Officers and command took the biggest hit," Delia added. "Right now, there's not much else in the way of details."

Back in Ramm, Sapphira sat quietly in a hangar. A'mi and other personnel were also present. Sapphira stood up and began to walk. Her eyes were looking down, and her composure was dead. A'mi knew where she was going, so she went to accompany her. "Sweetie?" she said gently. "It may be best not to go."

"I have to find him," Sapphira uttered.

"If anything, I can identify his body." A'mi reached into a pouch and brandished a small potion. She handed it to Sapphira, saying, "Drink it. It'll help." Sapphira took the vial and drank it as the two continued to walk.

They walked silently onward to command quarters. They passed the gruesome scenes along the way. Sapphira tried not to give any attention to the bodies and gore. A'mi took another of the potions. She drank it because it was essentially a numbing agent for the mind. They eventually came to the command and officer sector. They stepped over corpses and walked through blood all the way through the halls and various rooms. The two came to a strategy office. The scene was an absolute mess. There was one of the monster's corpses among the roughly two dozen personnel. Shell casings littered the bloody floor.

Voidkeeper

Stella, the voidkeeper, awoke from a two-day slumber after she had drunk the mana that Swae, the archangel, had given her. She had been flooded by the sounds of the battle at The Gate through the void and nether and had been unable to bear the phenomenon. She was in bed, naked, and awoke, wondering how she got there. Kora, the white mage, came into the room, saying, "Oh, you're awake! We were worried. You practically collapsed after you drank from that bottle. You were sweating a lot, too, so I figured you'd at least be cooler without your robes."

"Oh!" Stella replied. "Thank you. Have you been looking after me?"

"Of course," Kora answered. "You were frantic. You were covering your ears and were clearly distressed. Then you drank that liquid and passed out. Why wouldn't a healer look after you?" she asked kindly.

"I barely remember hearing screams," Stella said. "They were close by."

"There was an attack on our forces in Ramm," Kora affirmed, as she handed Stella a glass of water. Stella chugged the water and got up to get more. Kora looked over the glowing glass scars along Stella's body that were luminescent with a purple-pinkish hue.

"I wasn't aware of such a burden on you, dear. The void must be a heavy weight to carry," she said.

"I accepted it," Stella replied quietly.

"You're brave to have gone through what you have," Kora stated, "and still have a good mind and a good heart."

"I still feel so small," Stella replied. "It's like I'll never be able to do enough."

"You're just one person," Kora rhetorically said. Stella nodded. "Well, your contributions have already been enormous, and I've heard there are plans to not spread you so thin."

"Hmm?" Stella muttered curiously. Kora pointed respectfully at Stella's scars and asked, "What is the onyx crystal that your scars are made of?"

"It's a material that can be found on Harth, specifically beneath Asheya in Zuhetta. There are intentions to mine it since we have the means nowadays. Alliance leaders are planning to construct void-fusion generators in the major cities for power and supply."

"Who came up with this?" Stella inquired.

"Bree," Kora replied. "The assumption is that she's received this directive from a higher-up."

"How can it be mined?" Stella asked.

"Concentrated void rays," Kora said. "Cogs are already developing tools that can handle the task. They'll only need to be charged."

"Will a single charge be enough?" Stella asked. "Even the skyswords have to be recharged."

"Morgan will be going with whoever is selected for the venture to Zuhetta," Kora answered. "Her energy capacity will be more than enough for the instruments and tasks. You'll be staying here."

Stella slipped into some garments, saying, "I was worried about void energy being weaponized. I guess that was ultimately not my decision to make."

"Anything of this fallen existence will be weaponized, dear," Kora replied kindly.

"The trick is making sure the weapons are in the right hands." Stella nodded as her lavender eyes glanced down.

"There are plans for five generators: three in Zuhetta, one in Parraeysia, and one here," Kora added.

"I keep forgetting about Parraeysia," Stella said.

"Yana went there recently. I doubt that she'll mind making another quick trip there," Kora stated, "even if it's just to deliver a request."

"Powerful summoner and convenient mail courier," Stella said with a grin.

"Indeed," Kora replied in kind.

"Do you think I could go?" Stella asked curiously.

"I don't see why not. Parraeysia is a sanctuary. It's safe," Kora answered. There was a brief pause as the voidkeeper continued to gather a few items.

"May I ask something?" Kora inquired.

"Sure," Stella answered softly.

"Were you a natural necromancer?" the wolvyn asked. "You don't strike me as such." Stella smiled somewhat reminiscently.

"No, it was sort of slapped on me. Miri'el said it was needed."

"An angelic bestowment," Kora remarked. "You must have had quite a journey to get here."

"I was spared," Stella said quietly. "The Light pulled me from the twisted darkness that enveloped my home."

"You're a courageous one!" Kora said upliftingly.

"Everyone keeps saying things like that," Stella chuckled.

"Well, I pray the rest of your journey is more peaceful than its beginning," Kora stated.

"Thank you!" the voidkeeper replied, giving a slight bow of her head.

Elsewhere in the city, wolyvn rangers Jovuk, Shoshana, Holen, and Gif, the raven, had been directed to Azotus, the warrior chief, to report on their recent mission into Gol. "This is a nice place!" Gif commented, as he perched on Holen's shoulder.

"Can you believe that I never made a trip here while I was a human? People seem a bit glum, though." Indeed, it was easy to tell that something was amiss. The very mood of the city was heavy. The group headed east towards the highway that went into Ramm. Military vehicles passed by and were going in the same direction. Azotus was at a checkpoint at the edge of the city. He waved the group over as they approached.

The three wolvyn saluted their chief, as did their feathery companion. Azotus returned the gesture, although he raised his brow curiously at the raven. "Meet an escapee of Evermore," Jovuk said, gesturing to Gif.

"Only one to speak of, I'm afraid," Gif said casually. "Pleased to meet ya, sir."

"Your expedition was otherwise uneventful? The beacons are set?" Azotus asked.

"Aye," Jovuk answered.

"No problems," Holen added with a sigh.

"What happened here?" Shoshana inquired.

"There was an attack on our forces in Ramm," Azotus said, "an ambush at The Gate."

"Ambush?" Jovuk echoed. "How in the Light could there be an ambush?"

"It was the nature of the attackers--something we hadn't seen in such a capacity before," Azotus explained. "Given the limited records on these vile hunters and what information we've been able to piece together, the assumption is that the pit won't have enough of those monsters left for a similar assault. But, that doesn't mean their number is exhausted either."

"How many did we lose?" Shoshana asked.

"Four thousand, five hundred and nine over the course of roughly an hour," Azotus answered candidly.

"Only a handful of injured." Holen watched as more and more vehicles poured by, while numerous airships were en route over the mountains.

"We're taking something of a gamble," Azotus continued. "We are sending just about everything we have to see that the objective in Ramm is secured as soon as possible. King Amon is as pissed as the rest of us about the attack, but the decision to move forward was unanimous. A few thousand troops will remain in Shiro to continue with training and to assist with reconstruction efforts. We are simply praying against some catastrophe across the border and that we get a return on this investment."

"I don't know if the pit could launch anythin' too large scale, your furriness," Gif stated. "I know they're beefing up Evermore, but I haven't overheard ambitions to unleash more hordes anywhere else in the world."

"Overheard?" Azotus echoed with intrigue.

"Oh, yeah, that witch was always chattering on about things while she worked," Gif replied. "She talked a lot about the attack on Rime; that they needed another sacrifice and so on."

"Take your feathery friend to The Keep for debriefing," Azotus said. "We need to know everything he knows, no matter how trivial."

"Aye, sir," Jovuk answered.

Kora and Stella had come to Yana and Bael's residence around midday. Kora knocked on the door. Bael answered and bore a wide smile. Yana was standing closely behind him, kindly grinning. "You two seem to be in good spirits!" Kora remarked. Stella's eyes curiously shifted from Bael to Yana and then back to Bael.

"We just got some good news," Bael said. "What's up? It's not every day you two are poking around together."

"We have a request of your lovely wife," Kora answered kindly.

"Come on in," Bael replied, motioning with his head. The two entered, and Yana hugged each of them.

"That's a pretty necklace!" the voidkeeper complimented.

"Thank you," Yana, the summoner, answered with a smile.

"Bael has good taste," Kora added. Bael, the human warrior, winked.

"What can I do for you two?" Yana asked with a mild chuckle. "It must be important."

"Not really," Stella uttered.

"Well, it's an important matter overall, but our being here is rather cordial," Kora said.

"We need a portal," Stella said, "to Parraeysia."

"Of course," Yana replied.

"Really?" Kora asked curiously.

"That was easy," Stella added.

"I can't really say no to a voidkeeper," Yana kindly answered. "Gizmo mentioned bringing some Ma'ji to Shiro anyway. Maybe this will be good timing."

"Gizmo is the one we need to speak with as well," Kora said.

"Hopefully, not too much of his personality has rubbed off on the Ma'ji," she added with a sigh.

"So, we're really serious about these void generators I've heard about?" Bael inquired. "The general plan has echoed through reaper ranks, but it almost sounds too good to be true."

"Quite serious!" the wolvyn replied.

"Doesn't sound like some overnight job," Bael commented.

"Indeed not. Current projections put completion dates roughly at no less than two years from when our crews begin to mine," Kora said. "Our voidkeeper will have her work cut out for her here for a while longer."

"Not to mention the pylon in Mol'do. There's no telling how or when that will happen," Stella thought to herself.

"Well, I guess we should go then?" Yana said with a smile. Stella and Kora were a bit surprised. "Shouldn't we let someone know?" Kora asked.

"Nah," Yana replied. "I think it'll be fun to just surprise the city with a bunch of Ma'ji coming back."

"If you insist," Kora said. "Hard to think that she has more demon kills than any other hero on Harth, isn't it?" Bael joked, referring to Yana.

"A little bit," Stella replied.

Yana flexed her arm and winked. "Let's go to the backyard. It's covered and fenced. No one will see us there," she said.

"No one will think to question flashes of light coming from a summoner's property," Bael sarcastically said under his breath. Yana stuck her tongue out at her husband.

"You're so sneaky," Bael spitefully stated. Yana rolled her eyes and motioned for Kora and Stella to follow. So the three lasses went through the small house to the back and entered a rather lovely yard. Since Yana had created a portal to Parraeysia before, she was able to easily do it again. She performed the spell motions with her hands, conjuring the anomaly.

However,

When the three came into the dragonkin island, they found themselves in the middle of a sparring session between dozens of Ma'ji heroes. Lightning, fire, ice, nether, and all kinds of magic crashed and flew by them. Rushing bladedancers and warriors stumbled around them as they appeared, slamming into each other and tripping every which way. Kora, Stella, and Yana could not even react to the environment into which they had entered. There were elemental explosions all around them as well as a hefty melee.

Then...

THERE WAS A BLINDING FLASH AND A FORCE THAT THREW EVERY COMBATANT TO THE PERIMETER OF THE AREA. A protective barrier of nether encompassed the three from Shiro, and there was now a large figure standing in their presence. It was Uz'rel, fifth-born, a primordial dragonkin archangel and the crafter of Eternal weaponry. He was of massive stature. There was muscle upon muscle. His scales were pearlescent ebony, and his four wings shone like fire. His tail was armored and bladed. The three from Shiro could not believe their eyes as they gazed in awe at the being. Uz'rel chuckled, looking at Yana with fiery eyes, saying, "I dare say, your compass seems a bit off, child."

Yana, along with everyone else around her, was in utter awe of the being, not knowing what he meant or even how to respond. "You really are more of a mischievous lot than you put on," he added, glancing at Stella, the voidkeeper.

"We're always having to hold your hands," he playfully sighed. The barrier diminished among the awestruck Ma'ji, which caused some to barely take a step toward the center point. They mumbled and whispered amongst themselves as to the nature of this encounter. First, being as frightful as he was, they had to distinguish that Uz'rel was even an ally.

Uz'rel held out his massive claw towards Yana to help her off her behind. "You're getting a little too comfortable with your abilities, summoner," he said with a dragon's grin.

"With such an attitude, mishaps are bound to happen when conjuring portals as if they were a leisure item." Yana could only nod in agreement as she was helped to her feet. Uz'rel looked about the crowd of Ma'ji heroes, kindly hollering, "Come closer, children. I don't bite!" At that, the Ma'ji hurriedly gathered around the archangel and the three from Shiro.

Frankly, Uz'rel enjoyed such company. He knew his appearance was practically paralyzing to most, always crediting The Light for putting him together so well.

"I, I don't get it," Yana mumbled. "Why didn't we appear on the beaches like before?"

"Check your hand, little one," Uz'rel hinted, pointing to the summoner's left hand. Yana's eyes grew wide, and her stomach sank. She quickly unwrapped the ornate cloth around her palm, revealing that the scar had lost its glow. Yana gasped and was once again struck at a loss for words. Stella glanced at the scar, commenting, "I don't get it."

"It would appear that the destroyer truly does have a longing for this world," Uz'rel laughed.

"You look a little pale, Yana," Kora said.

Indeed, the summoner was a bit pale. "Bastard!" she uttered.

"Wait, so Deth is in your baby now?" Stella asked. Yana had a burst of anger, yelling and pointing at her torso.

"YOU SON OF A BITCH! THIS WAS YOUR PLAN ALL ALONG, WASN'T IT? HOW DARE YOU! HOW IS THAT PERMISSIBLE?" Many of the Ma'ji stepped back at the summoner's outburst. Kora laid her claws on Yana's shoulders, passing calming energy to the livid summoner. Yana actually staggered a bit.

"Oops!" Kora uttered. "Perhaps that was a bit too much."

Stella was perplexed about Yana's expression regarding the situation. Nonetheless, she reached out to help her. Uz'rel gave a hardy laugh, saying, "Humanity has always been entertaining in its own ways, but this is truly a first. I'll have to ask Dehza what he plans. I pray he tells me."

"You angels are about as odd a bunch as we are!" Stella remarked.

"I wouldn't argue with you," Uz'rel agreed.

"Can, can I protest?" Yana tiredly asked as she weakly shook her fist in the air.

"You can protest all you'd like, child," Uz'rel replied, "but it won't change anything." The Light permitted such an event to happen, so there must be great plans for your unborn. You should be thrilled," he happily explained.

Yana mumbled incoherently. "What did you do to her?" Stella inquired of Kora.

"A simple, soothing spell," Kora huffed, folding her arms. "I don't use my magic as much as I used to."

"It might be best had you given her a little less of the dose," Uz'rel said. "She's in a bit of an awkward spot. Her confusion is understandable."

"'Confused isn't the word I would've used," Stella remarked. "She seemed to uh, catch on quick."

"This sort of mingling is unheard of," Uz'rel humbly replied. "Our dear summoner will be a bit overwhelmed for some time, regardless of whether or not she shows or admits it."

Yana mumbled incoherently again. "I was going to go for a stroll around the island," Uz'rel said happily.

"Surely you have some reason for nearly getting sandwiched between steel and magic. Personally, I'd like to see Rayne, our new broodmother, while I'm in the neighborhood. I hear she's a dear friend of yours, Yana?" he asked.

"Mhm," the summoner replied, still hunched over a bit. So, the archangel began to walk, and the three from Shiro followed. The Ma'ji that crossed paths with the archangel were fearful at first sight but were soon reassured by a wave from the awesome being and by seeing Yana and the others in tow.

Yana was finally able to fully support herself and walk in a straight line. She smiled and graciously said to Stella, "Thank you." Stella replied with a cute smile of her own. Uz'rel looked about, saying, "The beaches haven't changed much, but I hear this

Gizmo has really done a number on the interior. I suppose this place had to modernize at some point."

"You don't get out much?" Kora asked.

"I forge the weapons of angels," Uz'rel replied. "It's a full-time job, though it may not seem so in this plane. The truth be told, too many of our kin are rather careless with their steel among the ethereal battlefields."

"So, why step away now?" Kora followed up. "Is Parraeysia your territory?"

"I won't be gone long. If need be, Jip'rel could always cover for me," Uz'rel answered. "And no, Parraeysia isn't my territory. It just seemed like a good fit."

"Who is Jip'rel?" Kora continued. Uz'rel chuckled, replying, "Leave it to the white mage to ask questions. Jip'rel is an armorsmith, a dwarven archangel, and my counterpart."

"I don't suppose we could make some requests?" Yana asked, pouting at her unusual circumstance.

"Hah. Our armaments would decimate the common mortal's anatomy," Uz'rel answered. "I suggest you continue to use your own artisans."

The group continued walking for a way, and a small crowd of Ma'ji was never far behind. As they entered the city within the mighty volcano, Uz'rel halted, gazing to the upper levels and observing the ever-developing network of engineered additions to the ancient sanctuary. There were lifts, a magical power grid, new bridges, and new pathways that arched back and forth. News of the archangel spread quickly, prompting a number of elders and hosts to hurry and see him.

Soon enough, Gizmo, the runt cog; Radagast, the wolvyn priest; and Zeit, the alpha wolvyn, were wading through the crowds towards the guests, as cheers and joyous whistles echoed from every level of the city. Radagast and Zeit bowed low before Uz'rel. Gizmo nodded his head at the archangel, saying, "You're definitely an impressive one." Uz'rel chuckled.

"Rise, young alpha," referring to Zeit.

"I'm not here on such formalities." Zeit rose, and Uz'rel looked him over, saying, "A marvelous kin of mine, a fine warrior to have survived. The honor guard of the broodmother, no doubt?" Zeit nodded once in affirmation.

"Surely there are countless dragonkin among the angelic ranks," Radagast uttered.

"You could only be the fifth-born." Uz'rel smiled.

"Is that special?" Gizmo asked.

"If you were to know the name of ONE angel, I would have expected you to know that of the eternal weaponsmith," Radagast huffed. Gizmo's ears perked up a bit.

"Perhaps Zeit can escort me to the hibernation chamber. These three are here for other matters," Uz'rel stated, motioning to the three from Shiro. Zeit saluted and began to walk with the archangel. Gizmo and Radagast turned their attention to the other visitors.

"Do you ever not make some sort of entrance?" Gizmo asked.

"It wasn't planned," Yana grumbled in reply. Gizmo looked at Kora.

"What's up with her?" he asked, referring to Yana.

"Umm, just a curious bit of news," Kora replied.

"Since when is there not some curious news these days?" Gizmo stated in an unimpressed manner. Stella began to wander off, wanting to explore the island. Gizmo and Radagast just sort of watched for a moment and then shrugged it off.

"What is the nature of your visit?" Radagast inquired.

"What is the status here?" Kora answered.

"Things are pretty much up and running. Why?" Gizmo stated.

"The alliance is moving forward with an energy plan for each major territory," Kora explained. "We could use you, Gizmo."

"Could use me or need me?" Gizmo asked candidly.

"Either?" Kora said.

"What's the gig?" Gizmo asked.

"Onyxium diamond located beneath an area of Zuhetta," Kora answered.

"The first portion of the plan is a massive mining and engineering endeavor. We'll need our best on site," Gizmo smirked.

"The alliance is moving into void energy production?" Radagast asked with intrigue. Kora nodded.

"Oh, my!" Radagast gasped.

"You should see the aircraft they've already started using in Shiro!" Kora remarked. "Time's unstoppable march has put us in a unique point of history."

"Yeah, yeah, history and stuff," Gizmo said. "You said aircraft? Like, with void engines?"

"Indeed," Kora affirmed. Gizmo smirked in such a way as to signal his interest and participation.

"This place could use a break from you anyway," Radagast added.

"A void will be left in my absence. You'll see!" Gizmo confidently rebuked.

As Stella strolled along the western beach, she was greeted by any number of Ma'ji. The breeze, the aroma, and the temperature helped put her somewhat at ease, a feeling she had not had for some time. She stopped and simply looked out over the water. *"It's* so quiet here," she thought to herself. Two Ma'ji children, a boy and a girl, came up to her. The little boy tugged Stella's robe, which drew the voidkeeper's attention.

"What happened to you?" the boy asked.

"Don't be rude," the girl stated. Stella smiled at the two and knelt down to meet them.

"Those are scars, right?" the boy asked, referring to the crystalline anomalies visible on the voidkeeper's skin. Stella nodded. The girl gasped.

"See?" the boy said to the girl. "I told you."

"They're good scars?" the girl asked. Stella laughed a little as she held out her forearms for the children to touch the diamond-like streaks. She replied, "Yes, they're good scars."

"Did it hurt?" the boy asked.

"Yes," Stella softly replied.

"But now you're super strong, right?" the boy continued. Stella smiled and tilted her head a bit, saying, "I suppose so."

"They're pretty," the girl said, noting the star-like glimmerings and twinkles of lightning. "Pink and purple are my favorite colors!"

"Yeah?" Stella answered kindly.

"You must like sunsets?" The little girl nodded.

"Our parents are heroes, too," the boy proudly declared.

"They'll get to fight the bad guys with Rayne, the broodmother. They tell us all kinds of stories." Stella hid her dismay at the fact that there was a war to be fought in the near future. She maintained a happy composure. Stella sat down on the sands of the shoreline. She looked at the boy and asked, "So, what kind of heroes are your parents?"

"Our dad is a warrior. They just finished making him an awesome shield that's as big as he is," the boy said excitedly.

"Mom is really good with bows. She can hit fish way out there with a tethered arrow," he added, motioning towards the sea.

"Are you a mage?" the girl asked of Stella.

"Hmm, I guess--maybe something like that," the voidkeeper pondered.

"Can we see some of your magic?" the girl eagerly asked. Stella chuckled and held out her hand with her palm facing up. An orb of void energy manifested in Stella's hand. Pink and purple were its most distinguishing colors, with flares of pearlescent light and faint traces of lightning.

"Wooooah!" the children uttered in awe, never having seen such power. Stella was happy to amuse the children so easily, but she felt some sadness at the same time. She had a fleeting memory of her decimated homeland.

That night, Yana, Kora, Stella, Gizmo, Twitch, and ten thousand Ma'ji were set to return to Shiro. By conjuring a portal 100 yards long and 20 yards high, Yana was able to perform spell motions that reflected the likeness of the Shiroan pasturelands. Soon enough, they were on their way to Shiro. As soon as everyone passed through the portal, it was closed.

The Original Sin

"The Pulse" was a place where Dom'rel went to coalesce and regenerate power. The walls were practically a living organism that glowed blue. Several tubes and chords hanging from the ceiling were connected to the devil's flesh. Dom'rel was residing in one of the chambers in the pit.

Vox'rel, the fallen archangel, stood across the room with her back to an exceptionally large door. It was quiet. Only the humming of the room could be heard. There was an echo from the side of the door as it opened and then quickly closed. As the sound came closer to the oculus of the chamber, faint sounds of a young girl weeping could be heard. Dom'rel lifted his head forward, seeing Vox'rel walking beside a trembling robed female.

Vox'rel halted the girl while she helped the dark lord to his feet. "Thank you, dear," Dom'rel uttered, his voice briefly distorted. Vox'rel said nothing, but she noticed that her master did not sway too much as he began to walk towards the girl. The girl's eyes met Dom'rel's. She turned and began to run. She was quickly paralyzed in place, as if a massive hand had wrapped itself around her. She was being pulled back towards the devil.

"Am I really so repulsive?" Dom'rel smirkingly asked. The girl looked back at him in sheer dread.

Vox'rel put a chalice in Dom'rel's right hand, which he held between himself and the young girl. He grasped the top of the girl's head, gripping it with enough force that her skull began to crack. She could barely scream before her head was torn from her body and her blood poured into the chalice. When the cup was overflowing, he chugged the blood. When he was finished, he handed the cup back to Vox'rel and resumed his reclined position.

"Shall I send to have the corpse removed, my lord?" Vox'rel quietly asked.

"No," Dom'rel replied with a relieved sigh. "I don't need anyone coming in here right now."

"As you wish," Vox'rel said.

"You know, you may not be as much fun as Vil'el, but you are certainly much more poised and reserved. I like that," Dom'rel said, closing his eyes. "Vil'el was motherlier, though."

"Is it my master's desire that I interact more with the children?" Vox'rel asked.

"No," Dom'rel scoffed.

"Look where that landed Vil'el. Further, at a minimum, Yojun, Kush'hera, and Herod are all dead from that bargain. The damned things are off playing with demons somewhere, for fuck's sake!" There was silence for a minute or two before Dom'rel spoke.

"Let me ask you something, Voxxie. Why did you join my ranks?" Vox'rel was a bit taken by his inquiry, not having thought of such times in eons.

"You, you were the first of our kind," she began. "You stood as commander of our legions, a cherished creation of The Light. Even celestials and guardians gave you reverence. You were the first being to be so closely created to The Light's own form. You were my commander, and so I followed you. I also believed in your words and even your criticisms. I have not observed as much of humanity as some, and I'm not envious of that. Among other things I admired about you was that you proved they could not handle the knowledge of good and evil because they were easily swayed in one direction. You proved others were capable of receiving worship and would likewise rebel."

Dom'rel chuckled mildly, saying, "See? In your own ways, you're refreshing to have around."

"Can I ask something, my lord?" Vox'rel inquired. Dom'rel tilted his head and looked at her as if to say, "Ask."

"Is it true that one of the angels of death retains its mortal body?" she asked.

"So, you ARE capable of snooping around," the devil answered.

"Here, I thought you just stood around like a statue even when I'm not around." Vox'rel quickly bowed low, with her hands and knees on the floor. Her eyes were uncharacteristically wide.

"Forgive me," she pleaded.

"There's nothing to forgive," Dom'rel scoffed in amusement.

"Which one?" Vox'rel asked as she remained on her hands and knees.

"Elo'el," Dom'rel replied with a grin. Vox'rel actually gasped.

"Don't worry, dear. He's been a very tame dog for quite a while now. Loyalty would be an understatement. Since I saved him from the fate of the others, control is probably closer to what I have over him. He's been useful a great number of times. However, as ironic as it is, time and deployment have taken its toll on him. Beings like Elo'el were made with a failsafe. They were without a harbor in Eternity. With the Celestial of Tide being destroyed, he and his lot deteriorate differently than the rest of us. I've had to practically rebuild him more than once."

"How have you kept him hidden?" Vox'rel asked.

"There are depths of this realm that even Bol'rel isn't foolish enough to dive," Dom'rel answered.

Into the Arms of Sorrow

One evening, Sapphira walked some distance from the base's perimeter, losing track of how far she had strayed in the cold. Her eyes looked down as she was beginning to sway and stumble a bit. She kept her grip on a half-empty bottle of whiskey she held in her right hand. Eventually, she just sank to her knees and began to sob, not caring for where she was or what could happen. She cried sorrowfully and, at times, gave a painful scream. Her body was unsteady, and her muscles were tense.

Her hand trembled as she threw the bottle aside and reached for her sidearm. The poor girl put the barrel of the gun against her temple, still sobbing as she looked to the dark sky. She pulled the hammer back and put her finger on the trigger; but as her finger began to pull back, the firearm was instantaneously disassembled. The pieces remained suspended in the air around her. Sapphira looked about confusedly when she heard an unfamiliar female's voice behind her. "I'm glad I got here when I did." Sapphira turned and saw Swae, the archangel, standing among the gentle snowfall. Feathers of her scarlet wings were gently waving in the breeze.

"Why did you stop me?" Sapphira asked, her voice quiet and somewhat raspy.

"Do you know that you mortals are the only suicidal species to exist?" Swae answered in the same manner as before. Swae approached the bottle that Sapphira had tossed aside. Sapphira just looked through her weary eyes at the archangel, who was now bringing the bottle back over.

"Aren't you supposed to tell me how I'm ruining myself with stuff like this?" Sapphira asked.

"You already know that," Swae smiled, handing the bottle over. "Besides, you deserve a celebratory drink, right? You're alive!"

Sapphira's overall demeanor was limp as she took the bottle in hand and took a sip. Swae knelt down, wrapping her arms and wings around Sapphira. Sapphira grabbed onto the archangel's arm and began to sniffle again, with tears returning to her eyes.

"I'm sorry, child. I know what it feels like for your heart to be in such pain," Swae said softly, "but this isn't the answer for you. Something like this has never been."

"What use am I to anyone?" Sapphira sobbed. "I have nothing left in this world. All that's left is just darkness."

Swae held Sapphira tightly, saying, "He can wait for you. Think of your friends and what news of something like this would have done to them. You are not alone in your loss, even though it feels that way. There is still Light, and I know that you know that. You are also a Light to others. You always have been." Sapphira did her best to stop her tears, breathing deeply as the archangel's energy warmed her. Swae dried the last few tears from Sapphira's eyes with the tip of one of her wings, saying, "Being in Ramm will take its toll on those stationed here. It is outside the bounds of protection that places like Shiro and Dan-hali enjoy. I need to know you can harbor this."

Surprised at the angel's statement, Sapph asked, "You think that I should stay?"

"Shouldn't you tell me to run back to Shiro and be comfortable?"

"I want you to turn this into resolve," Swae answered.

"No one knows what the future holds. Think of how far you've come. Did the angel Galai'el not eat and drink with you and your friends? Are you not the comrade of darkdancers? Have you not saved lives, Sapphira? You're not a bad soldier, but the war has truly struck you to the ground. Will you get up?" Sapphira was speechless.

"Come. I'll walk you back," Swae said, taking Sapphira's hand in hers. Leaving the bottle in the snow, the two began to walk back to the base.

Swae kept an illusionary spell about them in order to disguise their return. All anyone saw was wind, frost, and stone. The darkdancers were in their hangar, lounging about and doing this and that. Trova seemed to sense something as he stared out the open bay doors. He even forgot to take drags on his dragonskunk cigarette. The other darkdancers noticed the sensation as well but were somewhat less keen to what it was. Each sort of paused in what they were doing.

All of a sudden, Swae and Sapphira appeared in the hangar before the lot. "Holy shit!" Kasslow, the wolvyn, exclaimed in fright as he fell back in his chair. A'mi, the alchemist, jumped as well, fumbling the potions and elixirs in her arms. The darkdancers were simply awestruck by Swae's appearance--her four ruby wings, golden eyes, and powerful aura. Trova was the first to bow low, causing gasps throughout the room. Everyone else quickly did the same. Swae approached Trova, motioning with her hand for him and everyone else to rise, softly saying, "So, the shadows will continue to protect this side of the world. I suppose we'll make do elsewhere."

Swae turned to Enysa and smiled, saying, "Hello, again." Enysa returned the smile and rushed to hug the archangel. Swae, hugging Enysa back, laughed as the shadow embraced her.

"What are you doing here?" Enysa asked excitedly. Swae glanced at Sapphira, then back at the group, saying, "Just a friendly visit." Clearly, there was more to it than that, but it was also clearly confidential. Trova smirked at Enysa's mannerism with the archangel, saying, "You could have remained unseen. Why reveal yourself in such a way, wings and all?"

"Sometimes, I just like to remind our companions we're around," Swae answered casually, as she spread her wings wide. Everyone—each in their own way—was in awe at the sight of shimmering red feathers, pulses of electricity, and waves of red light.

Yes, Swae was showing off at this point.

Swae became stoic and stretched ever so gracefully, saying, "The people of Dan-hali are used to me. It's funny to think such brilliant shadows would be so taken aback." A'mi and Kasslow had ducked behind a couch. Kasslow whispered to A'mi, "This is totally awesome!" A'mi was simply fixated on the archangel. Light then came about Swae, and pieces of armor began to manifest on her. Each piece was primarily crimson and was adorned with gems, gold detailing, purple silk, white silk, blue silk, and scarlet silk. Her armor, all at the same time, was sleek, fierce, wicked, and gentle—her gold irises shone like lights through her dark visor. Even Trova took a step back at the sight of the transformation.

Seeing Swae in a way few mortals ever had, Sapphira was also amazed. "Come to me, shadows," the archangel said peacefully. The group was certainly curious at the request, each darkdancer looking cautiously at the archangel. Sij, Horus, Lua, Enysa, and Trova all approached Swae, kneeling down before her. One by one, Swae placed her hands on their heads, saying, "May the shadow go before the body and not behind." Runic lightning began to zip and trace from the archangel to and along the darkdancers.

Swae continued. "Shadows bend to the will of the Light. They dance to its flicker. Pierce the dark, weave through its storm, and carry your master. Carry the Light to the heart of darkness. Illuminate the blackness." With that, there was a gentle breeze that swirled about the place. Then, Swae's armor and her wings faded away. She resumed an appearance of a mortal. That is, she wore a red trench coat; her braided hair was tied back with feathers and beads here and there for decorations; and she conjured a pipe in her hand from velvet smoke.

"That was cool!" Kasslow commented to A'mi, both of them still behind the couch.

"I don't feel any different," Sij said.

"Check your right palm," Swae stated, beginning to puff her pipe. The darkdancers looked at their hands to find a glowing red glyph, an angelic symbol from ancient times.

"What is it?" Lua inquired.

"An 'Oh, shit' button for darkdancers," Swae answered. "Try not to use it too often and don't use it around regular people."

"A one-time thing?" Trova asked.

"Rechargeable," Swae said, "but it'll take a while since I'm normally so far away."

"I wanna push the button," Enysa uttered.

"No," Trova said plainly.

"Bad girl." Enysa pouted, leering at Trova. Swae looked at Lua and Sij, saying, "I'm glad to see elves in this chapter. I hope you are up to the task. You'll be around for quite some time. Can you endure? Can I count on you?" Sij saluted, valiantly replying, "I AM HERE FOR THE PROTECTION OF THE PEOPLE, FOR THE PROTECTION OF LIFE, AND FOR SHIRO. I WILL HELP HUMANITY WHEREVER THEY MAY NEED IT." Lua, rolling her eyes, looked at Sij with exasperation.

Swae smiled, saying, "The Light always chooses well. I'd be foolish to doubt. I look forward to our future encounters."

"See?" Sij declared to Lua. "Looks like we'll be 'heroing' it up for quite a while."

"They'll outlive us, huh?" Enysa asked.

"Yup," Horus stated. "Elvish lifespan plus the darkdancer modification? They'll be around a few thousand years."

"No, thank you," Trova said.

"That is a bit much," Horus agreed.

"What's so bad about that?" Enysa asked.

"Longevity brings the elements of time, little one," Sij answered rather upliftingly.

"The physical body is exposed to the sands and to pain and sorrow. You see and feel the world decay. You lose friends and loved ones if you have any. Immortality in a mortal world isn't as wonderful as most think." Enysa glanced over at a satchel of hers that contained the remaining blood vials. Trova, smirking at the thought he had, saw this but said nothing.

A portal opened behind Swae, revealing the likeness of Danhali through mystic mirrors and swirling light. "That simple, ma'am?" Trova asked.

"Remember that the world is a whole," Swae answered.

"There is so much in motion and so much at stake. Remember, there are Evermore people that have battles ahead of them. Also, remember how many fronts there are." Sapphira locked eyes with Swae as glimmers of light floated by.

"Be still," Swae said. "May the war part at you." Swae stepped back into the portal and was gone.

There was a certain moment and then a pause. All at once, the group fixed their eyes on Sapphira. Sapphira gave a half-smile, cleared her throat, but said nothing. "I won't ask," Trova remarked.

"Psh, I will," Enysa said. Lua gave a small zap to Enysa in the arm as if to say, "No." Enysa yelped a bit at the slight. A'mi began to come up to Sapphira to inspect her.

"I can smell the whiskey from back here. Were you partying with the archangel?" Kasslow asked. A'mi shined a light in

Sapph's eyes, felt her pulse, and asked her to hold her hands up at her waist, palms up. There was still a minor tremor in her hands.

A'mi looked caringly at Sapphira as though she knew what had or had almost happened. She nodded for Sapphira to follow her. The two walked into the nearby kitchen area, and A'mi had Sapphira sit at the table while the rest sort of just pretended not to watch. A'mi fetched a powder from her supplies, putting a pinch of it on the table.

"Snort it," she said plainly. "It'll keep you from getting sick or having a hangover. That's the last thing you need right now." Sapphira did what A'mi asked and took one quick inhale.

"Where's your sidearm?" A'mi quietly asked. Sapphira covertly pointed towards the open bay doors as if to say, "Out there." A'mi, smiling, shook her head and said with a sigh, "You and I are gonna be a bit closer now, ok?" Sapphira agreed.

"I didn't come all the way from that shitshow in Zuhetta to see people like you off themselves," A'mi said.

"We've had our fair share of that already." Sapphira nodded.

In the main area, Enysa leaned over to Trova, saying, "What do you think they're talking about?"

"Sapph was going to kill herself," Trova stated plainly.

"WHAT?" Enysa shouted. She ran over to Sapphira, bearhugging her from behind and lifting her out of the chair, and exclaimed, "No, no, no. It would break Yana's heart!" Sapphira was struggling to breathe a bit from the darkdancer's squeeze but smiled a little at the overall gesture. The rest of the group made their way over.

Fata Morgana

Even though Vega had been in Shiro for some time, the arrival of so many Ma'ji at once was still quite an event. Shiro, now harboring dwarves, was the most diverse place on the planet. Dwarves, common humans of various nations, Ma'ji, wolvyn, and trolls were sprinkled here and there. The limits of Rime were expanding, practically making the city Shiro a nation.

The truth be told, Shiro was becoming something that had not been seen since the first kingdom. Frankly, the Wolvyn are unnatural, so this was a little new to us as well.

On a particularly sunny day, Bree, the mother of the Christ child, was atop The Keep steps with the Child as Ma'ji were registering with the city census and being woven into Shiro's tapestry. Thulo was perched on Bree's right shoulder, and Thalis stood at her left side. Thulo entertained the Child by playing peekaboo as officials and military personnel coordinated with the Ma'ji.

"You're only entertaining to him because you're so round and goofy looking," Thalis remarked.

"You're just jealous," Thulo rebuked. Bree smiled, rolled her eyes, and said, "Has a representative or leader from them come forward?"

"No, Ma'am," Thalis answered. "Technically, their leader is back in Parraeysia," Thulo added.

"Rayne?" Bree affirmed. "I do hope I get to meet her one day. Surely there's a hero or someone among them who can speak for their community?"

"I'm sure we can find one," Thalis stated.

"None of them are being sent to Ramm?" Bree asked.

"We have more than enough firepower going into Ramm," Thalis chuckled. "We may as well just level the whole country."

"Only a few have inquired of the warfront here," Thulo added. "It seems that most of these travelers are simply travelers and new citizens for Shiro."

"That's good," Bree replied.

Elsewhere in Rime, a particularly beautiful woman was walking down the streets. Though she wore ornate robes of white, yellow, and orange, her figure could be readily noticed. She had angelic tattoos, irises like a sunrise, and sandy hair. She turned every head and especially the heads of the men she passed, but she never looked at anyone. Rather, she observed the buildings and environment around her. She had a spacey expression but was not clumsy in any sense.

Her name is Jezri'el. She is one of ours, an angel. At the onset of an ancient battle, she suffered a concussion, resulting in a level of forgetfulness and her otherwise spacey nature.

Gif happened to be perched in a nearby tree. Jezri'el was passing and called out to her. "Oye! Haven't seen you around here, and I think I'd remember someone like you." Jezri'el looked up and smiled, saying, "Oh, a talking raven! Aren't you the cutest thing?"

"Ugh," Gif grunted. "Seeing a lass like you makes me rue the day this happened."

"Come here," Jezri'el stated, holding her arms open.

"Oh?" Gif uttered to himself.

He flew into her hands. She held him against her chest, hugging the above-average-sized foul. If ravens could purr, he would be purring. "I take it back. I can live with this," Gif uttered. All the while, there was a decent number of onlookers, obviously curious about the woman's foreign origin and her interaction with one of the two talking animals in the region.

"What brings you here?" Gif asked, snuggling into Jezri'el's breast.

"I can't remember," she answered in an upbeat manner.

"Seriously?" Gif asked surprisedly. Jezri'el shrugged and smiled.

"Well, just keep walking. I'm sure it'll come back to you," Gif said contently.

"Maybe I was supposed to meet someone?" Jezri'el wondered aloud as she walked. "There was something about black crystals."

"Maybe go to The Keep?" Gif suggested, his feathers puffed and cozy.

"Maybe someone there can help?" Jezri'el gasped. "Which way? Do you know?"

"Of course," Gif replied. "Just a few more miles north and then west."

"Such a smart bird," Jezri'el said, embracing the raven. Gif melted and sighed against her breast.

The two continued towards The Keep. Men tripped over themselves and walked into various objects when they saw Jezri'el. She maintained a sort of blissfulness and did not take notice of how much attention she was getting from the people.

"So, are you some sort of enchantress?" Gif inquired. "A mage or something? You can't have eyes like those and not have a story."

"I'm an angel," Jezri'el kindly replied.

"Fair enough," Gif replied. "I've encountered all sorts of angels through this, but I'm yet to meet one of you. Do you all just mosey about fairly often?"

Jezri'el shook her head and said, "Mostly during times of stress in the world."

"Times of stress, she says!" Gif chuckled. "I suppose demons, monsters, and cataclysmic events are stressful?"

"Mhm," Jezri'el happily replied. "There are a few of us in the mortal plane right now, but I can't recall where my siblings are. I just know I have somewhere to go with people from here."

"Your memory always been iffy?" Gif asked.

"I don't remember anything before a certain point in our history. I've been told I took a nasty blow to the head in a battle," Jezri'el replied.

"I can't really imagine you in a fight," Gif stated curiously. Jezri'el shrugged and giggled. On their way, they passed by an eatery, where Yana, Bael, and Delia, the Aki'rah, were having a bite to eat. Even Bael, Yana's husband, glanced at Jezri'el for a moment too long. Yana gave him a hefty slap across the face.

The angel and the talking raven eventually came to The Keep steps, continuing up and inside. As they came to a corner, they could hear laughter coming from the other direction. Sure enough, Thalis, a human warrior, was walking with To'to, the troll, and was joking with him. Thalis walked straight into Jezri'el. Jezri'el had never been the shade of red that followed. In fact, he developed a brief stutter in trying to apologize.

"I 'tink dis be her if you can believe," To'to remarked happily.

"Talk about timing, mon." Jezri'el was overjoyed to know she had found the right place. "Wait. How did you know she was coming?" Gif inquired.

"Me have me ways," To'to replied.

"Oh, hush! Practically everyone knew," Thalis commented. "The Queen Mother of the Light incarnate resides here. It makes for an interesting place to be. There are plenty of messages coming in and going out."

"That's right. The Baby is here." Jezri'el gasped. "I was supposed to give him a present. Can you take me there?"

"Of course, milady," Thalis said confidently, motioning for the angel to walk with him.

Jezri'el handed Gif over to To'to. "Aw," the raven said sadly.

"Tell me about it, mon. Musta' been a comfy ride." To'to agreed. Gif sighed with delight, saying, "It was." Thalis tried to shield Jezri'el from the ongoing construction within The Keep by taking a longer route than it would otherwise be.

"It's nothing to be ashamed of," Jezri'el said kindly. "Scars will be scars. Even with my spotty memory, I remember the battle for this city. You impressed a number of our kin. Many fighters and civilians came to Eternity that day."

"I'm sure it's been a busy place since all this started," Thalis stated. Jezri'el shrugged, pondering aloud. "I mean, time and space are different there. There's lots of room, so I guess it never feels busy, at least not to me."

"In all honesty, you aren't quite what I expected for this assignment," Thalis remarked.

"Oh, yeah. Tell me. What's up?" Jezri'el answered.

"Well, soon, we're dispatching crews to Zuhetta to mine Onyxian shards," Thalis explained. "We're taking all of the proper precautions; but, apparently, someone thought we needed extra security."

"How fun! I knew it had to do with black crystals!" Jezri'el said excitedly. "To send for one of us, this must be important."

"'One of us?'" Thalis repeated.

"Celestial paragons," Jezri'el said casually. Thalis stopped in his tracks.

"That's an awesome title," he said with noticeable awe.

"I don't remember much of my time in the early years, but it's impossible to forget our training," the angel said.

"So, what's the difference between you and an archangel?" Thalis inquired. "A title like that has to come with some crazy power?"

"Mmm, mostly age," Jezri'el explained. "There are archangels in our legion too, and they do have the ability to access significantly more divine energy than we can. Think of it as layers of power. Each has a ceiling that must be broken through. Overall, our lot is like the heroes of Harth. We are diverse in capacity and in utility." The two continued to walk down the Hall of Shields, eventually ascending a spiral staircase to the top level of The Keep. Bree was in a lounging area with a glass of wine but looked up from her book when the two came into her line of sight.

Bree stood and greeted the two with a warm smile, saying, "You must be the muscle?" Jezri'el smirked and playfully flexed her arm.

"I put Iman'el to nap not long ago. He was around lots of people today. I think it tuckered him out a bit," Bree said.

"That's fine. I won't wake him, I promise," Jezri'el replied, "but I need to give him this before I forget." Bree showed the angel into the room, wherein she knelt by the cradle.

"A prince certainly needs a crown," she whispered. The angel held her hands open, and tiny lights and lightwaves became like a circle of planets. She motioned over the Child's head, and the crown stayed suspended just above his brow.

"It's beautiful!" Bree whispered.

"Starlight," the angel whispered back. "Each light was made by a different angel."

"Incredible!" Bree uttered with a grin. Jezri'el stood to walk back out of the room, and Bree gently closed the door behind them.

"Hopefully, he likes it," Jezri'el said.

"I have no doubt," Bree replied.

"Well then, I suppose I'll just wait for our marching orders," the angel said with a smile.

Later that night, Delia, Yana, and Bael went to Delia's estate, keeping something of a buzz going throughout the day. "I still don't know about you smoking," Bael commented, as he lit a skunkweed cigarette.

"That celestial bastard is in my baby. I'm sure he'll be simply fine," Yana answered, plopping down on a couch.

"I still can't get over the fact that you're expecting," Delia added. "Have you thought of a name?"

"Rook," Yana said, taking the cigarette from Bael.

"We're kind of betting it'll be a boy at this point," Bael said.

"I bet Dehza knew. That's probably why he went away all sneaky and shit," Yana huffed.

"We're just kind of hoping there aren't scales," Bael joked. Yana added nothing.

"I'm sure he'll be normal enough," Delia said with a smile. Yana simply crossed her fingers.

"On another note, I did hear from Sapphira," Delia stated.

"She sounded down, but who wouldn't be? But I was assured she has good company. I asked her if she wanted to come to Shiro for some rest, but she insisted on staying. She said, "I want to see the bombs go off." She works exclusively for our shadows now, and it sounds like they'll keep her close."

"I trust them," Yana said.

"We'll see her again." Delia nodded. Jeeves came into the area, joining the three. Bael greeted the skeletal caretaker with a fist bump, as did Delia.

"Did you show him that?" Yana asked in amusement.

"I actually learned such a greeting from my previous masters," Jeeves said, as politely and as calm mannered as ever.

"Ugh, I hate when you use that word," Delia sighed. "You don't consider me your master, do you?"

"I've learned not to answer that question," Jeeves replied. Delia rolled her eyes.

"I took the liberty of sending the rest of their apparel via a military courier," Jeeves added. "They left before it was finished."

"Turns out he can make magical armor," Delia commented, as she motioned to Jeeves.

"A craft I've perfected over the ages," Jeeves said.

"I thought you had a guy for that?" Bael asked.

"Horus is skilled, but we're talking about two different arts. The living cannot cast the enchantments," Jeeves answered.

"But, you're alive, right?" Yana asked. Jeeves replied with a simple, "Hah!"

"I'm just confused now," Yana muttered.

"My soul is fast asleep as long as these bones are active," Jeeves continued. "An angelic spell, if you must know."

"An angel did this to you?" Yana asked, as if offended.

"I volunteered," Jeeves answered.

"How the fuck has this not been told to me?" Delia asked, as if offended.

"Such language doesn't suit you, Lady Delia. I've told you that before," Jeeves said.

"Otherwise, I suppose it just hasn't really come up in our dealings." The group fell silent for a moment before Bael broke the silence by saying, "Yeah, let's see someone follow that up."

"So, what kind of armor are we talking about?" Yana inquired.

"Runic Polymorphous Plate," Jeeves replied. "Shadowsteel can be infused to change shape and is responsive to the wielder's energy signature. While on occasion it has been done to weapons, the spell is exclusive to solid plating. Rorik was the only one in the previous chapter house that used it, and that was because of his strength and size. This set was made to fit Sij. I also finished a few items for others on behalf of Master Horus. One can accomplish much without the need for sleep or nourishment."

"And what have you done lately, Delia?" Yana giggled. Delia playfully stuck her tongue out at Yana in reply.

The truth be told, even as well off as places like Shiro were, there was always this melancholy that echoed within each soul. The attack in Ramm was a heavy blow to many individuals, a sobering reminder of the times. The demonic fronts of Zuhetta and Mol'do took their own shapes, and the inevitable raid on Evermore was always in front of those surviving in Malene.

Yana found herself wondering how long she would have her child before facing Baaltha, the evil king's son, or how many nightmares awaited her in the fallen city.

Jezri'el's placement with the mortals going on the Zuhetta mining expedition was not just for show. Even if her being there proved uneventful, the security of this operation was key to humanity having any hope for a sustainable future.

On what would have been a starry night over Ramm, the sound of rolling tanks and airship propellers broke the deathly silence. Sapphira boarded her company's personal craft, piloted by Kasslow and accompanied by A'mi. The darkdancers had already taken point on each assigned front, helping ground forces to clear paths forward. Several destroyers preceded the darkdancers as they began their absolute bombardment of most major cities. The thunder of the eerie blasts could be heard in parts of Shiro.

Sapphira watched the distant flashes through slightly misty eyes as their craft remained stationary in the dark sky, some miles east of the base. "We're going to beat these fuckers!" Sapphira sniffled. "We'll push them back to the sewage they crawled out of."

"Damn right," Kasslow concurred. "It is worth enlistment just to experience this."

"Hard to imagine what Amon is feeling," A'mi noted.

"He'll get over it," Trova replied over the void comms.

"Eli told me stuff about the final goal here," Sapphira uttered, "…that no amount of airpower would count; that this army is in some vault."

"That is why WE are here," Sij said proudly over the comms. Kasslow leaned back, holding out a cigar box towards the ladies.

"Skunkweed?" he asked.

"You sly dog," Sapphira replied, taking one from the box. A'mi shrugged as she took one for herself.

"This is a cool moment," Kasslow said. "Getting to light up with some buddies while bombs are being dropped in the distance." The girls could not help but smile at their furry comrade.

"Our line is moving up," Horus said over the comms. *"About time. With all that armor, you should be ahead of us,"* Trova replied.

"It's because of the armor that we're slower on the roll," Lua interjected. *"Ass!"*

"In Trova's perfect world, all roads are made to easily accommodate massive tanks," Horus added.

"This is my perfect world," Trova answered.

"So dark and edgy," Lua joked.

"HA!" Sij bolstered.

"All glory to our dark and edgy leader," Enysa added mockingly. *"Too bad I knew you before you got your superpowers. You're a big softie at your core."*

"No less of an asshole, though," A'mi sighed.

Sapphira reached out of the bay door, firing a flare into the black clouds that signaled to forces further back that there would be movement. Other aircraft in similar roles did the same down a stretch of a dozen miles. "We'll be touching down to resupply at The Gate when the destroyers pass," Sapphira said with a yawn and a stretch. "They've been at it for a while now. I imagine they're about empty."

"No word of casualties," Kasslow commented. "I think this is a good sign."

"A few injuries," A'mi said. "Enough to let you know there's still activity down there."

"I'm sure there are lots of prayers around this," Sapphira uttered. "Any victory isn't much of a victory right now, anyway."

"War on all sides," Kasslow stated.

"Mhm," Sapphira agreed. "Sapph?" A'mi asked.

"Hmm," Sapphira answered.

"Did Eli ever tell you anything about Evermore? I've heard that name more than once," A'mi stated, hoping not to offend her friend.

"It's where everything started for us," Sapphira somewhat reminiscently explained. "Evermore is the epicenter of Malene's invasion. I suppose the end goal for this part of the world is to destroy whatever and whomever is there. Even with the scouting that's been done, there hasn't been much news. The most noteworthy thing always seemed to be that its main access would be via air. Honestly, Eli always seemed worried about a raid there. I think he tried not to talk about it because he knew Yana would be going there."

"Yana. I know this name," Kasslow commented.

"You are friends with the summoner, yes? See? This is a celebrity airship." Sapphira grinned. A'mi smiled as well, saying,

"I'm sure we can handle it." Sapphira nodded even though she still struggled with the idea.

As the destroyers eventually started coming back into sight, the second set of flares went off, indicating Operations should wrap up and convene at their respective locations. The crew set down in a town that was essentially a pile of rubble, using exterior lights of the airship to illuminate some of the areas around them. Sapphira stepped onto the cold ground and was struck with chills, uttering, "I wonder how many died here?"

Each darkdancer parted from their group to meet up with their comrades. Shadowstepping in Ramm was as easy as breathing. They were able to cover miles in less than a minute. Trova was the only one not to arrive in Ramm in a timely manner. The shadows, however, were in good spirits and completely unharmed. They exchanged kill stories and compared the sizes of their prey. Trova remained silent, not needing to boast about the destruction he waged against the swarm. A'mi seemed to hear something on her void comm and then said, "Sij." Sij proudly replied, "Yes?"

"There's a package making its way up the line for all of you. However, they have used your name specifically for receipt," A'mi explained. "Do you want me to see where it is so you can pick it up, or do you wanna wait? It should be delivered by midday tomorrow."

"It can wait. I won't be needing it just yet," Sij stated.

"Must be the gear that Jeeves was finishing," Horus commented.

"It'll be good timing to have it for this vault we're after." Enysa gasped.

"My surprise? I can go get it," she said eagerly.

"You can wait," Lua chuckled. Enysa looked away dejectedly.

"I'm surprised Trova hasn't just told her. It seems like something he could ruin," A'mi remarked.

"She needs to learn patience!" Trova rebuked. Enysa folded her arms and huffed.

"How long before you reach the city?" Kasslow inquired.

"Technically, I've already been," Trova answered casually. This was news to everyone. "At this rate, it'll be about 70 hours. The concentration of these bugs is exponentially higher there. If the surface of Lok'rom is any indicator of what's beneath it, it's going to be a hell of a party. The destroyers don't have to worry about blocking any routes. There's a highway that loops around the city that will get us to where we need to be. The more they can pummel the place, the better. We can pretty much avoid having to fight through the whole city and use a back door."

"I would assume Amon knows the best way in?" A'mi asked. "Is there any specific information we should relay?"

"Not really," Trova replied. "Light the place up and hit it hard and fast. My suggestion? We move in while the destroyers are overhead."

"Try and overwhelm an overwhelming enemy?" Lua pondered.

"There are multiple hive minds there, but if we strike everything at once, there will be a lag time in their responsiveness. We will likely be blinding their entire force momentarily," Trova explained. "I found some of the hive minds, and they're all in heavy bunkers. The destroyers won't hit them by just passing them by."

Trova pulled out a marked map and handed it to Sapphira. "I'm confident in this plan," Sij remarked hardily.

"You're confident about everything," Lua mumbled.

"Just take that map to Amon and be sure all of our pilots get a look at the hotspots," Trova concluded. Sapphira nodded in agreeance.

"So, I get my surprise in, like, how many hours?" Enysa asked. Trova sighed with exasperation.

"Did you hear any of what he just said?" Lua asked with a grin. Enysa shrugged, saying, "Hard and fast."

"Close enough. She'll be fine," Horus commented.

"Aww, thank you honey!" Enysa said, hugging Horus.

"Plus, we just got a perk from an archangel. If any one of us dies, it's just because you suck," Trova added.

"Yes, sir!" the other shadows answered.

The next morning in Rime, one of the groups, including Gizmo, Twitch, Morgan, a handful of cogs, and a number of hired workers, was gathering, and was set to depart for Zuhetta. They had been told that most of the supplies would be ready for them in Zuhetta, so each individual had only what he or she could carry. Morgan kissed Kira, saying, "I'll be back."

"You better be, love," Kira replied.

"So, who's left? Who're we waitin' on?" Gizmo asked. Twitch chirped and shrugged. Then there was some mumbling among the group as Jezri'el approached.

She was wearing pieces of sterling with ornate armor on top of her robes. She already shimmered in the dawning sun. She greeted the group with a loving smile. Then she saw Gizmo, who was beginning to fawn over the wolvyn runt. "Awwww, aren't you adorable," she said, as she crouched to pet him.

"Please, stop that," Gizmo uttered as Jezri'el smooshed his face.

"Please!" Jezri'el ruffled his ears and stood up. At the time, he was satisfied. Gizmo rolled his eyes. Twitch made some chirps that sounded more like laughter.

"Yeah, keep it up and see how long your legs stay bolted on," Gizmo replied to his companion. Kira was in awe of Jezri'el, to the point that Morgan slapped her on her butt.

"OW!" Kira exclaimed.

"Sorry, sorry, but I'm not so sure I want you going on a trip with someone that looks like her," she mumbled.

"Hush! There's nothing to worry about," Morgan assured. Kira held Morgan's hand and looked at Jezri'el, saying, "She's mine." Jezri'el smiled, replying, "I know. I'll be sure she comes back in one piece."

"Alright, let's get this show goin'," Gizmo stated, as he started up the path to the rainbow bridge. The group followed, eventually coming to the nexus. One by one, they stepped into the network and out of Malene.

Eye of the Swarm

The forces of Shiro have decimated the former dwarven kingdom. Pillars of smoke rose like burnt offerings from leveled cities and towns, and embers fought valiantly against the chill of the swarmlands.

*The men and women of Harth braved the campaign with outstanding success. I say, "Harth," because of the diverse composition of this army. This was not just Shiro or dwarves reclaiming a homeland. This was **one** among many of the battlegrounds of humanity. They all fought for a common cause. They fought a common enemy.*

This army marched as skyswords continued ripping through the Vae'yiri air and as their comrades across the seas faced off against the dark. Tanks and vehicles dotted the rocky terrain; formations rolled over the land, and airships continued their bombing runs. War is a glorious thing from certain perspectives. The mere sight of the theaters can be breathtaking.

Casualties were minimal en route to Lok'rom, though those who perished suffered bloody and gruesome deaths, which was, unfortunately, a testament to what was to come.

Forces were rallying at the parameters of the city as communications went back and forth from every level of the operation. It was the eve of the assault on the vault, an eve of mixed emotions and mannerisms. Some areas were lit up with cheer and merriment as they readied for either encouragement or the last party. Other sections were more somber, displaying quiet nods, smiles, prayers, or meditations. All the soldiers here interacted as though they were family. Even officers waived professional informalities.

Fires of all kinds beautifully speckled the area to the front of Lok'rom.

As King Amon finished meeting with his various commanders, he stepped out of a tent and into the cold. His eyes were tired as he silently looked over the massive highway they would be taking to the battlefield in some hours. He took a deep breath, clenching his fists so that his knuckles cracked. General Nix came beside King Amon, standing "at rest" and saying, "We won't fail." Amon sighed, replying, "I'm not concerned over failure. It's the red that I'm thinking of."

"How much has been spilt to get here?" Nix rhetorically asked.

"It's the pain, Charles," Amon answered.

"We mortals are but flesh and bone, fluids and fuckin' nerves. I never thought I'd see so much mortal blood in my lifetime, especially as things began easing up." Nix glanced down at Amon, staying in his stoic posture.

"Easing up," he said with a chuckle.

"You don't deny the societal issues then?" Amon lit a cigar and whistled to a soldier for a stein of beer.

"Malene has been in a state of melancholy for some time," Nix continued. "Darkness was always here because we were here."

The soldier returned with the beer, handing it to Amon and saluting before he resumed his post. "Don't go getting all poetic," Amon said. "You're insufferable when you get like that."

"They are soldiers and heroes, Amon," Nix stated with a grin.

"So are we? Regardless, pain is in our destiny. They know this. All we can do is roll the dice." Amon nodded and took a hefty drink from the stein. Nix checked his pocket watch, then said, "Don't forget to rest tonight, Amon." Amon nodded. General Nix put his hands in his coat pockets and strolled off, saluting as he passed the soldier who had retrieved the beer.

Elsewhere, Enysa could barely be contained as she waited for her surprise. Trova went out of his way to have the item in his custody. It was wrapped in dark cloth. "Gimme, gimme, gimme!" Enysa excitedly uttered, grasping in the direction of the shrouded object. Trova actually smiled. Being a bit high on remedy helped that. Sij was sporting his new pieces of polymorphic armor, trying them out some feet away. The armor rolled with Sij's energy. It flowed and compacted at command while spiking and curving at will.

"Let's see it," Lua said, sitting on a nearby crate.

"I'm actually kind of curious, too," Horus agreed.

"Here," Trova said, handing the item to Enysa. Surprisingly, Enysa unwrapped it rather slowly. The package revealed a runic gun blade. Enysa's eyes said it all when she saw the weapon. She was speechless.

"It's the same formula as Sij's stuff over there," Horus commented. "It can also likely polymorph."

The weapon was taller than she was. Needless to say, her assault rifle was now her secondary weapon. As a darkdancer, she could certainly wield it, but she would also have to slightly change her style.

The weapon certainly was beautiful. It was the work of artisan hands and design and still kept with the dark look. Enysa was quiet and in awe as she felt the metal. Red lightning was flickering between her skin and the steel. "I can kill something big with this," she uttered.

"That's the idea," Trova affirmed. Enysa took the hilt of the weapon in hand and was surprised by how light it felt. Sij, as curious as the rest, stopped working with his armor to observe this pairing.

Enysa smiled as she rather gracefully swung the gun blade. Sapphira, A'mi, and Kasslow were present across the way. "That is a big sword!" Kasslow commented.

"Let's just hope homegirl can swing it without cleaving our people," Sapphira said, placing a medicinal tablet under her tongue.

"I mean, I figured she would have accidentally shot someone by now, but she hasn't," A'mi added.

"I think she's good to go." Sapphira swayed a bit and leaned into Kasslow.

"You good?" Kasslow asked.

"I'm good," Sapphira replied with a content sigh.

Enysa finished a few twirls and thrusts with the towering gun blade, keeping control of each swing and coming to a pretty pose. "You good?" Trova inquired.

"I love it!" Enysa exclaimed.

"But how do I transform it?" she asked. Horus took out a small book from a pocket, thumbed through a few pages, and then said, "The spectrum for polymorphic weapons is broad, but it should respond to your energy as Sij's armor responds to his energy." Enysa pondered. Horus continued to browse his reference, eventually saying, "The polymorphic form is not predetermined. It locks in after the host's energy is synchronized. It's reactionary."

"Soooo, it needs to be in a fight?" Enysa asked.

"Pretty much," Horus replied. "I'm sure you'll figure it out," Trova remarked, taking a puff from a dragonskunk cigar.

"Just swing around in circles, and you're good," Lua, the terrani elf, said with a wink.

"With the right momentum of transfer and energy use, you can manage a sizeable radius. Think of it like physics," Horus commented. Enysa looked at Horus with a bit of a dumbfounded look.

"I'm sure you'll figure it out," Horus said.

"HAH! Physics tends to be broken all the time here," Sij added. "I will still protect the little one."

As Sapphira, Kasslow, and A'mi watched the darkdancers' exchange, they carried on in their own conversations. "I actually have kind of a good feeling about tomorrow," Sapphira said quietly, as she sat comfortably wrapped in a warm coat. "Yeah?" A'mi replied. "I'm still shaky about this sort of stuff."

"Stuff? You mean war?" Kasslow stated.

"It's ok to be chicken." A'mi leered at the wolvyn.

"I kid, comrade," Kasslow said. "You are a great asset to the effort. We all are, or else we would not be here. I will keep the ladies safe. Don't worry."

"I totally get why Eli picked you. It wasn't just for your inexplicable ability to operate aircraft," Sapphira said to Kasslow.

"Because I am awesome? And I'm cool?" Kasslow replied.

"Exactly," Sapphira said. "You would have complimented us from the beginning." Sapphira, silently looking away for a few moments, felt the scar on her neck. There would always be some level of sadness in Sapphira's eyes. Even now, she seemed to be reminiscing over past events, if only briefly.

"I was pretty lame before everything started," A'mi uttered. "I just ran a simple potion shack. Everything happened so quickly on that day."

"Now, you are an alchemical master. War gave you purpose and drive," Kasslow stated.

"Your people seem fond of war," Sapphira mentioned curiously.

"Chelsea was not a peaceful place," Kasslow affirmed. "Generations of battles with the dark left so many skeletons and the undead. Chelsea is a little place compared to here. There's less room to breathe in times of strife."

"Did you chew on skeleton bones?" A'mi asked with a mild giggle.

"No comment," Kasslow answered.

"That's cute!" Sapphira chuckled. "Would you chase a ball if I threw it?"

"We do not chase balls," Kasslow declared.

"We'll find you a nice bone, Kass," A'mi said playfully.

"That is unnecessary," Kasslow half-heartedly mumbled.

"What's all of this about bones and balls?" Trova asked, having snuck up and startled the three via shadow steps. "We're looking at a serious military operation in a few hours, and your minds are that far from reality?"

"I'm getting the hang of your sarcasm," A'mi said, brushing herself off after tripping from fright. "I guess we, regular people, are just exchanging war stories."

"I'm sure your past is ripe with heroism," Trova said, as he eyed A'mi.

"This one played like he ordered me executed," A'mi rebuked. "I had the barrel of a gun to my head."

"See? War can be playful," Kasslow commented. "He gets it," Trova stated.

"It wasn't funny," A'mi huffed. Sapphira resettled and laid down on a cot. She asked, "I heard you had to kill people over there. Was it crazy in Zuhetta?"

"Some disagreements had to be settled," Trova replied. "The rest was just bad timing."

"Or good timing," Kasslow injected. Trova shrugged.

"We're ready for tomorrow," A'mi declared.

"Yes, Sapphira will be on guns," Kasslow affirmed.

Sapphira waved from her cot. "I'm sure it'll be a hell of a show. Just don't get these two killed," Trova said to Kasslow.

"You got it, buddy," Kasslow confirmed with a thumbs up.

"I have a surprise for you!" A'mi said slyly to Trova. Trova was genuinely curious, raising an eyebrow at the notion. A'mi brandished a wooden box, revealing what looked like cigars.

"My own mixture, and it's coated with slayer's remedy," A'mi explained. "They're to share."

Trova took one from the box and ran it past his nostrils. "Smells like home." A'mi winked and replied, "Let me know how the others like them after the show, yeah?"

"I'll pass them around," Trova said, receiving the box from the alchemist.

"Could y'all have picked a bigger blade for her?" Sapphira sarcastically inquired.

"We didn't pick it," Trova replied.

"What Enysa has is like what Wolvyn Claymore has," Kasslow added. "The weapon will swing her."

"She'll be fine," Trova said, looking across the way at Enysa and the others.

Sleep came to some. It evaded others. Chemicals, nerves, and adrenaline kept those alert who could not sleep that night.

Dawn had barely come before destroyers were flying ahead of the ground forces and smaller airpower. They were to begin their bombing runs over Lok'rom. Engines, whistles, shouts, and the like resounded throughout the allied lines. It was a strange sort of morning.

Later history recalls this as "The Twilight Morning."

The ground shook as explosions began within the city, stirring up everyone within and outside the vicinity. Ground forces, accompanied by their close air support, would fire a few dozen rounds as they traveled down the highway. Bastion gunships, focusing on the points of interest that had been relayed, joined the destroyers in pulverizing the city. The massive structures of the city were collapsing as the bombs dropped. Fire, dust, and smoke filled the area. Smaller airships, providing sniper fire and spotting support, stuck to the outside of the city limits, still keeping with their teams on the ground.

The sight was astounding, comrades!

The destroyers, intertwining their flight patterns to have their targets constantly pounded, had been overloaded with munitions. Their speed was eerily slow as they left craters at certain points. Whatever responsibility did not fall to the bombs of the destroyers fell to the guns and cannons of the bastion ships that mingled with the destroyers in the skies. The battle was on.

Putrid flyers began to take to the smoky air. Many were cut down by machine-gun fire and cannons, but more still poured upward. Crews and heroes engaged those that landed on the aircraft while guns and flame turrets lit up the skies. All the while, the shelling continued on the city below.

Forward ground forces had made it to the breach and had set up firing lines for tanks and mobile artillery. Heroes and soldiers engaged the hellish bugs as more allied forces poured into the maw. While demonic blood and guts practically rained, the allies now felt the sting of their foe. Flesh was melted by acids, ripped by scythe-like appendages, and torn by serrated edges. Mortal blood once more flowed on the grounds of Lok'rom as monsters of all sizes--pierced, sliced, ripped, and smashed--thrashed about.

Warriors collided with rushing pit fiends, while their carapace and shield smashed together. Swords cleaved the insects, and the insects tore into the warriors. Gunslingers' barrels blazed and punched holes in the nightmares on both the ground and in the air. The insects fought back with acidic sprays, barbed webs, and ghastly projectiles from their own bodies. Spellflingers called upon every element across the lines, each casting powerful magic deep into the monsters' forces. Specialized specimens emerged that could produce flaming and lightning-laced bioluminescent beams. Bladedancers sliced and diced their way through the fiends like they were grass. Nonetheless, the fiends had snipers to stop them in their tracks.

On a smaller airship above, a ranger caught a glimpse of a Moriart demonic insect, clasped onto a towering building, releasing an explosive arrow at the six-legged thermo-camouflaged pit archer. Hitting it in the center of its six eyes, the monster burst into blood and goo that fell to the streets below. A young shield-bearing warrior was dueling with a pit mantis patriarch and was doing well to block its quick and hard swipes. The girl's shield took a number of rapid hits before she could get in an attack, but she was patient and disciplined. The duel lasted three minutes before the monster finally collapsed from the warrior's mortal strikes.

General Nix was with a group of infantries. He was partnering his mastery of ice with the heavy-hitting guns of his comrades. He froze entire portions of the enemy line by simply snapping his finger to shatter his victims. He was a class act and was with those who spearheaded a cold strike at the heart of the swarm inside the vault.

"Onward!" Nix shouted happily. "Let us see to the destruction of these abominations. Keep as warm as you can."

"Aye, sir!" those around him replied.

In the gunner position on their ship, Sapphira was having the time of her life as she blew away the pit fiends. A'mi was running munitions back and forth, as well as preparing alchemical rounds to be used. In order to support their comrades below, Kasslow kept the airship at an ideal altitude as he maneuvered well in the dusty air. "You like the gun?" Kasslow shouted down to Sapphira. Sapphira was jostling about from the firing of shells, but she loved it.

"You make aiming easy," Sapphira yelled back.

"Let's just hope one doesn't pop in on us," A'mi shouted, as she carried shells and reagents here and there.

"You better be a good guard dog, Kass." Kasslow replied with an affirmative and literal, "WOOF, WOOF!"

Below, the darkdancers, accompanied by thousands of soldiers and heroes, had made their way into the fray, now taking point to the doors of the vault. Horus, who had never seen the sort of engineering behind this massive construct before, asked, "Is there some sort of code?"

"Probably some lame kind of magical key," Trova replied, throwing one of his swords into the chest of a swarm brute. Artillery shells and poisonous projectiles were exchanged back and forth as tanks and siege beasts held their respective lines.

After cutting several infantry bugs down, Enysa pointed her gun blade at a siege scorpion. The weapon quickly morphed into a cannon, causing the girl to smile widely. "Sweet," she uttered. Enysa pulled the trigger that sent a ball of runic energy hurling forth. The recoil knocked her on her butt, but the resulting blast was remarkable. The monster at which she aimed was vaporized, along with anything else within a 15-yard radius. Sij laughed as he helped Enysa to her feet. "Be sure none of ours are downrange of that."

"That was so cool," Enysa replied.

"The king can open the doors," Amon said through the void comms, *"but since it has been insisted that I stay at the rear, there will need to be an overcharge of electricity to the system and a large enough pick to break the lock."*

"Big Burtha has the pick, sir," Skarg answered over the network. *"We're rollin' down the main street now. It shouldn't be too long."*

"Catch that, Lua?" Horus asked, fanning shots from his machine pistols into a number of putrid insects.

"Keep 'em off me, and we're good," Lua replied, as she cast powerful electrical pulses around herself that splattered dozens of bugs.

By now, millions of hell-spawn insects were coalescing from the entire kingdom to attack Lok'rom, a city in Ramm. Any and every monster not killed by now was moving from the outside to the inside. This was taken into consideration when the alliance planned their assault. Airships were to route their firepower in such a way as to create a bubble around a portion of Lok'rom. Soil and stone were kicked up by the melee below and from the projectiles raining down. The battlefield was practically its own earthquake.

Blood and tears fell as cries, hisses, shrieks, and roars were exchanged.

Lua and her allies continued their push forward, making it to the doorstep of the vault. The battle still raged in every direction. Death was still in every direction. *"Lua, you should see something like an eight-pointed star above the doors,"* Amon said over the comms.

"Hit that with everything you can. Also, ask for support from any other caster nearby that can conjure electricity." A resounding, *"Aye, sir,"* followed. Horus directed his shielding devices around Lua and threw a glyph-lined metal ball into the air between her line of sight and the star. Lua unleashed a torrent of lightning, hitting the ball and amplifying the energy's scope.

Electricity struck the star and dispersed it into the system. Bloodied and tired spellflingers came when they could to join with Lua's side. They conjured lightning bolts to add to the electrical surge. Some had to help others to even stand. Eyes had to turn away as the resulting beam became blinding. Electricity snaked through the doors and machines, prepping and activating various locks and systems. Lok'rom became sort of a star in and of itself from the amount of light that came from the location.

The slashing and gashing continued all the while, even aboard the airships.

This was no one-sided fight, comrades.

Airships burned as they fell. Some exploded in the sky. Bodies and body parts, as well as debris and gears, came from the darkened sky. Oil, dirt, smoke, and blood were all mixing together on the ground and in the air. The ambiance was deafening, maddening, and incredible. The Big Burtha tank was significantly damaged by the time it came to its position, but the main cannon was still operational.

"ARE WE READY TO DO THIS?" Lua cried over the comms. *"I CAN'T DO THIS FOREVER."*

"Aye, lassie!" Skarg replied. *"We're prepping to fire."*

By now, King Amon had been picked up by the smallest and most agile and well-guarded ship available. It was en route to the frontlines.

Skarg set some controls as the crew of Big Burtha began to leave the armor. It would not survive beyond one final shot from its main rail cannon. *"I need to be sure that you're getting out, Skarg,"* Amon said over the comms.

"Aye, sir," Skarg replied. *"Just makin' sure she'll go off."* Skarg finished setting the mechanisms and instruments, also prepping the trigger before leaving the massive tank.

"3, 2, 1," Skarg said.

Then...

The primary railgun fired. A flash of blue light left the barrel just before the tank began to explode. The projectile hit dead center between the mighty doors, resulting in a blinding light. When the explosion cleared, the doors became unlocked and drew enough apart for entry on foot. The beam of electricity ceased. Lua, almost fainting, was caught by Horus. The spellflingers, as well as all of the soldiers and heroes, were worn out by now. Mortality was beginning to reach its limits. But unfortunately, the battle had to continue in every direction and in every way.

The agile airship had come close enough to the ground for Amon to safely leap from its deck. He continued on foot into the darkened vault. Several heroes and soldiers went with King Amon as the fight burned behind them. "How does this work?" a warrior asked as he ran alongside the king.

"It'll take more than a drop," Amon answered.

Even King Amon was in awe of the dormant elemental mechanical army that they found within the vault as they came before Black Beard's legion. Indeed, the sight of the incredible monoliths took their breath away.

Amon stood before an opened upright sarcophagus. Those with Amon gasped when they came here. Now they grasped what was truly meant by the *blood of the king.* Amon did not hesitate. He climbed into the tomb after giving parting orders to those who had followed him.

King Amon's blood, becoming like energy, left his body. The monoliths glowed red with runes and energy as they came to life. Their awakening sent shockwaves in multiple ways from the vault.

Entire portions of the city collapsed as massive silos and bay doors opened to let the towering machines out. As it was, these walking armors were more than battle-ready. They instantly engaged the enemies of humanity. Black Beard's Legion was a legion of heroes. Each of the million elemental machines was unique in its output. The five-story goliaths easily relieved their mortal counterparts of their duty.

Jaws dropped across the battlefield as the legion came forth. Even Trova was astonished. The alliance had successfully cleared their objective.

The fog of war would clear from the eyes of those in Ramm. There was relief, but there was more than enough wounds to be mended. Two hundred and twenty-two thousand souls were lost in that battle. It took that much blood and the blood of a king to win back one of Malene's territories.

As airships settled in the aftermath, Sapphira crossed paths with General Nix. He had lost an eye in the battle but was otherwise on his feet. Sapphira stood at attention and saluted the general. Nix looked down over his grey moustache at Sapphira and grinned. He embraced the girl like she was his granddaughter.

Trova was leaning against a tank that was surrounded by the decimation. Enysa came beside him, playfully nudging him with her shoulder. "Hmm?" Trova uttered, not looking over. Baby girl did alright," Enysa said proudly. Trova let out a single chuckle, replying plainly.

"Yeah, you did okay." Meanwhile, Sij was carrying Lua as Horus walked alongside.

Lua had a spiteful look on her face, not liking that she was being carried by Sij. "You can't help that. Your legs have given away," Sij assured, smiling and nodding at other soldiers and heroes as they continued to walk. Lua said nothing. Horus sighed.

"I thought you were over this?" Lua said nothing.

"Terrani are so stubborn," Sij chuckled.

"Apparently," Horus agreed.

Kasslow was sitting with A'mi at their airship and was rolling a large skunkweed cigar. A'mi just laid back against the open door of the airship as she looked out over the destruction. "You want a puff?" Kasslow asked.

"Yeah," A'mi replied, somewhat in a daze. The wolvyn lit the cigar and handed it to A'mi, saying through a cloud of smoke, "This is pretty cool. We see big robots come from the ground; an entire city leveled; big dead bugs everywhere; and fire and anything else you can think of." A'mi let the smoke out of her lungs and shifted her eyes to Kasslow. "You're a good dog."

“I know,” Kasslow replied.

Across the World

Across the world, Swae was reflecting on their circumstances. She was lost in an archangel's train of thought. Xavus, king of Dan-hali, and Elsa, Xavus' wife, actually managed to sneak up on Swae as they came to a palace overlook to see her. The two of them were curious with respect to how they had caught the archangel off guard. Swae was just as curious as to why they had come to see her.

"How many would you allow to go to Tristen?" Xavus asked.

"Not many," Swae replied, as smoke from her pipe escaped from her nostrils.

"How many is that?" Elsa asked.

"Not many," Swae replied with a grin. Xavus looked at the archangel with exasperation.

"Why are you so curious all of a sudden?" Swae asked.

"I had a dream," Xavus answered, "a dream of dragons, fire, steel, void, and life energies." Swae sighed, saying, "It's not like I can walk alongside a hunting party."

Xavus leaned his forearms against the railings of the overlook, saying, "I know enough to know that you're needed here. Leave the fight to us."

"You don't need another battle," Swae replied.

"I know. You won't let us go far," Elsa said with a smile.

"We have the means to reconnect to the void network," Xavus added. "We have the people that can take on this quest."

"Did you seriously just say quest?" Swae replied.

"It *is* a quest," Xavus stated. "Mol'do cannot be like a severed limb to the rest of the world. I believe *our* window is opening."

"Xavus already has people selected," Elsa humbly said.

"They would only need your approval." Swae puffed her pipe as she contemplated what he said in her own way. A few moments passed until Swae finally said, "If Xavus selected them, they do not need my approval. Mol'do is the primary battleground between the Underworld and the Pit. You are talking about the last fallen celestial and the devil himself. Would anyone you plan to send have a grasp of the nightmare they'd be walking into?" Xavus nodded affirmatively. Swae looked up at the starry sky, saying, "I don't suppose you have a name for this group."

Xavus answered, "Omega."